NEMESIS: REIGN OF DARKNESS VOLUME .

First edition. November 8, 2023.

Copyright © 2023 Jeff Brown.

ISBN: 979-8215447376

Written by Jeff Brown.

Also by Jeff Brown

Aeolian's Quest
Aeolian's Quest Book I: Stormbringer
Aeolian's Quest Book II: Three Pretenders

Aeolian's War
Book I: Modal Shift
Aeolian's War Book II: Mysteries and Mayhem
Book III: Antiphonal Resolution

Reign of Darkness
Nemesis: Reign of Darkness Volume I

Slade Saga
The Return Slade Saga Book II

The Hunter
Bride: The Hunter Book I

The Last Mage
The Last Mage
In The Dark: The Last Mage Book II
Dawn of Night: The Last Mage III
Blood Sisters: The Last Mage IV

Vampire War
Vampire War: Ascension
Vampire War: Redemption
Vampire War: Resistance

Standalone
Refugees
Vampire War: Fallout
The Veteran
Thirst
Blurred Visions
\Another Slant/
The Princess Agenda: Complete Edition
Words In The Wind

Table of Contents

NEMESIS:
Reign of Darkness
Volume I

Jeff Brown

SPECIAL THANKS

Special thanks to the person who helped me through the process of completing this project. My editor, sounding board, critic, and support – Karen Bates.

ACKNOWLEDGMENTS

The following people have been instrumental in keeping me inspired and motivated. A multitude of thanks to them all.

DeAnna Allen, Jay Allen, Kevin Barr, Jo Renee Bass, Karen Bates, Lisa Bishop, Eldon Blalock, Penny Boyd, Ramona Burrow, Kim Chancelor, Paul Dancsisin, Wanda Faircloth, Georgia Fleming, Dee Freeman, John Goodwin, Ray Hamilton, Jerry Henderson, Monique Hibbs, Dorothy Howell, Melissa Jackson, Rochelle Jackson, Jody Johnson, Angela Jones, Jobina Khoo, Sharon Laird, Cleve Langston, Mary Larsen, Hal Maranto, Scott McGehee, Victor Merritt, Jennifer Miller, Pam Porcaro, Carol Price, Donna Rochel, Tim Rochel, Jacob Rosenthal, Braxton Rushing, Melinda Slemaker, Bonnie Stewart, Polly Varnado, Steve Vowell, Stacey Wilkinson, and Sydney Woodson.

NEMESIS:
REIGN OF DARKNESS
VOLUME I

PROLOGUE
Departure

"I'm done," Alex Chance growled as he stood facing the huge desk in the small office of Jonathan Cardwell, Director of the Domestic Security Agency Task Force he'd been part of for more than a decade.

Cardwell was seated behind the desk as Alex stood in front of him with his arms folded over his chest and said calmly, "It's over."

Alex, tall and massive, well over six feet tall with shaggy dark blond hair and steel gray eyes narrowed with the intensity of his mood, glared at Cardwell, a couple of inches shorter with short, light brown hair and cold hazel eyes that bore into Alex's eyes with a complete lack of expression on his narrow face.

"What do you mean?" Cardwell asked after a few tense seconds, his voice terse and low. "There's still work to be done."

Alex shook his head slowly, his jaw set firmly, and said, "Not for me. Davros has been destroyed. There is no Master. They don't have a leader and they're disorganized. It's all just mopping up the leftovers now. Besides, I'm tired, physically and mentally. I need a break."

"But we need you, Alex," he said, his voice still cold and even. "You're the team leader. They'll follow you anywhere and they work better when you're in charge."

Alex shrugged, "Bonacci or Deninger can handle it. They're good people and better soldiers. They have the background for it. The others will listen to them."

Cardwell shook his head, "It's not the same. They can't do what you can."

Alex leaned slightly forward and said, "You don't need what I can do anymore. It's all over. I just want to get out of here."

Cardwell frowned, stared at him for a few seconds, and said, "All right. On one condition."

"What's that?" Alex asked and stood up straight.

Cardwell sat back and said, "I want to be able to find you if something should change, if we're wrong about any of this."

Alex opened his mouth to speak, but Cardwell continued, "I know Davros is down and the power of the Master is gone, but we really don't know that much about all of this. It's a small possibility, but it's still there. We still don't know anything about their powers. I know the rest of the team is more than capable and they know how to take them down properly, but those abilities of yours have given us the edge. They're the only reason we got to Davros and took him out. So, if something changes, I want to be able to find you."

Alex nodded, "Okay. I guess I can live with that. I'll keep the GPS tracker active on my phone. I'll make sure Merina knows all about it and keeps it active on this end."

"Good enough," Cardwell nodded. "But where are you going?"

"I don't know," he shrugged and took a step back. "Maybe south."

"Back to Pine Ridge?"

"I doubt it," Alex said and shrugged again. "There's nothing there for me now. But I will keep looking for vampires no matter where I go. That should help a little."

"Yeah," Cardwell said and stood up, extending his right hand. "It will and I hope you're able to find what you're looking for."

Alex shook his hand and said, "I'm not really looking for anything, just a little rest. I need a break, time to process everything that's happened and try to figure out what's next."

Cardwell smirked, "You've been talking to Bonnie again, haven't you?"

Alex nodded slowly. Dr. Bonnie Stowers was the team's therapist and understood what their mission could do to a person.

"Yeah," he said rather softly. "But that's why she's here."

"True," Cardwell said and sat down. "But I didn't expect her to counsel you to leave us."

Alex took a step back, "She didn't do that. She did say I need to take a break, get my mind together, and figure out what to do with my life with the primary mission being over. I'll be available, but I don't know if I want to come back to all of this full-time."

"I understand," Cardwell nodded. "Just be careful."

Alex turned and looked over his shoulder, "I'll do my best."

Cardwell let out a low sigh and sat down as Alex turned and walked out of the office. Cardwell steepled his hands together beneath his chin with his elbows on the arms of his chair and stared at the door for several moments after Alex vanished from sight.

He didn't know what to do next, but he would try to figure it out.

CHAPTER ONE
The Long, Late Walk

Walking along the wide, five-lane street that connected the old and almost completely abandoned downtown district of Pine Ridge, Mississippi and the interstate creating the western border of the town was nothing new for Dana Richland. She'd walked the three-mile length, in both directions, twice a day and nearly every day for more than three years. She was accustomed to the trek, but it was growing more and more difficult with each passing day. Her body was no longer in the same shape it had been when she'd started the job at Harrison's Steak House almost a decade earlier. She'd been in her twenties then and had been physically fit. In ten years, the job had taken its toll and the long daily walk had only made it worse. With her older model car out of commission and being unable to afford repairs, the new motor it needed, or even a down payment on a newer vehicle from the most disreputable car dealer in town, she had no choice other than walking to and from the restaurant every day she was scheduled to work.

She walked slowly, her feet dragging and her shoulder slumped, but it wasn't only the exhaustion after a shift that had lasted more than twelve hours. It was the fatigue from years of the same routine and the depression that had settled into her soul. The accumulated grease left her long, dark blond hair matted and lank, almost plastered to her skull. Releasing it from the ponytail required by the restaurant hadn't helped ease the weight of it, but it did give her a faint sense of freedom. The uniform of a white blouse and black, knee-length skirt with black pantyhose felt like the chains of bondage, dragging her down and slowing her progress away from the prison of work. Her shoes, orthopedic shoes intended to ease the pain in her feet, legs, and lower back were old and falling apart, no longer doing their job. She needed to replace them, but the cost was prohibitive considering her meager budget. Her feet, legs, and back did ache and each step brought sharp pains through her heels, but she just accepted it as another part of her life and journey with not even a wince as it added just one more level of pain.

Dana Richland was thirty-four years old and felt her life was nothing more than a routine that had to be followed, a cycle of torment she would never be able to escape. It preyed on her mind, an almost fugue state of reflection locked onto her perceived failures. The cycle repeated itself each night as she trudged along the cracked and broken sidewalk along the south side of Michigan Avenue, named for the state and not the prominent street in Chicago.

First, though, she ran through her plan for the night. She was filthy after hours of rushing back and forth between the dining area of the restaurant and the kitchen, her hair and clothing coated with grease that didn't add much physical weight left an emotional burden that felt like the weight of the world. Once she reached her home, one side of a small duplex in an area close to the decrepit downtown district, she would strip off the greasy clothing, knowing from that the grease had soaked through to her underwear, and toss it all in the washing machine. She would then find something to eat and sit down in front of the TV until the wash cycle had finished. The house's water heater was rather small and couldn't accommodate both the washing machine and the shower at the same time. She would remain undressed, certain the windows were securely covered, then shower once the wash cycle was complete and the hot water reserve replenished. After the shower, sitting in front of the TV wearing only a worn-out old bathrobe, she would wait until the dryer had finished its cycle. It never completely dried her clothes on the first run and she would start the second before going to bed.

She tried to focus only on what needed to be done that night, but her mind drifted, as it always did, to the past and all the mistakes she'd made, bringing her from a bright, hopeful, and confident teenager to a depressed, defeatist woman that saw no future other than constant pain, permanent exhaustion, and being a lonely old spinster.

Her life had fallen apart not long after she'd graduated from Pine Ridge High School. She'd had great plans for her life, beginning with college and a degree in Finance. She'd seen herself as the CEO of a major corporation living in a major city, possibly on the West Coast, but it hadn't happened. First, her high school boyfriend, Alex Chance, had made some decisions that altered her life as well. Instead of joining her in college, first at the local community college, he'd enlisted in the Navy intent on becoming a SEAL. He'd gone through some physical changes during their last year of school that neither of them had been able to understand. He'd grown incredibly strong, much stronger than the daily workouts he'd gone through as a football player would've provided. His senses had grown sharper. He could almost see in the dark and could hear detailed conversations from more than a hundred yards away. He didn't sleep much, no more than three hours at a time, and felt just as energized as if he'd slept more than eight hours each night. He didn't understand the changes and he'd finally admitted to her just before he left that he'd received some advice from one of their teachers, Dr. Patrick Brewer, the one History teacher who wasn't also a coach. Dr. Brewer had done his best after Alex left to try and explain his departure, but he never gave her any real information, just saying that Alex needed to find himself and figure out what to do with his left. The military, particularly the service he'd chosen, would give him the opportunity to find out just how far he could go and what he needed to do with his life.

Of course, Alex had never returned to Pine Ridge. He'd kept in touch for a few months, but he'd stopped writing and calling once he'd completely basic training and had been accepted into the SEAL program. There hadn't even been a break-up message. He'd just vanished and her life had completely fallen apart. It had been the beginning of her depression which led to her leaving college and never returning to finish her degree. She'd started working, part-time at first, but had moved to full-time positions once her parents retired and moved to Florida, leaving her on her own. She refused to leave Pine Ridge should Alex return to look for her. She wanted to be where he would be able to find her.

She'd finally settled into the job at Harrison's Steakhouse and remained there, moving up the ranks to finally reach the position of head waitress. It was more money, but it demanded a lot more time. It also meant she was responsible for covering shifts when others didn't show up, which happened frequently.

The only bright spot in her life was the continued friendship with her high school best friend, Tiffany Gardner. She'd also remained in Pine Ridge and continued her relationship with Ben Mills, the guy she'd started dating their senior year. He was a couple of years older and had already been working full-time at an auto body shop making good money, but neither of them had been ready to settle down. Now in their thirties, Dana often wondered why Ben hadn't pulled the trigger and asked Tiffany to marry him. They were living together and she assumed it was all they wanted, a relationship without getting the government involved.

Over the years, Tiffany had tried setting her up with a few guys she'd met as secretary to the town's mayor. They had been mostly businessmen, contractors, or assistants and she'd gone out with a few of them, but none of them had felt right for her. After more than two years, she'd finally told Tiffany she wasn't interested and was still waiting for Alex to return. Tiffany hadn't liked the idea and thought it was holding her back, but she let Dana live her life.

She'd resigned herself to remaining single, until a few months earlier when she'd met a man who intrigued her. His name was Gerrit Jaeger, a German businessman intending to open a factory in Pine Ridge. They'd met when he visited the restaurant late one night when a majority of the day's traffic had subsided. He'd struck up a conversation with her and she'd been enthralled. They'd gone out a couple of times on her days off, also late at night due to his daily schedule in getting the details of his new business lined up, and she'd reached the point where she felt almost ready to enter a serious relationship, pushing thoughts of Alex and his return aside.

She'd hoped Gerrit would've visited her at the restaurant that night, but he hadn't and her hopes of not being forced to walk home were shattered. She walked slowly, tiredly, and kept her arms folded across her chest. She hadn't expected such a drastic change in temperature once the sun had gone down. She'd been without a cell phone for a couple of weeks, a prepaid phone that had run out of minutes and unable to purchase more until her next paycheck, and she had no internet access at home other than through a cell phone data plan. She felt like a relic, being one of the few people she knew of who still had a landline phone. She'd also been unable to pay her cable bill for the previous few months and didn't have access to any source of news or weather. With the sudden change in the weather, she'd gone to work without a jacket and she shivered a bit as she walked.

She wanted to walk more quickly, to generate some body heat, but her tired and aching legs with her level of exhaustion just wouldn't allow it. Her feet practically dragged the sidewalk and she stumbled a few times, her eyelids sagging as she fought to remain awake. Even the act of walking and moving forward wasn't enough to keep her fully awake. Finally, after more than an hour, she reached a darkened corner two blocks from the beginning of the downtown district, the lone streetlight above the intersection having long since burned out, and turned right, struggling as she climbed the shallow hill toward her home on the corner at the far end of the block, and on the opposite side.

Almost halfway along the block, as the hill reached its acme, she crossed the pitted asphalt and reached the top of the hill, just a couple of yards from the edge of the property she called home. There was a light in the front window of the house's left side, the half occupied by an immigrant family, but that meant little. She'd never spoken to them and had no idea about their habits. Dana paid no attention to that side of the house and focused on her own. Thankfully, she'd left the porch light on to give her a point of focus in the darkness. She walked toward the door as she fumbled in the large pocket of her skirt for her housekey attached to a small wallet-type leather pouch that also held her driver's license, more for identification than driving, and the little bit of cash she had, in case the restaurant manager wanted to be a jerk and not allow her to eat at least one meal from the kitchen.

She pulled the key from the pocket, the only key she had or needed, and prepared it for the lock. Pausing at the door, before inserting the key into the lock, she frowned and looked over her shoulder. A sudden feeling washed over her, like she was being watched. As she did, a lean figure stepped from behind the massive oak tree at the corner of the small tract of land and his bright blond hair was visible in the darkness and the tiny bit of available moonlight.

"Gerrit," she said tiredly and tried to smile, a weak smile at best. "What are you doing here?"

He shrugged, his dark clothing barely moving, and said, "I've been waiting for you, Dana. I think it's time for you to serve your purpose."

She frowned and faced him, "What are you talking about? What purpose?"

He continued moving closer, seeming to almost glide across the sparse lawn, and said, "I must confess that I approached you for a reason. You see, I feigned interest in you to draw you closer and hopefully, you will provide what I really need."

She felt almost heartbroken. She'd been counting on him to continue being the great guy he'd been since she'd met him. The addition to her depression was tinged with a bit of fear, the fear of not knowing what he wanted from her.

"What is it?" she asked, her voice weak and trembling. "What do you want?"

He moved smoothly out of the darkness into the pale yellow glare coming from the porch light and stopped a few feet in front of her, his sharp, angular face pale and magnificent in the dim light. His pale blue eyes seemed almost luminescent, as if there was a natural light behind them. His thin lips, frequently spread into a warm and inviting smile, were drawn tight, a faint line crossing his pale skin and his long hair, a pale blond so light it almost seemed white, fell around his shoulders looking like cornsilk.

"I want you to bring your boyfriend back to this town," he said evenly, almost coldly. "I need him here to complete my mission and you're the only one that can make it happen."

"Alex?" she frowned. "Is that who you're talking about? I haven't heard from him in over fifteen years and I have no idea where he is."

Gerrit smiled, a wicked smile, and said, "But he will know. He'll know that you're in danger and he will come back here."

She frowned and shook her head slowly, "What do you mean? How am I in danger?"

He took a step forward and said, "I am the danger, Dana. This is going to hurt, but it won't last long. I do care for you, but this must be done and I do apologize."

"What are you talking about?" she asked, her voice shaking with fear.

She wanted to turn and run into the house, but the door remained locked and she knew she would be unable to open it quickly with her trembling hands and get inside before he could reach her. She just didn't understand what he meant about her being able to bring Alex back to Pine Ridge.

"You see," he said and continued toward her, his voice smooth and even. "I need his presence to give me the power I need to complete my plan and he must be here, in this town, for it to be done properly. You are the only one that can bring him back. I need just one thing from you for that to happen. I need you to begin the process of becoming one of us."

"One of who?"

He didn't say anything, just took a large step forward and opened his mouth, impossibly wide, enough for her to see the brief glint of pale moonlight on the long, curving fangs that quickly extended from behind his perfect teeth.

He was on her in an instant and she didn't have time to scream until those fangs penetrated the flesh of her throat.

CHAPTER TWO
Tribal Issues

She rose naked from the large pond, moving slowly toward the shore where her aide and attendant Eldon Blake stood with a large towel in his hands while the three members of the tribal council stood to her left and watched almost reverently, all dressed in soft, tan, leather trousers and tunic, each of them holding a long pole with a burning torch atop it to provide a modicum of light in the clearing between the pond and the dense trees separating them from the tribal village less than a half mile away. To her right stood two others, one almost her equal and the other an outsider who had been welcomed into the tribe to represent a smaller faction with a similar purpose.

Danette Granger, the Chief Elder of the tribe, was fairly tall with long, jet-black hair that hung wetly along her back to brush against the tops of her firm, muscular buttocks, the result of years, practically uncounted years, of physical activity. Her body remained firm as well, with full breasts and lightly flaring hips, solid and muscular arms, and legs. Her narrow face, with thin lips and wide, dark eyes, showed no fear and no embarrassment as she stepped onto the shore and Eldon, his black hair short and neatly trimmed, stepped forward, moved behind her, and wrapped the towel around her though she didn't appear to notice the sharp chill in the night air.

Eldon stepped aside once the towel was wrapped around her, covering her from shoulders to mid-thigh, and reached for the neatly folded white robe resting on a small blanket a few feet away.

Danette waved him off with her left hand and took two steps forward then lowered herself to the ground, sitting with her legs crossed the folds of the towel draped across her upper legs. Placing her hands on her knees, the towel slipping away from her upper body a bit, she looked around at the others, her expression stony and unreadable.

Three members of the council stood stoically and watched her, waiting for her to address them. Two men flanked the single, shorter woman. The taller of the two men, Levi Gaston, stood on her right, his short, light brown hair seeming to almost glow in the firelight. On her right stood Carlos Montoya with long, perfectly straight, black hair falling halfway down his back. Melanie Parkman, her light brown hair, a shade lighter than Levi's, was even longer than that of both Carlos and Danette and framed her lean, narrow face with wide, bright hazel eyes.

Facing them, positioned just as far from Danette's position, stood the man known only as KJ, the tribal Shaman, his shoulder-length brown hair framing his narrow face to highlight his bright, green eyes. To his right stood Katrina Bentley, an outsider from a group recently allied to the Tribe. She was tall, taller than either of the other two women, with long, dark brown hair, neatly styled, and wide, dark hazel eyes set in an angular face.

"The situation has reached the point where we must decide on our stance," Danette said after a few seconds. "The treaty is in danger of being broken and our duty is clear should this become truth. We must oppose them before they reveal both their existence and ours to the world. That is the pact."

She scowled and continued, "The traitor is among them. He will continue to serve the unholy forces unless we intervene. KJ has seen the future and the traitor will be instrumental in allowing their plan to proceed."

"This plan," Levi said, frowning, and took a small step forward. "What does it entail?"

Danette focused her gaze on him and said, "The new Masters, the Virate, have taken the Book of Aranos and have begun following his plan for conquest. This must not be allowed to happen."

"What can we do?" Melanie asked, her gaze now intense with her strong jaw set firmly.

"Gather his pack," Danette replied. "Bring them to the council hall with his former betrothed. She will lead them to find him and they will return him to our land."

As they nodded, Danette stood up and let the towel fall to the ground behind her, fully exposed, and only Levi stared at her naked body.

With a glance at the robe resting on the blanket, she looked over her shoulder at Eldon and said, "Bring my clothing. I must prepare myself fully."

He nodded his understanding as she turned and began walking slowly toward the trees. Once she walked past the light of the small fires, Eldon scooped up the damp towel, robe, and blanket then followed her into the forest. The three members of the council followed with KJ and Katrina behind them.

They followed her in a single line along a narrow, winding path, a game trail, with only the light of the three torches. A few moments later, points of light began to appear through the dense trees. Eldon, the last in line, was also the last to see the end of the path as it opened onto a huge clearing filled with a variety of makeshift buildings, the homes constructed by the members of the tribe, those that had settled on tribal property at the base of an unnamed mountain in northern Colorado. The air was chilly, but not yet as cold as it would be, and Eldon marveled again at Danette's ability to withstand the cold. Even in the depths of winter, she would dress like anyone else would during the summer. In the chill of middle October, weeks before the temperature would drop below freezing and snow covered the land, Danette walked brazenly through the forest and into the village without showing any sign that the cold bothered her.

As they reached the edge of the village, the wide clearing typically used for meetings of the entire tribe, Danette turned around and focused on Eldon as she said, "I believe the robe will be appropriate now."

"Of course," Eldon said and hurried forward, tucking the blanket and towel under his left arm as he shook the robe out and prepared it for her to put on.

She turned again and held her arms out slightly as Eldon, eyes wide with the stress of the situation, rushed forward and held it in perfect position to slip into it. Once it was in place, he backed away quickly as she pulled it tightly around her and fastened it with a small leather strap at the waist.

"Now," she said and faced the group again. "Eldon, find the members of the pack and bring them here, Carmen as well. She will resist, but she must lead this mission."

"Of course," Eldon nodded and scurried away into the village.

Once he was gone, Danette looked to KJ and said, "Tell me more about the things you've seen."

The rather thin man stepped forward with a nod and said, "Moonshadow remains with the vampire. She still controls him, the one who claims a life debt. It will take a great deal to remove such control. They are currently in a small town in Mississippi, a place called Pine Ridge, and the vampires around her, the Virate claiming to have received the power of the Master divided amongst them, are planning something that will alter the course of history. It will also break the treaty and, as tribal law has stated, it will be considered an act of war between the vampires and the tribe."

Danette nodded, "We have fought the vampires before, but only to a standstill. We have not increased our numbers since replacing those we lost. The vampires, however, have created many more of them. Davros understood the pact and respected it. If he has been destroyed and his power has passed to these new vampires, it's impossible to know what they will do, but I suspect they will not honor the treaty."

KJ nodded slowly, "That's the impression I get from the visions. They're searching for an ancient power they believe will give them greater strength and greater control over the entirety of the vampire population."

"That cannot be allowed to happen," Danette almost growled. "But we need to be careful with our approach. First, the pack will do their best to restore Moonshadow to his true heritage. Once that has been dealt with, whether they succeed or not, they will do their best to oppose the vampires and their plan."

"We need to mobilize," Levi Gaston said, almost scowling. "Get the word out to every faction. We must begin preparing to deal with this situation. We must attack first."

Danette glared at him and said tersely, "We'll adhere to the wording of the treaty. We will not attack them and we will not reveal our presence until they've made the first move. The tribe will not be at fault when this war begins."

"Of course," Melanie Parkman agreed with a nod. "We must not be the instigators of the conflict, but I do believe it's coming, and pretty soon. I agree with Levi that we need to be ready, but we don't have the level of control the vampires do. We can't control all the individuals or the leadership of the factions. I think we should alert them to the possibility and have them prepare for it but with strict orders not to act until the word is given."

Danette nodded, "That's my intention. We spread the word and we prepare."

She then focused on Katrina and said, "I know our two peoples are different and we have yet to finalize a formal agreement, but we will definitely need to combine our forces to take on the vampires. Our separate numbers will not be enough."

Katrina nodded, "I agree. I was sent here to work with you for that very reason. We've noticed certain trends in the vampire community and we have heard of these supposed Masters, the Virate. If you're sending your pack to retrieve one of your own from their grasp, I'd like to travel with them and learn what I can so I can report to my people. We're prepared to go to war with the vampires and working with the Tribe has been discussed. Once I see these three that claim to be the Masters, I'll take it to my people and we will join you."

"Good," Danette nodded. "It seems only right for the Changers to all work together."

"They have arrived," Carlos Montoya said, nodding toward the cluster of buildings behind Danette as a group of six led by Eldon walked into the clearing.

Danette turned around and watched as the six, four women and two men, strode slowly into the clearing and spread out into a line with the women to her right and the men to the left. Eldon walked quickly back to the others and stood just behind Danette.

She looked them over for a moment then stepped forward, moving to the left, and stood in front of the first man. She looked him over carefully, sniffing lightly to commit his scent to memory, and looked him in the eye. He was tall, six feet tall, with a broad chest and massive arms. His thick, chestnut brown hair was a mess but seemed perfect for his almost blocky face and for his natural complexion that appeared to be constantly tanned. His name was Greyeagle, though Danette suspected it was an adopted name due to his bit of Native American Heritage.

She looked him over carefully then moved to the next man. He was a bit shorter, bald, with a thick beard and bright blue eyes in a soft face. He was Scott Cambridge, one of the last to be turned more than fifty years earlier, and had a similar build to Greyeagle.

The first of the women was the tallest, Holly Varden, a statuesque blonde with thick, loose curls that flowed halfway down her back and seemed to cascade over her shoulders. In human society, Danette could've seen her as a model with her height of six feet and a perfect hourglass body, a seductive body with a face to match.

The woman beside her, half a foot shorter, with long, perfectly straight, red hair and dark green eyes was Renee Bailey, a slim and quiet woman, but one that could be deadly in the right circumstances. Danette had seen her in action a few times and knew she was one not to be trifled with.

Beside her was Nora Burman, a bit taller, much leaner, and with dark brown hair falling to just below her shoulders framing her narrow face of sharp angles with thin lips and wide eyes almost the same shade as her hair with an intensity and a bit of crazy shining behind them.

The final one was the woman Danette was most concerned with. Carmen Pauling, fairly tall with a fantastic figure and shoulder-length hair so blonde it was almost white with a soft, almost round face with bright brown eyes and full lips, a touch of ego in the set of her jaw.

"Carmen," Danette said. "It's time for you to reclaim the past."

Carmen nodded, her jaw relaxing as she sensed the touch of anger in Danette's heart, "What can I do?"

"Moonshadow," she replied. "You are still his betrothed, despite what he has done. I need you to use that connection to bring him back to us, to break his connection with the vampires."

Carmen frowned, "He left me. He made his choice and decided to serve them. From what I gather, he's bonded to one of them and that's a different situation."

Danette nodded slowly, "You are the only one that can make any difference and, at this time, it's essential to our future. The war between vampires and lycanthropes is brewing and will undoubtedly begin soon. If Moonshadow, as part of this tribe, is seen as collaborating with the vampires, it will diminish our ability to lead the factions spread out across the nation. I'll lose my position s Chief Elder. This council of Elders will be disbanded. If we're going to take the lead in opposing the vampires and retain the ability to coordinate the lycanthropes, including the Feline families. You must find him and bring him back into the fold at all costs."

Carmen nodded slowly, "I'll do my best."

"Good," Danette said a bit more loudly and took a step back, looking across the line. "You will all accompany Carmen. Moonshadow is the true alpha of this pack and must return to his position."

She focused on Scott and said, "You've done an admirable job of taking over the position of leadership, but Moonshadow must resume the role. For now, Carmen will lead you. She will be able to find Moonshadow as his betrothed more easily."

Scott nodded once, "It will be as you say. We will follow her lead."

Danette nodded, almost smiling, and gestured to her left, "You will also be accompanied by Katrina, representing the Felines. She is to be included in every aspect of your search, which will also include learning as much as you can about the vampires, these alleged new Masters, and their plans."

"Of course," Scott said and nodded again. "We're ready to start immediately."

"Wait until morning," she said. "Rest tonight and be fully prepared. Eldon will make the necessary arrangements."

"Where are we going?" Holly asked, frowning lightly as she looked at Danette.

KJ stepped forward and said, "You'll be traveling to Mississippi. I have received a vision of Moonshadow in a small town called Pine Ridge."

Holly nodded and relaxed her expression as Danette said, "Now, go and prepare. I'll have all the details you need to be prepared for you by the time you depart."

CHAPTER THREE
After The Attack

Detective Neil Shafer stood at the corner beside his plain black, department issued, Ford Taurus with his hands stuffed into the pockets of the lightweight black jacket he wore over black jeans and dark blue t-shirt, what he'd first grabbed when he'd received the call from Chief Walt Baker about a vicious attack in the rough neighborhood adjacent to the downtown district of the town. He'd been reluctant to enter that area at night, just as the patrolmen refused to stop in that six square block area once the sun fell below the horizon. The flashing blue lights of the squad car and red lights of the ambulance parked along the broken sidewalk in front of the duplex were a bit painful as he watched the two EMTs, Jim Williams, and Erin Smith, do their best to work on the body of the woman lying on the sparse lawn in front of the house. The Medical Examiner, Mitchell Roth, had been called in only to find that the victim was still breathing. He remained, standing close to the ambulance in his ubiquitous black clothing and smoking a cigarette as he watched the scene unfold.

The two officers that had first responded, Hal Martino and Raquel Jackson, stood by their cruiser and watched the scene as well. Neil needed to talk with them and get their report on the situation before beginning his part of the operation, but he needed the reports from the EMTs and the ME first.

Neil was a tall man, just an inch over six feet, with a lean build, short, neatly styled light brown hair, and a sharp-featured face bearing an old scar from his days as a patrolman across his left cheek. It had happened so long ago, so early in his career, that he rarely thought about the jagged line of pale scar tissue until someone mentioned it.

A small crowd had gathered across the street, behind where Neil stood, but he paid them little attention after seeing there were only eight of them. If it had happened during the day, there would've been many more, people wanting to see the latest act of violence in the neighborhood. He did recognize a couple of them, two men who definitely weren't residents of that area, and he wondered what they were doing there. One was Ryan Sullivan, the fairly tall, pudgy, red-haired guy who worked for the local newspaper, but Neil knew the guy wasn't yet a reporter. He'd been with the paper for years and hadn't moved past being a proofreader and typesetter. That told Neil the guy either wasn't competent or had done something to stunt his professional growth. Either way, the guy was there with a small notebook in hand and was taking notes. The other was Dr. Patrick Brewer, an older man who remained in his position as a high school history teacher even though he'd been in the position for nearly thirty years. Neil didn't understand why someone would remain in the job after so long, especially considering the conditions prevalent in modern schools and the potential for disaster, but it wasn't his call and he'd let the man live his own life.

After several minutes, once the EMTs transferred the victim to a gurney, Mitchell tossed his cigarette to the ground, crushed it with the toe of his dark brown shoes, and started toward Neil, shaking his head. His car was parked just ahead of Neil's, pointed toward the highway that ran through the town and bordered the downtown business district, or what remained of it.

"I don't know why I was called," Mitchell said as he walked past shaking his head. "I expected a body, one that wasn't breathing. Waste of my time."

Neil shrugged, "That's the way this town works."

"You got that right," Mitchell said and kept walking. "I'm going home. See you later."

Neil nodded and looked toward the ambulance as the EMTs carefully rolled the gurney across the rough lawn toward the open doors at the back of the vehicle. Beyond the ambulance, the two officers slowly moved away from their vehicle, their gazes focused on the gurney, and Neil knew it was time to begin the process.

Drawing in a deep breath, he walked away from his car and focused his cold hazel gaze on the two officers. He knew them both rather well, though he typically worked the day shift and they were relegated to the overnight shift, the only two on duty, and it was rare for them to have something like the situation at hand.

Hal Martino was a fairly tall, somewhat muscular man who had been the owner of an HVAC company in New Orleans until roughly ten years earlier. His business had been bought out by a major company and he'd been forced out. Not wanting to remain in the area looking for work, he'd relocated to Pine Ridge and found his way onto the police force almost by accident. He'd been in the right place at the right time and he'd so far proven himself to be a competent officer. His partner, Raquel Jackson, was a fairly short, beautiful woman with long, dark blond hair and light hazel eyes that seemed completely out of place as a police officer and the dark blue uniform just didn't seem appropriate for her. She remained rather aloof and he knew nothing about her reason for joining the force. He wasn't going to ask and just settled his curiosity with the knowledge of her ability as an officer, equal to Hal, and that made them the perfect pair for the night shift.

"What's the situation?" Neil asked as he approached them, foregoing the niceties. It was too late at night for that.

Hal looked at him, faced him, and nodded slowly, looking down at the notes he'd taken in his small, leatherbound notebook, "The woman that lives here, Dana Richland, was attacked a little over an hour ago by an undisclosed assailant."

"Who called it in?" Neil asked.

Raquel nodded, placed her hands on her hips above the wide gun belt she wore, and said, "It was the neighbors, the Suarez family. The wife, Esmerelda, looked outside before calling. She claimed to only see the victim. No one else was around. She said she looked around, but the area was clear."

Neil nodded, frowning thoughtfully, "Okay. What do we know about the victim?"

"Well," Hal said, looking down at his notebook. "Her name is Dana Richland, a waitress at Harrison's Steakhouse, in her mid-thirties. She lives alone and stays to herself when she's home. The neighbors didn't even know her name. We had to pull her ID from her wallet to find out who she was."

"Suspects?" Neil asked.

"None," Raquel shook her head. "The neighbors saw no one and there's no one else around."

Neil nodded and before he could say anything else, the ambulance pulled away, the siren starting a few seconds after it turned the corner, heading toward the town's hospital close to the interstate on the western edge of the city.

"Okay," he nodded. "You two get back on duty and file your report before the end of your shift. Just leave it on Lana's desk, unless she's as early as always. Then you can just hand it to her."

Hal nodded and smirked, "I expect she'll be in before we can get back to the station."

Neil nodded and took a step back, "Probably so. I'm going to the hospital and check on her, see if she's able to tell me anything."

Raquel shook her head, "I doubt it. She was unconscious when the paramedics showed up."

"We'll see," Neil said and turned around.

As he returned to his car, two phone calls were made across the street. Ryan Sullivan was the first to act. He walked away from the small crowd, tucking his little notebook into the back pocket of his dark blue slacks then pulled a small cell phone from the left front pocket. He held it tightly in his sausage-like fingers until he was well away from the crowd. Glancing back every few seconds until he was sure no one was following or watching him. He then looked at the screen of his phone, tapped it with his thumb until it lit up, then opened his contacts and found the proper number. He tapped the screen button to initiate the call then held the phone to his left ear.

Once the call was answered, he said quietly, a conspiratorial tone to his thin voice, "The EMTs took her to the hospital. The cops didn't do much of anything. I don't think they have a clue."

He listened for a few seconds then nodded and said, "Of course. I know her. I'll go to the hospital and keep an eye on her. Yes, I'll be there tomorrow at sundown."

The call ended and he frowned at the screen for a second. There had been no recognition of what he'd done, It didn't seem right, but he knew who he was working for and the promise they'd made for his assistance and cooperation. One day, he would become something more than he'd ever imagined.

Patrick Brewer walked in a different direction, turning around and walking quickly away from the house rented by Dana, into the darkness of the wide street and toward his own home on the edge of that troubled section of town. As he did, he pulled out his cell phone and made a call of his own. Once dialed, he held the phone to his right ear and waited.

"Caroline," he said once the call was answered. "Yes, I know what time it is, but we have a situation. There's been an attack in Pine Ridge. The victim is Dana Richland."

He nodded and continued, "That's right. Alex Chance's high school girlfriend. She was attacked about an hour ago and it's apparently a vampire attack. I think it has something to do with Alex."

The raspy, sleepy voice on the other end spoke, "Are you sure?"

"Yes," he said sharply and continued nodding. "I don't know the vampire, but I believe there's a connection to the Virate, based in New Orleans. I think they're trying to draw Alex out for some reason."

"What do you want me to do?"

"Tell Cardwell," he said, almost scowling. "This is a major development. Alex needs to know as well."

"He's not here," she replied. "He left a couple of months ago. Merina has his GPS tracker active all the time, but I don't know how to find it. I'll have to get her to tell me."

"Fine," he said. "Just let Cardwell know what's going on and keep my name out of it for now."

"Okay," she said. "You're still my 'anonymous source' and he won't question it."

"Good," he said. "I'll be in touch."

He disconnected the call, slid the phone into a pocket of the gray jacket he wore, and continued on his way home. He had work to do and not much time to do it.

22

CHAPTER FOUR
Getting the Ball Rolling

As she replaced the out-of-date landline phone that Cardwell insisted upon for reliable communication should something happen to their cell or satellite service, Caroline Parrish leaped out of bed, kicked away the rough blanket provided by the agency, and stood up on the cold concrete floor of the facility, an old medical clinic on the outskirts of Washington, D.C. Cardwell had used a bit of funding to convert into the headquarters of the unnamed DSA task force. The living quarters were sparsely furnished and Caroline saw no reason to spend any of her salary on something to decorate the small room that had at one time been a single patient's room, a protected room on a level that was below ground. It was always cold and the floor seemed to actually project cold rather than absorbing heat by the laws of physics. At least the room's sensors were functioning and the light fixtures at the top of the wall across from the bed flared to life and gave her enough illumination to see what she was doing, though she did squint for a few seconds as her eyes adjusted to the brightness.

She shivered as her feet touched the cold floor and gooseflesh rose on her bare legs and arms. Clad only in a pair of black panties and a matching sports bra, comfortable sleeping attire that would leave her prepared for a contingency such as what had just happened. She dressed quickly in the black trousers and long-sleeved black shirt Cardwell had them wear in the office to match the combat gear the insertion team wore almost constantly, minus the body armor, though it was available for them in case of an attack. Still, she doubted it would do much good if even a single vampire entered the facility.

She sat on the edge of the small bed, little more than a cot, and added black socks and a pair of black shoes with soft soles, essentially running shoes, then stood up and moved to the door, a thick steel door with a closing mechanism akin to that of a submarine hatch, another of the security measures, but this one had been installed under the auspices of their security chief, Steve Wolverton. He was good at his job, and knew his way around the equipment and technology, requiring only one assistant to make sure the facility was completely secure. He and the other security specialist, Nicole Jennings, alternated shifts and Caroline believed Nicole was on duty that night, but she wasn't sure.

At the door, she faced a console mounted to the wall beside it that protruded just over four inches and was a rectangle roughly the size of a standard hardback book. It was divided into two sections. The upper half being a small video screen and the lower a touchscreen pad. A simple tap on the lower screen brought it to life and she tapped a control in the upper right corner that connected her terminal to the facility's main computer network and triggered the public address system.

"This is Caroline," she said brusquely and quickly. "This is an all-hands call. I have received vital intelligence that must be dealt with immediately. All hands to the conference room."

She tapped the screen again, disconnecting from the public address system, and took a deep breath then walked to the small dresser across from the bed and ran a hand through her shoulder-length white-blonde hair. It wasn't perfect, but it was good enough. She also took a second to check her face. Without makeup, she felt a little overexposed and vulnerable, but there wasn't time for her to apply any. Her smooth, lean cheeks showed a few splotches of red, almost like blush, from her sleeping position and her full lips were pale, but her brown eyes were open wide and she was fully awake.

Grabbing her cell phone and tablet, she used the wall unit to unlock and open the door. As it swung open wide enough for her lean frame, she slid through the doorway into the corridor outside. As she entered the hallway, overhead lights came on and she moved quickly toward the stairs at the end closest to the central portion of the facility. As she reached the door to the stairwell, she heard the sounds of other doors unlocking and opening behind her, but she didn't look back and hurried up the stairs to the main floor of the facility.

The conference room on the first floor was a large room adjacent to the building's lobby, the former emergency entrance of the clinic, and the main desk, stretching across the wide lobby with a door on either end, remained in place. The plexiglass wall above the desk had been replaced with a thicker polymer that was impact-resistant, thanks to the work of Dr. Sydney Lawson, the task force's R&D Director. The conference room was to the left as Caroline arrived from behind it, past the small offices along the hallway leading to the reception area with one slightly larger office at the end that had been a triage room and was now occupied by Director Jonathan Cardwell. As Caroline strode past, the office door was closed and no light appeared at the base of the door, meaning that Cardwell had retired for the night and she'd awakened him, hopefully, with her announcement.

She was the first to arrive and opened the door easily; it remained unlocked, trusting the exterior security measures to keep it safe, and the lights came on as she pushed the door open. Inside, she found a large rectangular table with eight chairs on each of the longer sides and one each on the shorter ends. Each person residing in the building was given a specific seat, assigned seating as if they were still in high school, but it worked for the meeting typically held in the room. The wall to her right, facing the front of the building, held a massive video screen with a thin column of small speakers on each side. Another table, much smaller, rested against the wall below the screen. With no scheduled meeting, there was nothing prepared, and Caroline knew she would be called on to essentially begin the discussion.

She took her seat, on the right with her back to the door, the first seat beside the head of the table where Cardwell would conduct the meeting. As his Administrative Assistant, he wanted her close at hand. Logistics Director, Paul Sandusky, would be seated across from her with the five remaining members of the Insertion Team along that side of the table. Merina Janek would be seated beside her with Sydney Lawson next in line, Lab Tech Jana Hendricks would be next with Security Operatives Wolverton and Jennings taking up the next two seats on that side and the team's Therapist, Dr. Bonita Stowers, referred to as Bonnie, occupied the final chair on that side. Their military liaison, Colonel Martin Vincent, would sit at the end of the table, opposite Cardwell. That would leave two chairs on the opposite side, one intended for Alex Chance, the former leader of the Insertion Team, and one for a potential visitor, though there hadn't been any in quite some time and Caroline doubted there would be any in the foreseeable future.

She sat down and placed her hands flat on the table, her brow furrowed as she began planning what she would say. The idea of an attack happening in such a remote location, the small town of Pine Ridge where Alex had grown up, just didn't seem likely and, at least to her, it meant something major was taking place there. It was a little confusing, trying to fit the pieces together, but she wasn't given time to figure it out. A moment after she'd taken her seat, Paul Sandusky strode through the door.

He was a tall man with short, graying hair and pale blue eyes set in a face that had once been sharp and angular but had started to sag. His gaze remained intense as he entered, a little more intense than his normal intense expression.

"What's going on?" he asked, his voice deep and gruff, as he walked over to sit across from her. "You called this meeting, and said it was an emergency."

She looked at him, her eyes narrowed a bit as she struggled to make sense of what she'd been told. He sat back in his chair, elbows on the arms of the chair with his fingers laced together across his stomach.

She let out a sigh and said, "I received a call from one of my contacts. There's been an incident we need to be aware of, but I'd rather talk about it with everyone else here, so I don't have to repeat it."

"Understood," Sandusky nodded. "It shouldn't be long."

It wasn't. They began filing in and taking their seats just a moment later. They entered with a little grumbling, but they were in place quickly. Cardwell, as Caroline had expected, was the last to enter, having taken a little extra time to dress properly in his standard dark gray suit with a white shirt and dark blue tie. The only thing missing was the tan trench coat he preferred once the weather started turning cold.

He took his seat and all eyes were on him as he leaned forward, intertwining his fingers on the table as he looked at Caroline.

"Okay, Caroline," he said in his usual emotionless tone. "What's the emergency?"

She nodded and said, "I received a call from one of my contacts, a Dr. Patrick Brewer in Pine Ridge, Mississippi. He informed me of a vampire attack in the town."

"Right," Cardwell nodded. "We've been working our way westward and we've expected more attacks in that region."

"You don't understand," she shook her head. "He said the victim was a woman named Dana Richland."

Cardwell sat up and gripped the arms of his chair, his eyes opening wider, "Alex's high school girlfriend. That could be significant."

She continued, "He believes this attack is somehow connected to the Virate, the Masters that have shown up in New Orleans."

Cardwell frowned, "That name has come up, but I don't know anything about them. I assume this Brewer thinks it's connected to Alex because of the victim, and I can see that. What else?"

"He said there's something going on in New Orleans," he replied. "He thinks they're looking for something there, something to help with whatever plan they have."

Cardwell sat there, silent, for a moment, thinking it through, then sat up straight and nodded.

"Okay," he said and looked to his right, to the members of the Insertion Team. "This is what we'll do. It's about five hours until sunrise there. That should give us time to get there and find out something before the day begins and the vampires all go to ground. I'm not sure about this possible connection with Alex, but we need to let him make that decision."

He focused on the tall man with short, brown hair seated beside Sandusky, turning his chair slightly, and said, "Bonacci, you and Deninger take Chopper One and find Alex. I don't care what you have to do, but get him to Pine Ridge."

"Will do, boss," Bonacci said with a curt nod.

Cardwell shifted his gaze a little farther and said, "Dyson, Parker, and Coleman, you'll come with me. We'll take Chopper Two to New Orleans. If we leave in the next half hour, we'll arrive in plenty of time."

Melissa Dyson, a woman of average height with shoulder length, mostly straight, dark blond hair, and deep hazel eyes, nodded and said, "I'll have the chopper ready in fifteen."

"Good enough," Cardwell said and looked at Merina, a small woman with long, black hair framing a tawny face that held just a hint of her Asian heritage. "Merina, set up whatever it is you need to set up so they'll have access to Alex's GPS tracker."

Merina nodded and said, "That'll take just a couple of minutes."

He then turned to Sandusky and said, "Make arrangements for us to have a car ready when we reach New Orleans."

Sandusky nodded, "What about backup?"

Cardwell shook his head, "I think we have what we need."

He looked to the far end of the table, the largest man at the table, Thomas Coleman, and said, "Coleman, make sure we have all the weapons, ammo, and gear we'll need. Take extra, just in case."

"Yes, sir," the bald Black man said with a nod.

"Good," he said and turned to his left, looking at the two tall, beautiful women seated between Merina and Steve Wolverton, Dr. Sydney Lawson with her long, curly chestnut brown hair, and Jana Hendricks, a bit shorter and thinner with long, dark blond hair. "Sydney, I want you and Jana to stay here and put some more effort into that serum you've been working on. It might be needed with this situation."

Sydney shrugged and said, "We'll do that, but don't expect a miracle. We've been trying for over a year and haven't had any real successful results. I have an idea, but it's pretty drastic."

"I don't care what it is," he replied. "We need to take some drastic measures around here. I have a feeling this is going to be much more than we're thinking."

Sandusky shook his head, "Those feelings are usually pretty accurate."

Cardwell glared at him for a second then looked over the others, "The only thing left is this place. I want you all to be on your toes. Steve, Nicole, I want you both patrolling until we get back."

Steve nodded, "We'll handle it."

"Merina," he said. "Stay on top of the tracking and communications. We'll need to stay in touch at all times."

"I've got it," Merina replied. "I'm still working on the new gear, with Sydney's help, but it isn't quite ready yet. It should be by the end of the week. But what we have will do the job."

Cardwell nodded and looked at Caroline, "Get your source on the line and let him know when the first group arrives. We'll want to talk with him."

Caroline nodded, "I'll do my best."

"Okay," he said and pushed his chair back. "Let's get started."

The others began to stand and Cardwell turned toward Sandusky. As the taller man started to rise, his hands on the arms of the chair, he paused and waited.

"One more thing, Paul," Cardwell said. "The President is scheduled to visit tomorrow."

Sandusky sat down and frowned, "Is there a reason for the visit?"

"Funding," he said. "She's coming with the senator in charge of the funding committee. They're going to look over the operation and see if they can find more funding for us. I doubt I'll make it back by then, so you'll have to take care of it."

Sandusky shook his head, "She's your friend, Jonathan. I don't know if I can get the same response."

"You'll do fine," Cardwell said and rose to his feet. "But we have to get moving."

"Right," Sandusky said and stood up, following Cardwell from the room.

CHAPTER FIVE
The Cabin

H e walked slowly through the sparse trees surrounding the cabin. Dressed in black tactical gear, without body armor or protective helmet. His dark blond hair, just a shade too light to be called brown, and his fairly dark complexion were the only things standing out in the dark. Armed only with the massive .50 caliber pistol in a holster at his right hip, Alex Chance looked around carefully, cognizant of the special sense he'd developed years earlier, one that would alert him to the presence of vampires within a hundred-yard radius of his position. At the moment, with the cold air of northern Alabama filling his lungs, he sensed nothing.

It was late, well past one in the morning, and he planned for it to be his last perimeter search of the night. He'd been up since four the previous morning, but he no longer needed much sleep. Three to four hours was more than enough, but he started feeling a little tired after more than twenty hours of being awake and active.

The night was clear, the moon at its smallest, just a sliver of white in the sky, and neither the moon nor the stars provided much light. Alex, with his enhanced vision, had little need for sources of light. He could see clearly in the dark, as clearly as he could in the daylight. The lack of light just left things appearing almost as shades of gray, with very little visible color. He did see a faint source of artificial light, the light coming from a pair of oil lamps in the small cabin at the top of the hill in the center of the property he'd purchased. In the months he'd been there, he'd cleared the top of the hill, leaving a wide open area around it, allowing the other person living in the cabin, one without his unique night vision, to see anyone approaching the cabin, vampire or otherwise.

He'd met DeAnna Jones two months earlier, just before he'd decided to settle in the state rather than going back to his hometown where nothing waited for him, that he knew of.

It had been a hot night in late July when he'd discovered a nest of vampires, one that was larger than he'd anticipated. He'd taken out most of them but three had survived and he'd been forced to flee the old barn where they'd been hiding. They'd chased him to a truck stop just off Interstate Twenty. It had been late and there were thankfully few people there. Only the lone cashier, DeAnna, two people working in the diner portion of the truck stop, and two customers, old men having a really early breakfast. He hadn't been able to sense the vampires when he'd entered the place and hoped he would have enough time for a brief meal, depending on how quickly the cook could prepare a cheeseburger.

He'd talked to the two old men sitting on the stools at the diner's main counter, each of them sipping on a cup of coffee, and tried to relax a bit, resting while he could, and the food arrived, giving him just enough time to wolf down half the burger before the familiar sensation, a tingling at the base of his skull, told him the vampires had found him. Shoving another bite of the burger into his mouth, he'd gone to the main part of the building to confront them before they could do much damage.

When the three vampires entered the store, two men and a woman, dressed as if they'd stepped out of an eighties punk movie, spotted him and attacked. He'd regained enough of his energy to take care of them, but they'd spread out he thought they would've threatened the tall woman with long, black hair behind the counter, but they acted as if she wasn't there. She'd even moved from behind the counter and came close to one of them, the woman, but the vampire had no reaction to her presence and Alex found that strange. When it was over, all three vampires were destroyed and returned to the level of decay they would've reached had they remained dead, Alex looked at her and asked how she'd been able to do what she'd done. She didn't understand it, either, but she was intrigued by his fighting ability and the fact that he knew they'd been vampires the instant they walked in the door, if not before.

Fearing that more might be arriving, some that he hadn't located in that particular nest or from a nearby hideout, he'd asked her to leave with him for her own safety. He would see her home and make sure she was safe.

Then, when she'd agreed and picked up the Bible and silver crucifix on a thick strand of leather from behind the counter, along with her small purse, Alex began to have an idea. Once they reached her home, riding on his black motorcycle, she'd invited him in to eat and finish the meal he'd been unable to finish at the truck stop.

While she cooked and while they ate, she told him about herself and it struck him that it was her unshakeable faith that had protected her from the vampires, had rendered her invisible to them. She didn't understand it, but she accepted it and decided to join him in his quest, believing this ability might help. That was when he'd bought the cabin and started training her.

She wasn't quite ready for full combat with vampires, but she was getting there and was capable of at least holding her own. It wouldn't be long until she was ready to go in actual combat, but he hoped that wouldn't happen.

He concluded the circuit around the property and headed toward the cabin, focused on the small points of light to guide him. Without having sensed the presence of vampires, he felt safe walking a bit more quickly and worrying less about moving silently. It took little effort for him to do so, but it allowed him to relax and consider the idea of actually sleeping once he reached the cabin. DeAnna was still awake; he was sure of that, but they would both be going to sleep before long, once he set the cabin's defenses.

He drew closer rather quickly, but he didn't use the additional speed he'd acquired long ago, along with greater strength and heightened senses. He was a bit tired, but not that tired. He just liked the isolation and time alone, the feeling of the cold air, though it didn't exactly bother him. He felt the temperature, hot or cold, but it didn't affect him.

A few moments later, he reached the edge of the clearing surrounding the cabin and stopped. He saw motion off to the right, almost behind the cabin. It took a second for him to focus his vision and by that time, the source of the motion had vanished behind the cabin. He still didn't feel the presence of a vampire and wondered who could be stalking his cabin. He walked quickly toward it, picking up the pace quite a bit, his hand hovering over the grip of his pistol.

When he was within twenty yards of the cabin, the shadowy shape appeared at the corner of the wooden building and his eyes focused, seeing clearly.

He stopped and relaxed, frowning as he said, "Krista? Is that you?"

"Yes," Krista Deninger said and walked forward a little more quickly and confidently. "We need to talk."

Alex continued forward, slowly, and shook his head, "It's over, Krista. I'm done."

"Alex," she said and moved toward him. "Cardwell sent me to get you. We need your help."

"No," he said and continued to shake his head. "The whole thing is over."

She nodded toward the cabin's front door and said, "Let's go inside. We really do need to talk. Things have changed."

He drew in a slow breath, closing his eyes for a second to show his frustration, then shrugged and said, "Fine. Let's talk."

He led her into the cabin, opened the door, and entered the dimly lit living room, a small room furnished only with a small sofa and a pair of recliners, all covered with dark brown leather. A small fireplace in the corner to the right of the door crackled with the fire burning low inside it, giving the room a comfortable warmth.

As they entered, Alex gestured toward the sofa and said, "Have a seat. Let's hear it."

She moved toward the sofa and he walked around it toward the recliner farthest from the door as DeAnna Jones entered from the back of the building, from a small hallway leading to the pair of bedrooms and single bathroom on one side of the rear half of the cabin. The other held the kitchen and a small laundry room.

DeAnna was dressed similarly to Alex, but instead of the pistol, she wore a sword at her left hip, angled to be drawn by her right hand. She was a tall woman, approaching six feet, with long, gleaming black hair hanging down her back and across her shoulders. Even through the black tactical gear, Krista could tell that the woman was in great shape and had apparently been working out with Alex. Her lean face held the remnants of a summer tan and her sharp features, wide, dark eyes, slim nose, and full lips held an air of both intensity and mystery.

"Who is this?" Krista asked as she entered and stopped a couple of feet past the entrance to the hallway.

Alex nodded to her and said, "This is DeAnna Jones. She's been training with me for a couple of months. And she has a rather unique ability that could prove highly beneficial."

Krista sat on the sofa, leaning forward, as Alex sat in the recliner facing her.

"You'll have to tell me about it later," Krista said. "This is a little more urgent."

"Fine," Alex said and sat back, his hands resting on the arms of the chair. "Tell me."

Without speaking or being asked, DeAnna walked over and sat in the other chair after taking off the narrow leather belt holding the sword and placing it on the floor beside the chair, ready to be grabbed in an instant.

"Alex," Krista said, ignoring DeAnna. "There was a vampire attack in Pine Ridge."

He frowned and shrugged, "I've been keeping track. They're moving to the west. It's expected."

"No," Krista shook her head. "The attack happened earlier tonight. The victim is Dana Richland."

His eyes opened wide and his breath caught in his throat. He hadn't thought about her in several years, figuring she'd moved on and forgotten about him. It was a surprise to learn she was still in Pine Ridge.

"It could've been just a random attack," he said and sat back.

"I don't think so," Krista shook her head. "Neither does Cardwell. He thinks it has something to do with you."

"I don't get it," he said. "I haven't seen Dana since shortly after high school graduation and haven't been in contact with her since about a year later. It doesn't make sense."

"Look," Krista said and placed her hands on her knees, gripping them tightly. "Caroline received a call from one of her sources, a man named Brewer in Pine Ridge."

Alex sat up straight, eyes wide, "Not Patrick Brewer."

"I think so," Krista replied, frowning. "You know him, don't you?"

Alex nodded, "He was my high school history teacher and the only one I talked to about my abilities as they were developing back then. What's he got to do with this?"

Krista shrugged, "All I know is that Caroline said he was part of some organization that kept track of vampires and their history."

Alex shook his head, "That doesn't make any sense. He never said anything to me about it, but he knew what was happening with me."

"I don't know anything about that," she shook her head. "I just know that this man claims that the attack on Dana is directly connected to you. There's a reason behind it and Cardwell thinks that bringing you in, at least to consult on it, is necessary."

He continued to frown as he thought about it. He hadn't thought about Dana in years, especially since he'd joined the task force and became integrated with the entire operation. His focus had been on the mission, the goal of defeating the vampires, and he'd thought it was all over with the defeat of Davros, the Master.

"There is something else," Krista said when Alex remained silent for a moment.

He looked at her and asked, "What is it?"

"Cardwell believes the power of the Master was transferred before you defeated Davros."

He gasped. The idea had never occurred to him. He'd been so proud of having defeated the Master. It had seemed like the culmination of more than a decade of work, something only he could have done, but it began to make sense as he replayed the incident in his mind. He'd gone into the final fight with the Master completely confident in his abilities, believing he was strong enough to take him down. The fight had lasted quite a while and Alex had sustained numerous injuries, though none of them close to fatal, and he'd finally destroyed Davros. Thinking back on it, Alex realized that, while Davros had been an exceptionally strong and powerful opponent, he hadn't been as strong as they'd all been led to believe the Master could be. It made sense after so many years that Davros had relinquished the power and had sacrificed himself so that the plan of the vampires could continue without more interference from the task force.

"Where is the power?" he asked, looking at Krista again.

She shrugged and replied, "We're not exactly sure. There's a rumor that the power was given to a trio of vampires that call themselves the Virate. We don't have any idea about the name, what it means, or where it came from."

"It's stupid," DeAnna said, her voice rich and smooth. "It's an abbreviation of the word triumvirate, with a little different pronunciation."

Krista and Alex both looked at her, frowning. She shrugged and said, "There's three of them, right? It makes sense, but it's still stupid."

Alex nodded slowly, looking at her, then shifted his gaze to Krista, "What does this mean? Do we have a new Master, well, Masters?"

"I think so," Krista said. "There's definitely something going on."

"Okay," he nodded. "I guess that means I'm back in the game."

"Good," Krista nodded firmly and sat up straight. "Bonacci is waiting in the chopper about a half mile away."

Alex frowned, "Why didn't he come here with you?"

"He thinks there might be trouble," she said with a shrug and a slight smirk. "And he wants to keep the chopper ready to go. It's going to take a while to get to Pine Ridge."

"A couple of hours," Alex said. "The hard part will be finding a place to land. There's not a lot of air traffic in that little town."

"We'll figure it out," Krista said. "But we should get going."

As he nodded, a familiar tingle flowed across the back of his neck and his eyes opened wide, his back straightening.

"We have company," he said. "There's three of them and they're heading this way from the south."

DeAnna was instantly on alert, standing up as she grabbed the sword and returned it to her waist.

"What are we doing?" she asked, looking at Alex.

He stood up as well and said, "We're getting out. Grab what you need and leave the rest. We're abandoning this place."

DeAnna nodded and hurried to the back of the cabin as Krista stood up and looked at Alex, frowning.

"What are you going to do?" she asked, knowing all about his abilities, particularly his ability to sense the presence of vampires.

He looked at her, a familiar stony intensity on his face, and said, "We'll draw them in, get out the back, and blow the place."

"You have your home rigged?" she asked, her hand on the small 9mm pistol tucked into a concealed holster at her right hip.

"Yeah," he replied. "I wasn't exactly planning on this, but it's been a possibility since I moved in."

"Fine," she said and took a step forward. "What do we do now?"

He nodded over his left shoulder and said, "There's a door in the kitchen leading outside. Go there and wait. I'll get what I need and set the charges. It'll only take a couple of minutes. DeAnna should be there in a moment."

He started to turn, but Krista moved forward and grabbed him by the arm, a dark scowl on her face as she said, "First, tell me about you and DeAnna. Have you forgotten Sydney so soon?"

"I haven't forgotten her at all," he said. "DeAnna needed training. She has a great ability and I'll tell you all about it once we're in the air. Now, let's get moving."

Krista shook her head as Alex pulled away and hurried into the back of the cabin while Krista made her way into the kitchen. She found the door easily, halfway expecting Alex to have come up with some sort of camouflage to confuse anyone, particularly vampires, trying to get in. While she waited, she checked her gear. The pistol was loaded and ready, with a bullet already in the chamber. All she had to do was take the safety off and it would be ready to fire. She had two blades with her, two knives, each blade coated with silver, one thing that would cause great harm to vampires and could possibly destroy them, though they'd never actually seen that happen. The longer and larger of the two was in a sheath at her left hip, turned to be gripped with her left hand, and the other was in another sheath attached to her right ankle inside her black tactical boot. Three additional clips of ammunition, ten rounds each, were attached to the back of her belt, also angled for easy retrieval.

She began to grow anxious about the presence of vampires in the area. She wasn't exactly afraid of them, especially with Alex being there. She'd dealt with and destroyed more vampires than she could count, but there was always an element of risk when not knowing the level of power the vampires possessed. She was fairly certain none of them were close to the power of the Master or the very old, but they were still stronger and faster than any human, except for Alex. He wasn't quite on their level, but he was closer than any other person on the planet.

After what couldn't have been more than two minutes, DeAnna entered the room, now dressed in body armor over the tactical clothing she'd been wearing. The sword remained at her waist, but a pistol larger than the one Krista had was now attached to her belt on the right. Her hair was pulled back into a ponytail and she had a black leather pack strapped across her back.

"Alex is coming," she said as she entered the room. "He's setting the charges."

Krista nodded, "How long will we have to get away?"

"What we need," DeAnna replied, almost coldly. "Alex has a remote trigger."

"Good," Krista said and cut her dark green eyes toward the door. "We'll have to get past the clearing fast. We don't want to be in the open too long."

"Of course," DeAnna said. "But you'll have to lead us to your helicopter."

"We'll head due north," Krista said, almost matching DeAnna's tone. "It's on a ridge about half a mile from here."

"I know the ridge," DeAnna said. "We shouldn't have any trouble getting there."

"If we take care of the vampires," Alex said as he entered the room.

He still wore no body armor or helmet, but he had added a large pack with a sword between the pack and his back, angled over his left shoulder. His slate gray eyes were narrowed slightly, an intensity in his gaze not otherwise evident on his face.

"Let's move," he said and continued toward the door. "Krista, lead the way."

Krista nodded, opened the door, and walked out of the cabin into the cold air outside.

DeAnna followed her with Alex behind them, closing the door. Krista walked quickly across the clearing, heading directly toward the waiting helicopter, looking around the best she could in the darkness. Without the night vision goggles she should've brought with her, she saw little and drew her pistol after just a few steps. Behind her, DeAnna did the same. Alex, able to see clearly, kept his pistol holstered while holding a small device, the remote trigger for the explosives filling the cabin, in his left hand.

"They're coming from the south," he said once they were several yards away from the cabin. "The cabin is between us."

Krista nodded and began to focus on their path rather than looking for the vampires to reach them. Knowing she would see nothing if she looked back, her eyes remained on the path leading them to the chopper and only glanced back to make sure DeAnna and Alex were behind her.

After a moment, before they reached the line of trees at the edge of the clearing, they heard the sound of splintering wood as the vampires broke into the cabin. Alex gave them a few seconds, long enough for them to enter the cabin and begin their search. Focused on their escape, he couldn't quite identify their specific locations and hoped they were all either inside the cabin or within the blast radius. As Krista reached the tree line and moved fluidly between two large trees, with DeAnna two steps behind her, he depressed the single button on the remote and was rewarded an instant later by a loud, low whump of the initial explosion. The first explosion collapsed the integrity of the cabin, causing it to fall in on itself. The second, taking place two seconds after the first, erupted with a loud clap and a ball of flame rose from the center of the cabin and rapidly expanded both upward and outward in a perfect circle. Debris began to fly, bits of wood and a few rocks, and clattered on the ground around the edges of the clearing. Alex didn't break stride and entered the forest as the light of the explosion showed him the landscape around him clearly for a handful of seconds.

As the rumble of the explosion filled the air, followed by a wave of hot wind, the tingle in the back of his mind went away, telling him that all three vampires had been caught in the explosion and completely destroyed.

CHAPTER SIX
New Orleans

"They say New York is the city that never sleeps," Jonathan Cardwell said almost absently from the passenger seat of the dark blue Cadillac SUV parked in the massive lot beside the Jax Brewery just a few blocks off Canal Street. "But New Orleans is the city that only takes the occasional nap."

Melissa Dyson, seated to his left and behind the steering wheel, nodded slowly and said, "I guess this is one of those naps."

"I hope so," Cardwell replied and drew in a slow, deep breath. "We really don't need to be noticed and it's almost time."

He reached to his left ear and lightly tapped the device placed snugly in it then said rather casually, "Are you ready?"

The crystal clear voice of Alvin Parker replied almost instantly, "We're in position. The alley is clear."

"Good," Cardwell said with a nod. "The operation commences in two minutes. Stay alert and keep your eyes open."

"Roger that," Parker replied and Cardwell broke the connection with another tap to the device.

"Okay," Cardwell said and looked at Melissa. "Hold position here and keep the motor running. We'll keep comm open so you'll know when to move. And when you do, move fast. There won't be a lot of time. I imagine I'm going to say something to piss this guy off."

"Got it," Melissa said with a sharp nod. "I'll be ready."

He looked at her for a second then opened the door and climbed out. The air was cool, but not close to as cold as the air in Washington. Still, he wore his standard tan trench coat over tactical clothing, but he opted to forego the body armor, knowing it would do nothing other than slow him down in a physical conflict with a vampire. He was armed only with the .44

caliber pistol that had become his favorite weapon. The .50 caliber Alex used was more powerful and did more damage with similar rounds, but Cardwell felt it had too much kick for him to use in close-quarters situations like the alley he was about to enter.

He crossed the remainder of the lot quickly and exited through a narrow gate in the high iron fence surrounding it. The wide sidewalk outside the fence was practically deserted at that time of night, but for a few pedestrians, mostly drunk partygoers working their way slowly back to their hotel rooms or to a place where they could make use of the public transportation system. He barely noticed their presence as he focused on a small side street across the wide street in front of him. There had been little traffic since their arrival almost half an hour earlier, telling Cardwell that the nightly party was winding down, but he still had to wait for a car to slowly roll past, heading toward Canal Street to his left, the crossed the wide street and walked past a chain restaurant on the corner just before he turned right onto the dimly lit side street that would take him deeper into the area known as the French Quarter. He wasn't going that far, only about twenty yards to the narrow alley running behind the businesses, primarily restaurants and bars with a couple of gift shops for tourists, and served as a place to dispose of their trash. He wasn't exactly looking forward to walking through it all.

As he reached the opening of the alley, he paused and looked around for any sign of his contact having brought backup, but he saw nothing. He actually expected to see nothing, The vampires would remain out of sight, concealed in the shadows, until it was time to make their presence known.

"Okay," he said softly, the comm unit easily picking up his voice. "I'm going in. Be ready,"

Melissa and Parker responded with their single-word acknowledgment and he resumed walking, entering the alley despite the trepidation he felt. His eyes remained open wide, quickly adjusting to the even dimmer light. His heavy boots, part of his tactical clothing, thudded against asphalt, damp with a variety of fluids from the bursting black garbage bags spaced along the walls close to the back doors of the businesses. He let out a sigh and moved forward, doing his best to ignore what he was stepping in. The place reeked, a combination of rotting garbage, stale beer, and just a hint of urine. Breathing shallowly helped a bit, but it wasn't perfect. He kept moving forward and soon reached the spot he recognized as the place where he'd been instructed to meet, an intersection with another alley, one running perpendicular to the one he was on and leading only to his left. He stopped there and waited, glancing up to see the rounded shapes of tactical helmets belonging to Parker and Coleman. Knowing they were in position provided just a little hope that he would survive the encounter, but he knew how vampires could react, how strong they were, and wasn't sure those two, as good as they were, would be able to help him escape if it came to that.

He didn't have to wait long. With a brief rushing sound, like that of a sharp gust of wind, his contact appeared in a blur of motion too fast for the human eye to see clearly. The dark blur stopped suddenly and the figure of Dorian Thibodeaux stood in the alleyway to his left. He wasn't overly tall, a couple of inches shorter than Cardwell, with shoulder-length light brown hair and small eyes the color of seawater. His skin was pale, telling Cardwell instantly that he hadn't fed since awakening. With only a couple of hours before sunrise, he wondered if Dorian planned on Cardwell being his next meal. He was dressed in black, like the stereotype that had been seen in numerous movies over the years, but his jacket was black denim, a little nod to a portion of the local population.

"What do you want, Cardwell?" Dorian asked, sounding perturbed and just a little angry.

Cardwell turned to face him and said, "I need to know a couple of things. Tell me first about the Virate."

Dorian shook his head, "Those three are bad news. They're ancient, and I mean really ancient, close to two thousand years old. They're claiming to be the new Masters, that they've shared the power of Davros. They're old and powerful, but I'm not exactly sure they are Masters."

Cardwell nodded, "Last I heard they were operating here, starting on some sort of plan."

"Yeah," Dorian replied, his arms folding across his chest with his feet at shoulder width. "They were here and they were working on a plan. They've been building numbers here and the rumor is that they're using the Book of Aranos."

"What's that?" Cardwell frowned.

Dorian shook his head, "Man, you don't know much about vampire history. Aranos was an ancient Master, more than five thousand years ago. He wrote a book detailing his plan to take over the world. Of course, at that time, the world was a much smaller place and it doesn't seem like it'll work."

"I'm guessing they have this book," Cardwell said, continuing to frown.

Dorian nodded, "They have one copy of it and they were looking for the second copy. There are only two. But they haven't been able to find it."

Cardwell shook his head, "Then how are we supposed to figure out what they're doing?"

Dorian leaned slightly forward and grinned, showing just a hint of his fangs, "I know where it is."

"Tell me," Cardwell said firmly.

"Okay," Dorian straightened up and lowered his hands to his hips. "But this has to be the last time, Cardwell. Whoever's in charge of this city will find out and that'll be the end of me."

"Okay," Cardwell nodded slowly. "The last time. I promise. Tell me where to find this book and where to find the Virate."

Dorian took a step back and said, "The book is in the home of a priest, Father Bruce Tourigney. He's an old man, in his eighties, and lives in a little house beside the cemetery behind the St. Louis Cathedral."

"I know where that is," Cardwell said. "We'll find it. Now, where are the Virate?"

"Not here," Dorian shrugged. "They left weeks ago. Word is that they've headed to some little town in Mississippi called Pine Ridge."

Cardwell's back straightened and he gasped lightly, "There was an attack there earlier and it's connected to one of my operatives."

Dorian shook his head, "I don't know anything about that. If they're involved, you're in real trouble."

He took a step back and held up his hands as he said, "Look, Cardwell, I'd planned on taking you down tonight, to end all of this, to stop you from coming to me for information, but I see that you're going to end it, all of it, and I think that might be for the best. So, take this as a gift. I haven't fed tonight and it's getting late. I might not be able to control myself much longer. Get out of here. Fast. I'll give you three minutes. If you're still around here, I might have to take you down anyway."

"Okay," Cardwell said and took a step back. "Thank you, Dorian. I won't bother you again."

"See that you don't," Dorian said and Cardwell turned, almost running along the alley.

He heard the rush of wind, a distinct sound, that told him Dorian was already gone, most likely moving to a position where he would be able to attack more easily, and moved faster.

"Let's move," he said, knowing the comm unit was still active. "Parker and Coleman, get to the street. Dyson, meet us at the corner."

Trying to keep track of the time, counting down the three minutes Dorian had given him before attacking, Cardwell moved quickly to the end of the alley, splashing through the rancid puddles of unknown liquids, and reached the side street in a moment. He didn't believe it was far enough in the open to deter the attack and kept moving. He was within ten yards of the main street when the car screeched to a stop at the corner. A second later, the door was flung open and he saw Melissa behind the wheel, her normally sedate expression replaced with one of intensity and fear. He'd never before seen that expression and it spurred him into a quick jog.

As he reached the car and climbed into the passenger's seat, Alvin Parker and Thomas Coleman practically sprinted along the sidewalk with huge rifles angled across their chests. Parker reached the car first and pulled the door open sharply, almost diving in as Coleman pushed him roughly, tossed his rifle to the floorboard, climbed in, and closed the door behind him.

"Go!" Coleman almost yelled. "Go!"

Melissa moved her right foot from the brake pedal to the accelerator, almost stomping it, and the car shot forward, pressing them all into their seats.

"Where are we going?" Melissa asked once they were away from the corner, thankful that there was no traffic at that time of night.

Cardwell shifted in his seat, sitting up straight, and said, "St. Louis Cathedral. We're heading for the cemetery behind it."

Melissa nodded, "I'm familiar. We'll be there in less than ten minutes."

As they sped through the streets of New Orleans, weaving around minimal traffic, Cardwell pulled his cell phone from a pocket inside his coat. He activated it and began a call.

"Merina," he said once the call was answered. "Get Caroline on the line, pronto."

"She's right here," the rich voice of Merina Janek replied.

A second later, the voice of Caroline came to him, "Yes, Mr. Cardwell."

"Caroline," he said. "I need you to get in touch with your contact, this Brewer person. We need information on something called the Book of Aranos. Hopefully, we'll have a copy of it shortly and we'll be heading for Pine Ridge once we do."

"Okay," she replied. "I hope I can get him. Do you have any idea when you'll get there?"

"Not a clue," Cardwell replied. "I don't know how long it'll take with this priest we have to see. It should take us an hour or so after that. I'm pretty sure it'll be after sunrise by the time we can get there."

Caroline replied, "I'll try to get him and let you know."

"Good," he nodded. "Thanks. Put Merina back on."

A second later, Merina was on the line and asked, "What can I do?"

"Have you heard from the other team?" he asked sharply. "Have they located Alex?"

"Yes," Merina replied. "Bonacci checked in about ten minutes ago. They have him, and another that's been training with him, and they're on the way to Pine Ridge. He estimates they'll arrive in just under two hours, close to sunrise."

"Good," he said. "We'll probably need more down here, but I'm not positive yet. I want Sydney, Jana, and Bonnie ready to travel once the meeting with the President is over. I'll let you know the details when we have something figured out."

"I'm on it," Merina replied. "I'll let them know and I'll check with you after the President has left."

"Good enough," Cardwell said and ended the call abruptly.

He drew in a slow breath and returned the phone to its pocket, staring straight ahead as he did his best to figure out what to do with the information he'd received from Dorian.

A few minutes later, the car slowed to a stop at the curb in front of a small, ramshackle house at the edge of the cemetery. It was surrounded by a low iron fence, each slim pole was topped with a rusted cross with a gate hanging by one hinge at the end of the narrow, overgrown walk leading to a warped wooden porch. The small yard was overgrown with grass and weeds that threatened to encroach on the cracked white paint on the house's walls. A single lit, a dim yellow, burned in the dirt-encrusted window to the right of the single door at the top of three wide steps leading to the porch, telling Cardwell that the house's inhabitant was either awake or had left the light burning through the night.

They sat in the idling car for a moment, staring at the house as Cardwell made a plan.

"Okay," he said after a moment. "The car stays here. Dyson, you're coming with me to talk to this priest. Parker and Coleman, patrol the area, but don't go too far. Keep your comm active. I don't want any surprises."

Almost in unison, they opened the doors and climbed out of the car quickly. Melissa walked quickly around the front of the car, making sure her 9mm pistol was secure in its holster and ready to be drawn. Coleman hurried around the back of the car and joined Parker with their rifles ready.

Cardwell walked quickly along the narrow walk then carefully climbed the three steps to the warped porch. His weight caused the boards of both steps and porch to creak, undoubtedly alerting the person inside the house to their presence, and Melissa followed him carefully. He approached the door and raised his hand to knock, but it opened quickly before his hand could touch its surface.

The old man standing in the doorway with a small pistol in his right hand, aimed at Cardwell's chest, scowled with his soft brown eyes open wide with fear. His slate gray hair, seeming to almost stand on end, surrounded a soft, round face and a grizzled chin.

"What do you want?" he asked gruffly with an accent Cardwell associated more with the northeast than south Louisiana. "You aren't one of them."

"No," Cardwell said calmly, his expression remaining cold and intense. "We're human and we need your help, if you're Father Bruce Tourigney."

"I am," he nodded once. "And who are you?"

"I'm Jonathan Cardwell," he answered and nodded over his shoulder. "This is Melissa Dyson. We represent a Domestic Security Agency task force and we're working on stopping a major vampire plan."

Tourigney stared at them for a couple of seconds then leaned slightly to his right and nodded as he saw Parker and Coleman standing vigil on the other side of the car.

He took a step back and lowered the pistol as he said, "I guess I'll take your word for it. Those two outside seem like they're ready for an attack."

"They are," Cardwell replied. "May we come in?"

"Of course," Tourigney said and backed out of the way.

Cardwell and Melissa entered, Melissa closing the door behind her, and Cardwell led them into the small, sparsely furnished living room. He walked slowly to a chair in the far corner of the room, positioned to face the door. The only other furnishing in the room was a small sofa against the wall facing the front of the house. Tourigney eased himself into the chair as Cardwell and Melissa sat on the sofa, Cardwell closest to the old priest.

Tourigney looked at Cardwell and said, "I assume you're here because of the Book of Aranos."

"Yes," Cardwell nodded. "That's the information I was given."

Tourigney nodded, "It's here and it's the original, written in the language of the vampires that hasn't yet been completely translated. The one taken by the Virate is a copy, the only copy known to be in existence."

"What is it?" Cardwell asked. "Other than the writings of an ancient Master."

Tourigney sat back, the pistol still in his hand resting on the right arm of his chair, "It's a collection of his writings, yes, but it also contains a plan to take over the world. Of course, it's a few thousand years out of date. The world is a much larger place now."

Cardwell frowned, "Then how can they use it to take over the world now?"

"They believe it can be adapted," he answered. "In the hands of the Master, or Masters in this case, they can alter it to fit the world as it is today. But that's not the most important thing contained in the book."

"What is then?" Cardwell asked, shaking his head slowly.

Tourigney drew in a slow breath then said, "There are supposedly details on locating an ancient power, one even older than Aranos, that will give the Master much greater power, the power to control and coordinate every vampire on the planet and make them practically invincible. That's the only part that has been completely translated, and it's incomplete. We don't know where this power is located, but their current activity suggests that it's somewhere in this town of Pine Ridge."

Cardwell nodded slowly, "The Virate are there and there was an attack earlier. The victim is tied to one of our former operatives, Alex Chance."

Tourigney's eyes opened wide, "The Nemesis? He worked with you?"

Cardwell frowned and turned more toward the older man, "You know about Alex?"

Tourigney shrugged, "I know of him thanks to one member of the Morte Society."

"What's that?" Cardwell asked, Melissa, leaning forward to look at the old man as well. "This Morte Society."

Tourigney nodded, "The Morte Society is an organization almost as old as the vampires themselves. Its purpose is to record vampire history and keep track of their prophecies. I am part of this group and have been since shortly after I became a priest and there is another member that has transcribed a portion of one book of prophecy. It explains a bit about the Nemesis and his purpose in what is being called 'The Final Solution.' He's supposedly the one that will have the power to defeat the Master and remove that power from the Earth forever."

"And who is this person that has transcribed it?" Cardwell asked.

"His name is Patrick Brewer," Tourigney answered. "He is a teacher in Pine Ridge."

Cardwell nodded slowly and sat up straight, "This is all starting to make a little sense. The pieces are there. We just need to put them together and get to Pine Ridge."

"You'll need the Book of Aranos," Tourigney said and leaned slightly forward, ready to stand up. "I fear that the vampires will soon get in here and I would much rather have the book in the hands of someone, a human, that's trying to stop them than adding to what they already have."

He stood up and said, "Give me a moment. I have it hidden in my bedroom."

As Cardwell nodded Tourigney turned toward a door to the left of the entrance.

Cardwell's comm unit clicked and the voice of Parker filled his ear.

"Vampires approaching," Parker said. "Six of them walking down the street. There may be more."

"Engage them," Cardwell replied. "Take out as many as you can and get out if it gets too hairy. We have some vital information and we'll get out through the cemetery."

"One moment," Tourigney said as Cardwell and Melissa both stood up and drew their weapons. "You'll need the book."

As Tourigney entered his bedroom, Cardwell moved to the front of the room and looked out the window, pulling a yellowed blind back just enough to see the situation outside as the two operatives opened fire. His first instinct was to rush outside and join the fight, but the mission quickly took precedence and he stayed his ground.

A moment later, as Parker and Coleman continued to fire, backing away as the vampires drew closer, absorbing heavy damage from the powerful weapons, staggering and slowing as the silver embedded in each round. Cardwell knew it wouldn't be long before the two men were overwhelmed by a handful of vampires without backup, but there was nothing Cardwell could do. He had to get the book out of there and to this Patrick Brewer in Pine Ridge. His hand tightened around the edge of the blind and his jaw set firmly, but he remained where he was. The mission took precedence over the lives of any involved, including his own.

Tourigney returned after a moment with a large, leatherbound tome in his hands. He stopped just a couple of steps into the room, a calm expression on his face.

He held the book out and said, "Take it. This is what you need. Go out through the kitchen. The back door opens on the cemetery. It's holy ground and the vampires can't cross it. Besides, it's less than an hour until sunrise."

Cardwell took the book and said, "You're coming with us."

"I'm afraid not," Tourigney said. "I can hold them off a few minutes. I have a decoy book in the bedroom as well. They'll try to get the information from me before trying to kill me. That should give you time to reach the other side and be ready to leave when the sun comes up should there be more waiting on that side."

Cardwell shook his head slowly. He understood Tourigney's plan and appreciated his sacrifice.

"If we get into the cemetery, they won't be able to follow us," he said. "It makes no sense for you to sacrifice yourself."

Tourigney smiled wickedly and said, "I have another reason for doing this. I'm too old to continue this fight and my purpose in protecting the book is done. In my final act, I can at least aid you in your escape. Go now, before they get past your men."

Cardwell stared for a second and glanced to his left as the firing stopped and was almost immediately followed by a painful scream.

"Go," Tourigney said and waved toward the kitchen.

"Thank you," Cardwell said. "We'll do our best."

Tourigney nodded slowly as Cardwell turned and said, to Melissa, "Let's move."

She nodded and followed him through the open doorway beside the sofa and into the kitchen. As they left, Tourigney slowly crossed the living room and returned to his chair.

CHAPTER SEVEN
The Old Hotel

Kim Chandler paced the floor of the large room on the top floor of the old hotel on the south side of Pine Ridge, a decrepit structure that barely remained standing, her bare feet making no sound on the threadbare beige carpet and her naked body, pale flesh, seemed almost luminous in the pale light coming through the open window on the east side of the room, a window that had been covered with black-painted plywood to block out the morning sunlight once it had risen. Her long, blonde hair fell almost limply around her soft shoulders and her hands were clenched into fists. The expression on her rather wide face was a combination of anger and fear.

The conflicting emotions were brought about by her partner, the man who owed her a life debt, and had been on the prowl most of the night rather than sharing her bed as he'd done nearly every night for more than thirty years. She appeared to be no more than thirty herself, but the immortality granted to her when she'd awakened one night and found herself with a massive thirst for blood, human blood. She'd become a vampire more than two hundred years earlier, roughly the same time the United States had officially become a nation without foreign rule.

She'd been in another part of the world at the time, waiting in Scotland for a way to reach this new nation and begin her own reign of terror there. Unfortunately, it had taken her another twenty-five years before she'd been able to cross the Atlantic Ocean, in the hold of a cargo ship run by a group of former pirates that still had a taste for rum. She'd survived without feeding on any of them, not wanting to reveal her presence to any of them and possibly having it revealed to others, potentially the entire world, and had arrived in the port of Boston.

After spending a few years in the old city, she'd decided to move on before she was discovered. Years later, after visiting the west coast and viewing the Pacific Ocean for the first time, she'd begun traveling toward Missouri and had been crossing the desert when she'd encountered Moonshadow, a lycanthrope in dire straits. She'd taken him to shelter and provided him with food and water until he'd recovered. Her plan had been to just walk away, but he'd been adamant about remaining with her, doing his best to serve her and repay her kindness.

In more than thirty years, he still felt as if he hadn't repaid her. The bond between them had grown and he'd fallen under her thrall, taking him away from the tribe of lycanthropes that were the sworn enemies of the vampires, but an ancient pact remained in place preventing them from actively opposing each other. She wasn't completely sure how that worked or what it would take to break the treaty, but she had a strong feeling that her connection to Moonshadow, both as her lover and as one under her control, would cause problems before long.

She knew the sun would be rising soon, in an hour or so, and it was unlike him to not return so late. Her fear that something had happened to overpower him and either reveal his true nature to the locals or kill him, though that was a long shot.

She was growing anxious, hoping he would return soon, and continued pacing, her pale blue eyes narrowed and focused solely on what was ahead of her. Her back was turned to the door and she was walking away when a knock sounded on it, a fairly soft knock, but it was enough to draw her attention. She turned around and walked back to it, her jaw setting angrily at the interruption.

At the door, she unlocked and opened it, pulling it toward her, and was rewarded with the sight of Jade Hyson, one of the younger vampires brought in by the Virate, one dedicated to serving the one Kim considered physically the strongest and mentally the weakest, a massive red-haired man from Scotland named Colin McFadden. Jade was a couple of inches shorter than Kim with long, flowing soft brown hair framing a narrow face with large brown eyes that always seemed to hold a hint of fear in them. Her lean body was clad in black, as Gerrit, the ersatz leader of the Virate, had ordered for them all.

"What is it?" Kim asked, her voice a rich contralto. "It's almost sunrise."

Jade nodded and said, "Yes. Gerrit has called a meeting in the lobby. He has some details that need to be addressed before daybreak."

Kim nodded and opened her mouth to respond when a dark form shot through the open window. A massive black wolf landed almost silently on the floor and instantly transformed, taking just a couple of seconds to rise on its hind legs, the dark hair quickly retreating into the flesh beneath it, and became the naked form of Moonshadow, a muscular man with tawny skin, long, black hair, and sharp, angular features. Both Kim and Jade looked at him and Kim let out a light sigh of relief.

"It's about time," Kim said, almost scowling at him.

He shrugged and said, "Sorry. There's not a lot of game around here."

Jade took a step into the room, her expression hardening, and said, "Gerrit is waiting. We must hurry."

Kim looked at her and said, "We'll be down in a minute. Let us get dressed."

"Fine," Jade said and backed away. "Just hurry."

She turned and walked away quickly as Kim turned to face Moonshadow, an intense glare in her eyes and a firm set to her jaw.

"Where have you been, really?" she asked, placing her hands almost defiantly on her flaring hips. "I expected you back hours ago."

He looked at her, his black eyes, as dark as his hair, narrowed slightly and he asked, "Have you fed?"

"Yes," she replied. "Hours ago. Now, where were you?"

"Hunting, mostly," he replied and backed away, toward an old chair with dark clothing draped across it. "But I did scout the town a bit. It's bigger than we thought and there's a lot more going on. There shouldn't be a problem with you feeding."

He stopped at the chair and picked up the clothing, beginning to dress himself as he continued, "They're oblivious. They don't pay attention to their surroundings and never see what's really going on."

She moved to the small dresser against the wall by the door where her clothing, a black robe, lay neatly folded as she nodded and said, "That's interesting, but you could've let me know what you were doing. I was worried."

He pulled on a pair of black leather pants and said, "You weren't worried. You wanted me here to play with before the sun comes up."

"That's part of it," she said and slipped into the robe, pulling it around her body. "But this situation with the Virate is different. There's something going on that they haven't told us about. We need to be careful."

He nodded as he pulled on a thick jacket, the companion to his pants, and sat in the chair to pull on his boots, "Maybe Gerrit will tell us."

"I hope so," she said and moved slowly to the open door. "But we'd better get down there. You know how he gets."

"Right," Moonshadow nodded and stood up, starting toward the door.

Kim turned and walked out of the room, entering the upper hallway of the hotel, and turned right toward the wide stairs leading down to the spacious lobby.

It was a large open space, once luxurious and glamorous, but it had fallen into such disrepair that it felt like stepping into an old haunted house, the way humans would imagine it for some Halloween activity. The old furniture, several wide sofas and low coffee tables, were covered with thick layers of dust. The carpet, matching the carpet in the rooms, was also faded and dusty. A long counter occupied almost the entire wall to the right at the base of the stairs, also covered with dust, as were the small squares mounted to the wall behind the counter, small cubby holes intended for guests to receive mail and to leave their keys when they left the hotel for a while. The main entrance, double doors with more plywood covering the ornate glass ovals at the center of each one, making it look somewhat tacky to Kim, but she understood the need for the plywood, providing safety for their kind when the sun was in the sky. Just to the left of the stairs was the opening to a narrow hallway leading to the kitchen and a door set into the wall at roughly the halfway point along its length opened on the dining room that was almost as large as the lobby. Kim knew it had been cleared out for use as their conference room, though only six vampires and one lycanthrope were currently in residence. She knew Gerrit planned on growing their numbers, but that part of the operation hadn't yet begun.

As she reached the point of the curving staircase where she could see the lobby clearly, she saw that not all of the group was there. The first she noticed was the massive form of Dylan Ambrose, a young vampire, less than thirty years since his turning, standing six and a half feet tall with broad shoulders, thickly muscled arms and legs, and soft brown hair hanging almost to his waist. His eyes, a chocolate brown, were fairly small and remained narrowed most of the time. He stood behind the sofa facing the stairs where two of the Virate sat, seeming relaxed and confident. The tall, red-haired man was Colin McFadden and the woman on the right, almost as tall as Colin, was Rachel Thanatos, having been turned less than a decade after their presumed leader, Gerrit Jaeger, had been turned in the region now known as Germany. Rachel was a native of Greece and the heritage showed in her matte black hair and matching eyes, cold eyes, like those of a serpent and Kim knew she most definitely had many similar attributes with a viper.

The fourth one in the lobby was Jade Hyson, now standing behind the two members of the Virate and rather close to Dylan. She looked up at Kim descending the stairs with a light smirk on her face, a cocky expression that showed that she thought she knew more than Kim. It was possible and actually rather likely considering the nature of the trio that claimed to be sharing the power of the Master. They all liked to tell others that they were revealing secret information, part of the plan, but it never turned out to be anything significant. Kim, having been with them for more than a year, had learned her lesson and took anything said to her by one of them in private with a grain of salt.

At the base of the stairs, she turned toward them, angling across the thin carpet, and took a seat on a second sofa, a longer one, perpendicular to the one where those two sat.

Rachel looked at her as she sat with Moonshadow close beside her, and a wicked smile crossed her face.

"I see the wolf is still with us," Rachel said, her voice silky smooth with only a hint of her native accent. "I believe it is almost time for him to perform his duty to us."

Moonshadow nodded slowly and said, "I will begin once the sun has risen and you have taken to your hiding places."

Rachel scowled as Colin laughed, a hearty laugh, and said, "This renegade wolf isn't going to put up with your nonsense, Rachel. He is his own man."

"Yet he follows this sycophant like a little puppy," Rachel said and the smile returned to her face.

Kim bristled at the comment and her back straightened as her eyes opened wide to glare at Rachel.

"I'm no sycophant," she said. "I'm here to serve the greater cause, that's all."

Rachel gestured toward Moonshadow with her left hand as she said, "And yet you bring this ancient enemy into our midst, claiming that he will obey your commands. He has done as we've asked, but I have yet to see you issue a command to him. Perhaps he is not so completely under your control as you think."

Before Kim could reply, the double doors of the dining room swung open as Gerrit Jaeger strode through confidently and continued forward.

"Whatever his position at the moment, he will become something much more," Gerrit said as he walked over to the group and stood in a position where they could all see him clearly.

He looked them over for a second then smiled and said, "Our day is coming. The future of the vampire race, its very destiny, is at hand. The pieces of the game are falling into place and doing exactly what we need them to do. We will soon have all that we need to complete the first step in conquering this world."

"I'm ready," Colin said, grinning broadly, showing his teeth through his thick, red beard.

"Not yet," Gerrit said and looked at him, his smile fading. "There are many pieces to the puzzle and we must connect them slowly and carefully. The first has taken place. The first love of the Nemesis has begun the conversion process and he has received the information. He will soon arrive and do his best, with the help of his pathetic little team, to cure her and stop us, but they will be able to do nothing. We will continue to follow the Plan of Aranos, adapting it to the modern world, and we will eventually control everything. But we must be patient. This will take time, but we have all the time in the world, literally."

They all nodded at that, bringing a smile to Colin's face, and Gerrit continued, "We must wait through another day. The sun will rise soon and we must rest. When darkness falls again, our servant will arrive with information. He is watching this woman and will tell us everything taking place around her. She has been hospitalized and will most likely remain so for at least two days, possibly longer. We will take that time to solidify our position in this town and begin creating converts."

He looked at Moonshadow and said, "You, our shape-changing ally, it will be your mission to locate suitable subjects and bring them to our attention. Do not bring them here, to us. This location must continue to be forgotten by the residents of this town. Any activity will draw their attention and that could jeopardize our plan, or at least alter it in such a way that it will take even longer."

Moonshadow nodded, "I understand."

"Rachel," he said and looked at her. "You will continue your work in translating the Book of Aranos, specifically the details of his plan. We must have the next steps before we can progress."

She nodded, "I'm doing the best I can. Aranos reigned as Master for a very long time and the language changed quite frequently during that time. It is a struggle to decipher it since he has combined many of these languages in each sentence."

"Understood," Gerrit nodded. "Do your best, but don't waste time."

"I will give it my greatest effort," she said.

Gerrit turned to Colin and said, "Our new home is secure at the moment. I wish it to remain that way. It is your responsibility and I will hold you accountable."

Colin nodded, a touch of anger in his deep green eyes. They shared the power of the Master and Gerrit acted as if he was the sole possessor of that power. He could accept it for the moment, but he knew he wouldn't be able to hold his tongue forever.

Gerrit shifted his gaze to the two behind the sofa, "Dylan and Jade, our newest converts. You will continue as you have, protecting this place and preparing what is needed."

They both nodded and Gerrit shifted his gaze to Kim, "You served Davors and now you serve us. Once Moonshadow has located suitable subjects, it will be your responsibility to bring them to a place where we can feed."

"Of course," Kim nodded.

"Good," he said and took a step back. "We will continue working toward our goal and I expect you all to pull your share of the weight. If so, we will succeed and this world will be ours. Now, the sun will rise shortly and we must prepare. Go to your resting places."

He turned and walked back into the dining room. There was no conversation following his departure. There was nothing to discuss. The four seated rose from the sofas and moved away from the center of the lobby, moving in different directions, as Dylan and Jade followed Kim and Moonshadow to the stairs.

CHAPTER EIGHT
Shift Change

Lois Cashlin sat behind the desk in the front office of the Pine Ridge Police Department, having arrived for the morning shift an hour or so earlier, and she was bored as she watched two of the day shift officers, Evan Barker and Monia Halpern, wait for the return of Hal Martino and Raquel Jackson to officially relieve them and allow them to go home.

Evan was fairly tall, standing just under six feet, with a lean build and short, dark blond hair framing a face that almost always had a mischievous smile that caused his deep brown eyes to narrow quite a bit. Monica was nearly a foot shorter, barely reaching five feet tall, with long, platinum blond hair, an obvious dye job to Lois, a narrow face, sharp features, wide brown eyes, full lips, and a soft, voluptuous body that often made Lois wonder if she and Evan had something going on the side, or if they neglected their duty for a while to engage in some sort of carnal activity while on the clock. She had no proof, but the way they interacted was enough for her to consider it a possibility.

Lois didn't pay attention to their conversation. She didn't want to know any more about their relationship or what they did during their off time. Like most of the others, she just wanted to do her job, finish her shift, and go home. Of course, there was no one waiting there for her and she would spend the night alone. She wanted someone to go home to, but there really weren't many options in Pine Ridge at that time. It was getting boring and the loneliness seemed to build each night she spent alone, making her a little more desperate, but she had enough sense to stay away from the guys that would undoubtedly cause trouble and make her life miserable, even more miserable than it was being alone.

She tried to focus on the computer facing her, angled slightly toward her from the right, but she couldn't help seeing the motion of the two officers pacing the lobby of the building. Evan had a cup of coffee in his left hand, sipping occasionally as he walked back and forth across the wide room. Monica sat on one of the hard plastic chairs against the front wall, each a different color and connected to a long metal bar beneath the seats. She watched Evan as he walked and spouted some nonsense about how things were going terribly wrong in the town and the force needed to hire more officers.

Monica knew Chief Baker had been trying to hire more officers, qualified and capable officers, but the few applicants that had shown up were far from either. She was thankful that he wouldn't hire just anyone, and wouldn't accept less qualified personnel just to fill the vacant spots. It gave her faith that he was the competent and professional law enforcement officer he seemed to be, but she also knew there was something else there that had reduced the force to the four patrol officers and the small staff. She assumed the force had been larger before her hiring, roughly six months earlier, but no one was talking about why the others had left. She wanted to know why so many people had left the department, but she was afraid to ask.

Evan had been there longer, for almost ten years, and she'd tried bringing up the subject with him, but he wouldn't say anything about it. There had to be something major, some huge reason why the department had fallen apart, and the curiosity remained with her no matter how much she tried to just get over it and do her job.

Lois finished everything she could on the computer and no longer had an excuse to ignore the two officers and their conversation. She didn't want to get involved in what they were talking about, but she knew, as usual, that it would soon land on her desk and she would be forced to respond. It actually took only a moment for Evan to sense that she had no more work to do and was available.

"What do you think?" he asked, turning and walking slowly toward her with a sly smile, a lopsided one, on his face.

Lois leaned forward, resting her elbows on the desk, and asked, "About what?"

He stopped a few feet from the desk and said, "The way the shifts are run. Shouldn't we alternate days and nights? I mean, I'm getting tired of waking up at the crack of dawn."

Monica rose to her feet and approached the desk as well, scowling at Evan, then looked at Lois and said, "He's an idiot. I'd rather get up early every day than have to work double shifts during the change. It's bad enough working twelve-hour shifts as it is. I damn sure don't want to work twenty-four."

Evan looked at her over his shoulder and said, "But then we'd have a full day off when the shifts change back."

Monica shook her head, "It's just not worth it. Hell, I'd probably sleep through the whole day just to get ready to go back to work. I don't want that."

"She's right," Lois said and shrugged. "That's a lot of effort for no real rewards."

"Whatever," Evan said and backed away, shaking his head.

Monica looked at Lois and said, "He doesn't make any sense, but he's a good man under the surface of an idiot."

Lois chuckled and smirked, "I guess you'd know better than I would."

Monica started to say something, but she stopped with her mouth slightly open. After a second, she backed away and turned toward Evan just as the front door opened and the shift change began.

Hal held the door open for Raquel as she strode forward tiredly, shaking her head slowly. Hal followed her in and they stopped near the center of the lobby as Evan and Monica turned to face them.

"That was one hell of a night," Hal said through a tired sigh.

Lois nodded, "I heard about the attack. What happened, exactly?"

Raquel shook her head and took a slow step forward. Her normally bright hazel eyes seemed rather dull with the trauma and intensity of the episode. Her full lips appeared strange with a frown instead of her usual smile or the tightly pressed look of her "business face." She looked afraid and that was something Lois had never seen from the woman.

"It was horrible," she said. "We received the call and arrived at the address less than five minutes after the call. She was laid out on the front lawn, spread out with her head turned to one side. At first, we thought she was dead, but I checked and she was still breathing. I did the best I could to check her vitals and her pulse was a little slow, but she was still alive. There was blood all over her throat, her blood, and we couldn't find a cut or anything. It was weird."

She stopped at the desk and placed her hands on the edge, the typically manicured fingernails looked a little rough, as if she'd done quite a bit of manual labor, and she looked Lois in the eye.

"The EMTs showed up and took over, but Shafer was there, and the ME. Roth didn't stay very long, though. He thought he was there to declare her and was pissed off when he found out she was alive. Shafer stayed until it was all over and she was taken away. We really didn't do much after checking her out, but it was the worst thing that's happened in a long time."

Lois frowned, "Where was she injured? Where did the blood come from?"

Raquel took a step back and shrugged, "No idea. The EMTs checked her out and they couldn't find an injury. That should've been a good thing, but it was just too weird and creepy."

"Who is she?" Lois asked, her eyes widening slightly.

Raquel shrugged, "They took her to the hospital and we haven't been to check on her yet. We had a few other calls, but nothing major and no arrests."

Lois nodded, "I assumed that. There weren't any reports on my desk this morning."

Raquel shrugged, "We haven't gotten around to filling out the report yet."

"Yeah," Hal said and stepped up beside her. "We've been a little busy."

"Yeah, well," Evan said and took a step toward the door. "I guess that makes the shift change official."

"Pretty much," Hal said and glanced over his shoulder. "Have fun."

Evan waved over his shoulder as he moved to the door. Monica followed him, shaking her head at him once again, and said, "You guys take care."

Hal and Raquel looked over their shoulders and nodded almost in unison as Monica looked away and walked out the door, following Evan.

Once they were gone and the door closed, Raquel moved closer to Lois and asked, "Have you heard from the chief? Is he coming in?"

"Of course," Lois replied. "He's running a little late and stopped to get breakfast."

Raquel nodded, "Okay. I'm going to get out of this turtle shell."

"Yeah," Hal agreed, stepping up beside his partner. "Me, too."

Lois just nodded as they moved to the end of the counter and opened the door set in the corner of the lobby, entering the main portion of the station.

Once the door closed behind them, Lois sat back and began the process of assimilating the information she'd received. She didn't have all the details yet, but she was sure either one of the two officers or the chief, Walt Baker, would let her in on the details soon enough. They did so every time. Besides, she was not only the receptionist, she was also the secretary, notary public, and sounding board.

It wasn't long before the front door opened again, but it wasn't the arrival of the chief. Lois was a bit surprised to see the department's sole investigator, Neil Shafer, walk through the door. He looked a little rough around the edges, as if he hadn't slept well and was still dressed in what he'd worn the previous day.

"Morning," she said as he entered slowly, his shoulders sagging with exhaustion.

His pale blue eyes were narrowed and his face was tight with either exhaustion or anger. He shook his head as he walked slowly across the lobby toward the door where the other two officers had entered.

"Morning," he grumbled, his voice thick and raspy. "Chief in yet?"

"No," Lois shook her head. "He's on his way."

Shafer nodded slowly, "I'll wait in the back. I'm sure there's coffee."

"Yep," she replied as he reached the door. "As always."

"Thanks," he said tiredly and walked through the door.

He found the coffee brewed and waiting in the large room considered the squad room, though there was no real squad to use it. The only officers on duty would be on patrol for most of their shifts and would be there only long enough to write out and file their incident reports, if there were any to be filed. The night shift squad car, one of three the department owned, was parked outside, in the last space in the building's overly large parking lot. Shafer didn't know if there wasn't that much crime or that many issues in Pine Ridge, but the lot designed to hold a large number of vehicles was rarely used and never anything approaching capacity.

He poured a cup using one of the ceramic mugs placed upside down on a towel beside the machine and drank it black, savoring the bitter taste and the brief rush the caffeine brought to him. It wasn't enough to fully wake him up, but it was a start.

He stood there, slowly sipping the hot liquid, and reflected on the events of the previous night, the disturbing nature of the situation that had kept him from a decent few hours of sleep. He was still thinking about it, running through the events in his mind, when the Chief of Police, Walt Baker, entered the squad room with the unexpected presence of May Jay Downing behind him.

Walt Baker was a tall man in his mid-sixties with neatly trimmed and styled gray hair framing a craggy, lined face with narrow blue eyes that at times appeared almost white. He was dressed in his dark blue uniform, but he carried no sidearm. He didn't feel it appropriate for the chief, representing the department at public functions, to be seen carrying a weapon. Shafer didn't agree with that, but Walt was the chief and it was his call.

The mayor stood a good three inches shorter than the chief, a bit rounder with softer features and short, mouse-brown hair and heavy jowls. He wore thick, wire-framed glasses and wore a dark gray suit with a white shirt, maroon tie, and shiny black shoes.

"Mr. Mayor," Shafer said and lifted his mug toward the man. "Chief. Good morning."

Walt stopped several feet from Shafer, between two rarely used desks, and placed his hands on his hips, his growing gut stretching his uniform shirt a bit, then said, "I'd hardly say it's a good morning, Shafer."

"Right," Shafer nodded. "Just habit, I guess."

Downing stopped just behind the chief, a bit to his right, and looked at Shafer, "I heard you were involved in this incident last night."

"I was there," Shafer nodded and took a quick sip of the coffee. "I'm on the same redial service as the patrol officers. I heard the call and responded. Martino and Jackson were already there when I arrived. So were the EMTs and they were already working on the victim. The ME was there as well, but he didn't stick around very long."

"I see," Walt nodded slowly. "Tell me what you saw."

Shafer shrugged and said, "It wasn't much. The victim was unconscious and the only details came from the neighbors. The duty officers took their statements. I didn't talk to them. I stayed until the EMTs loaded her in the ambulance and took her to the hospital."

Downing frowned, "Didn't you follow them to the hospital?"

Shafer shook his head and looked at the mayor, "No, I didn't. There was no sense in it. They'd get her there and the emergency room staff would deal with her and that would take a while. I assume she was admitted, but I haven't checked yet this morning."

"Do that," Walt said. "Call the hospital and, if she's there, go get a statement. I'll talk to Martino and Jackson and get their report. Just keep your phone with you and answer it when I call this time."

"I will," Shafer nodded and took another sip, the coffee starting to cool.

Walt then nodded, dropped his hands from his hips, and started forward, "The mayor and I have a few things to discuss. We'll be in my office for a while, but I'll have my cell with me."

"Will do, chief," Shafer replied as Jay Downing followed Walt toward the back of the station.

"Good to see you, Mr. Mayor," Shafer said with a nod as the shorter man walked past.

Downing only nodded in response and walked quickly after Walt. Shafer drained the last of the coffee, placed the mug on the towel beside the coffee maker, knowing Lois preferred to wash them herself, then turned to his right and walked toward his office at the corner of the squad room to begin his day's work.

CHAPTER NINE
The Hospital

The old black pickup entered the parking lot across the wide street, Bender Street, that ran in a pair of curves around the semi-circle driveway at the front of the massive building. The truck's roaring engine and distinct rattles of something loose beneath the chassis drew attention from the few people walking around, pedestrians moving toward either the hospital, the new pharmacy to the south, or the small shopping center to the north that held a medical supply store and a gift shop with slightly cheaper prices than the hospital's gift and provided floral services as well. It entered the lot from the narrow street behind it, separating it from a small clinic and a store selling medical clothing at discount prices, and rolled slowly to a parking space close to Bender Street. It sat there for a moment, idling roughly, before the driver shut off the engine and the driver's door opened.

Ben Mills, tall and muscular, with short brown hair, an almost swarthy face, and small, brown eyes, wore a tight black t-shirt beneath a red-and-black flannel shirt open and the front with the tail hanging well below his waist, covering the faded jeans with a few oil stains here and there. His black work boots, scuffed and faded from nearly two years of constant use, thudded against the asphalt of the lot as he dropped from the tall truck.

On the other side, the passenger's door opened slowly, almost carefully, and Tiffany Gardner, short and lean, with long, neatly styled light brown hair and wide, hazel eyes, was dressed in jeans and a loose, gray t-shirt almost hidden beneath the dark blue jacket she wore zipped up almost to her chin. The jacket was a little tight and showed off her figure rather well. She was proud of her body and how far it had gotten her, especially claiming Brad as her one and only.

Tiffany dropped the asphalt, her knees bending in a practiced way from having done so on many occasions and her pristine white tennis shoes helped absorb the shock as well. She held a small purse against her side with a long, narrow strap slung over her right shoulder and stood up as she landed then turned around to close the heavy door. She hated the massive truck and hated being so short it was difficult for her to climb in and get out, but it was Ben's baby, one he'd been working on for almost three years, refurbishing and upgrading. She just hoped he would eventually get finished with it and maybe spend a little of the time he'd been spending on the truck with her.

She walked around the front of the truck and found Ben standing there, waiting for her, but the look of impatience on his face told her again that he didn't want to be there. He didn't like Dana, thought she was a pitiful excuse for a woman, and needed to just get her act together and find the right man instead of waiting on a high school boyfriend who had deserted her years earlier and definitely wasn't coming back. He felt she was stuck in the past and wouldn't accept that life moves on, and the world moves on. Tiffany didn't agree. She and Dana had been best friends since high school and they'd all known Alex. Ben had never really liked him, thought he was too arrogant and proud, but Tiffany knew Alex's attitude came from his time as a football player, the attitude the coaches instilled in the players and the recognition the players received from most of the students and a large portion of the public. Alex hadn't quite been like the rest of them, and had seemed a little more normal, but Ben hadn't seen that.

Still, Ben supported Tiffany the best he could when it came to Dana. She'd tried over the years to help her get over Alex and convince her that he wasn't coming back. No one in Pine Ridge had heard from him in over fifteen years and Tiffany was certain he'd moved on, found another woman, and settled down somewhere. She'd tried setting her up with guys she met, either at work or at the bar she frequented at Ben's insistence, but none of them had measured up so far. Dana had told her about a guy she'd met at work, a foreign businessman who was in the process of setting up a company in the area, but Tiffany hadn't met him. Dana had seemed to be completely enamored of him and thought they had a future together. If that was true, she figured he would be at the hospital sooner or later to show his support.

Ben took her hand as they met at the front of the truck and started toward the hospital's front entrance. He didn't say anything as they crossed in the wide crosswalk, stopping the flow of traffic that was always fairly heavy along Bender Street, leading from the end of the new business district on the west end of town and the mall a little over a mile to the north. Once across, they moved to the entrance and entered the building, making their way to the elevators at the back of the lobby without consulting the volunteer hostess at the desk to the left of the entrance. Tiffany knew which room Dana had been given and didn't need assistance in locating it since she'd been in the building on numerous occasions.

As they entered, Tiffany focused on the elevators and Ben looked around the spacious, lushly decorated lobby and the openings to a couple of hallways to the right, one leading to small offices and payment counters with the gift shop at the far end with the other leading to larger offices and the cafeteria. As he turned his head to look along the second one, with its rear wall also containing the twin elevator doors, he saw someone move, backing away from the corner and he frowned as he recognized the pale, flushed face and mop of unkempt bright red hair over a soft body.

"What's he doing here?" Ben asked, shaking his head.

"Who?" Tiffany asked, looking around.

"Sullivan," Ben replied and nodded toward the long hallway. "I saw Ryan Sullivan over there. You think he had something to do with what happened to Dana?"

"No," Tiffany shook her head and pushed the button to call the elevator. "I'm sure he still has a big crush on her, but he wouldn't hurt her. He wants something different."

"Yeah," Ben smirked. "And he's not going to get it."

Tiffany just shook her head as a light ding sounded with the arrival of the elevator and the opening of the door.

As Tiffany and Ben entered the hospital, Dana Richland lay on a narrow bed with a thin sheet pulled up almost to her chin. Beneath it, she wore only the standard hospital gown and a pair of panties, the same ones she'd been wearing when attacked the night before. She was awake but felt tired and groggy. Her hair felt nasty, remaining unwashed since leaving work the previous night, and clung to her skull, pulled back from her face which was now pale and gaunt. Her eyes stood out more than usual, but she couldn't see. There was no mirror available and she didn't want one. She didn't want to see how she looked. Besides, she was too tired and sore, especially the left side of her neck.

Part of the night, the last part, was a blur. She remembered the long walk home and the sudden appearance of Gerrit as she'd approached her front door. She remembered bits of their conversation and an impression of fear and loss of trust, but she couldn't recall the details. The last thing she could remember was him moving closer to her and opening his mouth wide, almost too wide, as he moved in to kiss her neck. He hadn't done that before, hadn't kissed her before, but she liked the idea. There was a brief memory of pain, a sharp and piercing pain, and nothing else after that.

She'd been left alone in the room since shortly after being admitted, after the doctors and nurses in the emergency room had done all they could. Of course, nothing was really explained to her and that left her more frightened than anything else. She began to think of how much else could go wrong in her life. A hospital stay would just add to her monthly bills and, without the proper insurance, she would be paying on it for years. With no one to talk to, her thoughts ran wild and she wondered if she was dying, how long it would take, and how painful it would be. If she wasn't dying, the pain would last for years, the pain of paying even more bills, including the hospital stay, follow-up doctor visits, and most likely a huge amount of pharmaceuticals. There was no way she could ever be able to afford all of that and her recovery, without those things, would take years, probably more years than she had left.

The attending physician, Dr. Ross Brinson, had entered the room with a nurse, Angelica Norris, not long after the sun rose and she'd awakened. Dr. Brinson, a short, stocky man with graying dark brown hair cut short and brushed back from his high forehead, pulled a chair to one side of the bed while Angelica, nearly the same height with dark brown hair just as short, framing a diamond-shaped face with a broad, almost flat nose, widely spaced brown eyes, and thin lips creating a straight line just above her sharp chin, moved to the other side of the bed and began checking her vital functions.

As Ross sat down and let out a tired sigh, his dark, red-rimmed eyes narrowed with the tiredness he felt, he shifted the chair a little closer and said, "Ms. Richland, I'm Dr. Brinson and I'll be looking after you. I've been reading your chart for the past half hour and I just can't figure out what happened to you. You lost a lot of blood, but there's no sign of injury, no wound where the blood could've escaped. To be honest, it's really confusing me. I've never seen anything like this."

Dana nodded the best she could, her neck not quite cooperating, and said, her voice little more than a croak, "I don't know. I can't remember."

"That's understandable," he nodded. "Your neighbors said you were attacked and such trauma can affect your short-term memory."

She nodded slowly, carefully, and he continued, "We've given you a transfusion, but you still seem rather anemic. I don't understand that, but we'll run some tests to see if we can figure out a cause for that. In the meantime, we'll keep you on an IV. I hesitate to give you any sort of pain medication, not knowing how your blood chemistry will react."

"It's okay," she croaked. "I'm not hurting, just tired and weak."

Brinson nodded and sat back, "Okay. We'll give it a day or so, let you rest and recuperate a bit, then we'll try running some tests. We're also assigning an occupation therapist to at least give you some options once you're discharged. Her name is Gina Filmore and she's good at her job, but she will seem a little, I don't know, flighty."

He smiled at that and she did her best to return it, seeing the little bit of humor in his statement.

He leaned forward then, starting to stand, and said, "I guess I'll let you get some rest, unless Ms. Norris has something to say about it."

Angelica finished taking her readings, looked at Brinson, and said, "I'm finished. It all looks pretty good, but blood pressure and body temperature are a little low."

"That's to be expected," Brinson said and stood up, looking from Angelia to Dana. "You just get some rest and I'll check on you later."

As he backed away from the bed, giving her his warmest reassuring smile, the door swung open as Tiffany and Ben entered the room.

Brinson and Angelica excused themselves and left the room as Tiffany and Ben moved closer to the bed. Tiffany sat down beside the bed in the chair where Brinson had been sitting and Ben moved to the other side of the room and another chair positioned beside the door that led to the small bathroom in the corner beside the entrance.

As Tiffany began doing her best to console Dana and started asking questions about the attack that Dana couldn't recall, a small, gray car pulled into the lot across the street, parked near the center of the lot, and four people climbed out. Scott Bonacci and Krista Deninger exited the front seat while Alex Chance and DeAnna Jones climbed from the back. Alex, the tallest of them and the one forced to endure cramped riding conditions, stood up and stretched before the quartet started for the entrance.

As they walked, Bonacci and Deninger leading the way, DeAnna walked beside Alex, almost matching the length of his stride, and looked at him as she said, "This victim was your high school girlfriend."

"Yeah," he replied. "That was a long time ago and I really don't want to talk about it."

DeAnna nodded, "I understand. I'm just curious if that's our only reason for being here."

"No," Alex looked at her, scowling. "You heard the report. It was reported as a vampire attack. That's why we're here. It doesn't matter who the victim is."

DeAnna nodded again and fell silent. They crossed the street quickly and walked along the wide concrete walkway at the center of a grassy area leading to the covered drive at the front of the building, and through the automatic sliding glass doors of the entrance.

As the doors closed behind them, Alex took the lead, vaguely remembering the layout of the building, but it had been almost sixteen years since he'd been inside and it had changed quite a bit.

"The elevator should be straight ahead," he said, pointing forward with his left hand. "Unless they've redesigned the whole place."

"Alex?" a voice said from the side. "Is it really you?"

Alex stopped and turned to his right, frowning, then his eyes opened wide at the sight of a shorter man walking toward them, a familiar face, though older and with hair having gone almost completely gray.

"Dr. Brewer?" he asked. "Is that you?"

"Yes," Dr. Patrick Brewer nodded and grinned, walking a little more quickly. "I expected you to show up for some reason."

Alex drew in a sharp breath and nodded, "You know what's going on."

"Yes," Brewer nodded as he stopped in front of Alex. "I've known since you were in high school and the changes started happening. I wanted to tell you, but I was forbidden."

Alex stared at his former teacher for a few seconds then said, "We don't have time to get into that right now. We need to check on Dana and make sure it was an attack."

"Of course," Brewer nodded. "She's on the fifth floor. I believe Tiffany Gardner and Ben Mills are with her now."

Alex shook his head, "Wow. I haven't thought about them since I left. I guess Dana and Tiffany are still best friends."

"Of course," Brewer nodded as they resumed walking. "I've seen them at several football games. They still keep to their old traditions and still support the school."

The other three were already at the elevators and had one of the two sets of doors open. Bonacci stood in the doorway, keeping doors from closing, and tilted his head to the left as he said, "Come on, Chance. I can't hold this open forever."

Alex shook his head and the two of them walked quickly to the elevator and entered the car as Bonacci stepped back and allowed the doors to close.

Introductions were made on the brief ride and that left no time for any discussion of the situation. The doors opened on the fifth floor and they left the elevator quickly. There was a bit of confusion on three of their faces as they looked around to figure out where to go next until Brewer stepped forward and gestured down the wide hallway.

"This way," he said. "Her room is near the end on the left."

They started walking with Brewer leading the way. They'd taken just a few steps when the cell phone in Alex's pocket began to ring. He scowled and quickly pulled it out, looking at the screen and the caller ID flashing across it.

"Cardwell," he said and stopped as the others stopped and looked back at him. "You go ahead. I'll talk to him."

Bonacci nodded and resumed walking with the others following suit.

Alex tapped the screen then held the phone to his ear and said simply, "Yes."

"Chance," the voice of Cardwell came to him. "Where are you?"

"Pine Ridge," he replied. "We just entered the hospital and on our way to Dana's room."

"Good," Cardwell said. "Dyson and I are about twenty minutes out of Pine Ridge."

Alex frowned, "Just the two of you?"

"Yes," Cardwell answered after a brief pause. "Parker and Coleman were taken. I don't know if they were killed or if they're being turned."

"Not good," Alex said. "What should we do?"

"Stay there," Cardwell said coldly, all business. "We'll come to you. I'm calling Sydney, Jana, and Merina to come in tonight. I don't know if anything Sydney has will help Dana, but it's worth a shot. Things seem to be centering on that town and we need to be there and ready. Also, Caroline gave us some information from a contact in Pine Ridge, a man named Brewer. We need to track him down and get more info from him."

"He's here," Alex said. "He was in the lobby when we walked in. He's an old friend."

Cardwell was silent for a second then said, "Okay. Keep him there until I can talk to him. I'm probably going to need Caroline as well. Hell, we should probably just bring in the whole team."

"Right," Alex nodded. "But I think it might be best to leave someone there to keep the place secure. We can handle things here."

Cardwell replied, "Okay. I'll have the security team remain in place and I don't think we need the military response just yet, but everyone else will come to us. It'll be later. The President and the senator chairing the committee that's funding us are visiting this morning. They'll be free to leave once that's over. Now get in there and talk to Dana. See what you can figure out."

"I'll do it," Alex said with a nod. "And we're on the fifth floor, by the way."

"Right," Cardwell said and Alex could almost hear his curt nod in the response. "We'll be there in about thirty."

Alex ended the call and returned the phone to his pocket then walked toward the room at the far end of the hall. He felt a bit of trepidation about seeing Dana for the first time in almost sixteen years. He knew he owed her a huge apology for the way he'd just disappeared and hoped she would understand once he told her everything that had happened, especially if the attack on her was what they believed it to be. It was going to be tough facing her after so long, but he was no longer that eighteen-year-old kid who had run away to the military because he didn't know what was going on with himself at the time. Thinking about his departure from her and the town of Pine Ridge all those years ago and his reasoning for doing so made him realize that he'd done the same thing when he'd walked away from the task force after the death of Davors, the Master of vampires. He'd wanted to get away, to try and live a life that had nothing to do with vampires, but it hadn't turned out that way and he'd now returned home, to both of his homes, and he had to face the consequences of both.

He reached the room at the end of the hall and could hear a few voices inside. He paused at the door, took a deep breath, and pushed the door open. As he crossed the threshold, he saw Dana, the one-time love of his life for the first time as an adult.

"Alex," she said, her voice weak and barely above a whisper. "You're really here."

"Yeah," he said and moved slowly forward, letting the door swing closed behind him. "It's about time I tell you everything that's happened."

"I'm ready," she said. "Tell me everything."

"Come on," Dr. Brewer said, standing on the left side of the bed beside Tiffany and Ben with Bonacci and Deninger on the right side. "Let's get out of here so they can talk."

With nods, they began moving toward the door.

As he passed Alex, Bonacci looked at him and said, "We'll be in the hall if you need us."

Alex just nodded as they left the room and the door closed behind them.

Then he sat down beside Dana and told her everything.

CHAPTER TEN
The Visit

The motorcade of four shiny black vehicles with darkly tinted windows pulled up to the front of the old building that was home to the DSA task force. The first vehicle, a massive SUV, pulled past the entrance and stopped with the long limousine behind it stopping at the entrance with a third SUV stopping behind it and the fourth pulling alongside it. The vehicles idled for a moment then the engines of the three parked directly in front of the building while the fourth remained running.

Once the engines stopped, the doors of the SUVs were flung open and a Secret Service agent leaped from each open door. The first out was Martin Raymond, the Presidential detail's lead agent. He stood up wearing a black suit with matching tie and white shirt. His eyes were covered with dark sunglasses and a translucent, coiled wire ran from his right ear to the small transceiver attached to the belt at his waist. He was a tall, massive African-American man with a tight cap of black hair, cut above his ears in military fashion. He'd been part of the detail for over a decade and the lead agent for almost three years, since President Memory Hutchins had been inaugurated. She'd personally chosen him over others with more seniority and he was not going to let her down.

The visit to this decrepit facility, home to a DSA task force he'd barely heard of, seemed like a bad idea. It was in a fairly deserted part of the city, on the outskirts to the south, and he feared those who disagreed with the President's policies might use the opportunity and the remote location to attack her. They might attempt to attack, but he would let it get no further than an attempt.

The President was the first to exit the limo with her Chief of Staff, Stephanie Kenton, following and they both moved forward as the other two began climbing from the vehicle. First was Senator Theda Howland and last was Kevin Burns Director of the Domestic Security Agency. As Martin looked around, checking out their surroundings, he couldn't help taking a glance at his four charges.

The three women were all roughly the same height, no more than an inch separating any two of them. The President and Stephanie were both blondes, long hair flowing over their shoulders, the President with dark blue eyes set in a soft face with wide lips providing an even wider smile. Stephanie was a bit thinner, her face narrower, and her eyes a dark brown. Both were dressed in sensible dark blue dresses, almost matching. Theda Howland was older, well into her sixties, and had been part of the senate for almost thirty years. Her body was growing soft with age, but there was still fire in her soft brown eyes and an intensity on her wrinkled face. Her short hair, a steely gray, just fit her perfectly as did the pale gray pantsuit she wore beneath a long, black sweater.

But it was Kevin Burns that drew Martin's attention and respect almost equal to that of the President. He was also a tall Black man, dressed in an expensive dark blue suit with a silk tie that probably cost more than the amount of Martin's monthly paycheck.

Once he finished scanning the area and seeing no potential threats, he looked to Memory for his next move. As he did, she nodded and smiled.

"Lead the way, Martin," she said.

"Yes, ma'am," he said and started for the building's entrance with the foursome behind him.

As they walked, he triggered his transceiver with a small device in his right hand and said, "Set up a perimeter on the entrance. Mobile unit, begin patrol."

When the other agents, all twelve of them, replied, he relaxed just a bit and focused his attention on the potential for trouble waiting inside the building.

As they approached the entrance, the door swung open and a tall man with graying hair held it open.

Paul Sandusky nodded and smiled the best he could as he said, "Welcome, Madame President. Please, come inside, all of you."

Memory nodded her reaction and they entered the building, Burns nodding to Sandusky as he walked past.

The lighting in the building's lobby was quite a bit dimmer than the sunlight outside and it took a moment to adjust. As Sandusky closed and locked the door behind them, the President's entourage faced the eight members of the task force.

Burns looked around quickly then focused on Sandusky, walking to join the others, and asked, "Where's Cardwell?"

Sandusky stopped beside Caroline, at the end of the line, and said, "He's on assignment. There's a situation brewing in an area close to New Orleans and he left suddenly to speak with a contact there."

Burns nodded, frowning, and Theda Howland shook her head sharply, "That's one hell of a note. We come to see this supposedly vital organization Cardwell created, to think about giving him more money, and he's not even here."

"I'm sorry, Madame Senator," Sandusky said as pleasingly as he could. "It couldn't be helped."

"Never mind all that," Memory said, waving her left hand dismissively. "Tell me who we have here. I'm just sorry Penny couldn't be here to meet everyone as well. The Vice-President is looking after things while I'm here."

"Of course," Sandusky said with a sharp nod then moved along the line as he introduced each one. "Caroline Parrish is our Administrative Assistant. She's also part of our intelligence operation. Merina Janek, our Technical Director and inventor. She keeps our equipment up to date and sometimes more advanced. Dr. Sydney Lawson is our R&D Director. She works with Merina in developing new technology as well as researching a possible cure for this situation we're facing. Jana Hendricks is our primary Lab Technician and she works closely with Sydney in several aspects of our operation. Dr. Bonnie Stowers is our resident Therapist and shoulder to cry on. She's kept the insertion team functioning for much longer than we thought would be necessary."

Memory interrupted, "I'm familiar with her work. Bonnie and I have met before."

Bonnie nodded to the President, smiling warmly.

Sandusky then continued, "Our primary Security Officers, Steve Wolverton and Nicole Jennings. They keep this facility safe and secure. And finally, Colonel Matthew Vincent, our liaison with the military. He aids us in acquiring the equipment we need."

"I see," Theda said and nodded slowly. "This is where the money goes and still you have to beg, borrow, and steal from the legitimate military."

"It's not quite like that," Sandusky replied, looking at her, his expression growing a bit cold. "We do occasionally borrow some equipment and we always return it, unless it's been damaged. Then, we either pay for repair or replacement."

Theda glared at him for a second then asked, "Where is this insertion team? Shouldn't they be here, ready to go into action when the vampires attack?"

Sandusky chose to ignore the verbal barb and said, "They're in the south as well. An incident occurred in a small Mississippi town and they're in the process of dealing with it."

"What sort of incident?" Memory asked, frowning as she leaned slightly forward.

Sandusky nodded and replied, "There was an attack on a woman in the town of Pine Ridge, the hometown of our lead operative, Alex Chance, and the woman happened to be his high school girlfriend."

"So," Theda said loudly, her head tilting back slightly. "You send this entire team to some little town just so this Alex Chance can go spend time with his girlfriend."

"No," Sandusky shook his head. "It's not like that. Alex hasn't seen or spoken to this woman in over fifteen years. He's there to assess the situation and determine if there's actually been a vampire attack."

"There hasn't," Theda said. "Vampires don't exist. It's as simple as that. You people are wasting our time and the taxpayers' money. I think this entire operation needs to be shut down."

Memory turned to face her and held up her hands, "Let's not be hasty, Theda. We don't have all the facts."

Theda glared at Memory and said, "You allowed this to happen. You let this Cardwell talk you into funding this thing so he'd have a job. He must've been some sort of paper pusher before this."

"No, ma'am," Kevin Burns said and stepped forward, looking at her. "I've known and worked with Cardwell for years. He's a decorated DSA operative and leader. I haven't seen any hard evidence that vampires exist, but I take Cardwell at his word. I believe there is something going on in this country and perhaps his investigation into vampires will lead us to the truth."

Memory then looked at Sandusky and said, "This is what I'm going to offer. I'll give you a month to provide hard evidence that vampires exist and that they're a threat to this nation. When you do, I'll approve all the funding you could ever want."

Sandusky nodded, "We can't ask for anything more."

"Sure you can," Theda said and smirked. "You could ask for the run of the country, but I'll go along with the President's idea. You provide the proof and we'll provide the money."

"Thank you," Sandusky said and looked from Theda to Memory. "Thank you both."

"Okay," Memory said. "Now show us around the facility so we can see what we're working with."

Sandusky turned his upper body toward the line and said, "Caroline knows the facility and she'll show you around then bring you back here if you have any questions or other concerns."

"That'll be fine," Memory said and smiled at Caroline. "Show us what you have."

Caroline stepped forward, smiling, and said, "If you'll follow me, please."

Caroline walked away down the wide central hallway and the President's entourage followed closely. Once they were out of earshot, Sandusky turned to the others.

"I received a call from Cardwell a few moments ago," he said. "Things are apparently getting rather heated down there and they need help. We're all going to Pine Ridge to help with this situation."

He looked at Steve and Nicole, "You two will remain here and keep the place secure."

They nodded in agreement and looked at Matthew, "I'm sorry, Matt, but he doesn't think you'll be needed just yet. He wants you to stay here as well and be ready to get things going when he needs them."

"I can do that," Matthew responded with a sharp nod.

"Good," Sandusky said and Sydney took a step forward, turning to face him.

"I guess he's counting on the serum to help this woman," she said, frowning lightly. "But it isn't ready. What we have doesn't work."

"I don't know," Sandusky shrugged. "All we can do is go down there and see what we can do."

She nodded slowly and stepped back.

As she did, Merina looked at Sandusky and asked, "How much gear should I take?"

"No idea," Sandusky shrugged. "I'd suggest whatever you think is essential. We'll be leaving shortly after this little visit is over, so let's get started."

CHAPTER ELEVEN
Unofficial Meeting

P resident Memory Hutchins sat at the head of the small table in the cramped quarters of the small room reserved for private meetings, typically between her and a foreign diplomat, but the room was soundproof and was devoid of any electronic surveillance devices. Her Secret Service detachment, particularly the lead agent, Martin Raymond, made sure of that. Considering the room, she felt it perfect for what she needed to talk about, mainly the situation with the task force and what Jonathan Cardwell thought was happening.

Seated to her right was Vice President Penny Kramer, a slightly taller woman with a mass of loose light brown curls cascading over her shoulders and down her back like a waterfall that framed a lean, narrow face and highlighted her sea-green eyes. To Memory's left sat Chief of Staff Stephanie Kenton, the woman who served as more than a coordinator. She had advisors, but she trusted the instincts of Stephanie more than the knowledge and intelligence of any advisor.

Beside Penny sat Kevin Burns, as stoic and as patient as anyone she'd ever known, and across from him was Colonel Matthew Vincent, an Army officer assigned to provide access to military equipment and potentially personnel for Cardwell's task force. He'd changed from his standard work uniform to a full dress uniform, complete with ribbons and citation medals, for a meeting with the President. Memory appreciated the effort, but it hadn't been necessary.

She'd called the meeting to discuss the situation with the task force. She wanted more details on what they were doing, how they were operating, before she allotted more funding for them.

"Okay," she said to begin the meeting, leaning forward with her fingers laced together and her forearms resting against the edge of the table. "There are a few things I need to know and you have some of the answers to my questions. I want to talk about this DSA task force run by Jonathan Cardwell."

As they nodded, she focused on Burns and said, "Mr. Burns, as Director of the Domestic Security Agency, this task force is your responsibility. We've let them go on without any serious oversight or supervision for quite some time. I think it's time we at least know what they do and, more importantly, how they're spending taxpayer money."

Burns nodded slowly, sitting back in the chair with his hands folded together in his lap as he looked at her and said, "I understand, Madame President. When Cardwell came to me over a decade ago, as one of my field operatives, with a fantastic story about vampires, and ancient books of prophecy floating around, I was more than a little skeptical. The very idea of vampires actually existing and living secretly in the modern world made no sense. I didn't believe him then and I'm not sure I believe him now, but I do believe in him. He was a tough, competent, and serious field agent, especially after an incident in a small Texas town near the Mexican border while pursuing a former DSA field director who had vanished with some information we felt was essential to national security. He returned from that mission with a hard edge to him and almost a zeal for this idea of hunting vampires."

Memory nodded, "So, do you think he's delusional? Does he have any mental issues?"

"No," Burns said firmly and shook his head slightly. "Jonathan Cardwell is one of the most competent people I've ever known. He's a realist and takes every situation at face value. I've never seen a vampire and I still doubt they're real, but Cardwell says they are and that's enough for me to give him the benefit of the doubt."

"I see," Memory nodded slowly and sat back, sliding her hands from the table and onto her lap, almost mimicking Burns' posture. "But do you believe this project deserves additional funding?"

"That's hard to say," he replied. "Without proof, I would say no, but Cardwell has been given the task of providing the proof and I believe he will."

"I see," Memory said, her eyes narrowing slightly. "But what can we expect from this task force, particularly his insertion team, if they have more funding."

"I'm not sure," Burns said and shifted his hands to the arms of the chair, anticipating a heated discussion, if not an argument. "I believe he would likely use the funding to upgrade their equipment and weapons."

Penny frowned and looked at him, "But they already have equipment and technology that's far above the norm."

"True," Burns nodded and turned his head toward her. "But it's mostly thanks to Merina Janek. She's absolutely brilliant when it comes to technology. She's been building what she needs from scratch and parts of other equipment. I've even mentioned acquiring a patent on some of these devices and licensing them, but she refuses. She's not interested in getting rich. She just wants to complete their mission."

"And what is their mission?' Stephanie asked. "It seems like a lot of nonsense to me."

Burns looked at her, almost glaring, and said, "Cardwell has explained their mission statement as the complete eradication of a vampire presence on Earth. I don't have any details beyond that."

Stephanie frowned, "That's not much of a mission statement without a detailed plan or any proof."

Burns shrugged, "I believe Cardwell has a more details plan, but he hasn't explained it to me, and I haven't asked. I've let him run his own show and there haven't been any real problems as of yet."

"Do you think there will be problems?" Penny asked, her gaze growing intense.

"I don't know," Burns replied and looked at her again. "He seems to think this incident in Mississippi has the potential for something major, something that could possibly affect the entire nation. He could tell you more about it, but I don't think he would reveal very much. He doesn't like the idea of having information revealed to very many sources. He likes to keep the details rather close."

"I can understand that," Memory said and sat forward again as she looked at Matthew. "Now, how does the military fit into this operation?"

Matthew looked at her and shrugged, "It's a little complicated. I was assigned to the task force as military liaison by my commanding officer, General Nathaniel Hamrick. He explained that he'd worked with Cardwell previously and had encountered Alex Chance previously, during a retrieval operation in Italy more than a decade ago. He was so impressed with Chance, and with Cardwell, that he agreed to provide them with any assistance they required. I was informed when given the assignment that I would be under Cardwell's command, but I still reported to General Hamrick."

He shook his head and continued, "I don't quite understand how the chain of command works in this situation, since Cardwell isn't a formal member of any military branch. So, I just do as he orders and relay it all through General Hamrick's office. I haven't actually spoken with the General in more than two years. I've been dealing with one of his subordinates and everything Cardwell has asked for has been approved."

Memory shook her head slowly, "That's not a good way to run things. I'd like to see some paperwork on that."

"So would I," Stephanie added. "It also needs to go through the accounting office."

Burns sat forward and said, looking from Matthew to Stephanie, "I believe there is a paper trail for everything Cardwell has requested. I'm sure Paul Sandusky or Caroline Parrish can provide it."

Stephanie nodded firmly, "I hope so. I'll be sending a formal request later today."

"Okay," Memory said and let out a sigh. "I'd still like more information, but it appears the only one able to provide it is Jonathan Cardwell, and I can't very well call him into this office while he's leading a mission."

She looked at Burns again and said, "Mr. Burns, I would like you to inform him that there will be a partial audit once he has returned to Washington. However, I believe in the sincerity of his beliefs, but my hands are tied right now."

"Not exactly," Penny said and looked at the President, leaning slightly closer. "It is possible to extend emergency funding for a brief period, no more than six months, upon your approval."

"That's right," Memory nodded. "I can do that. I'll get it started a little later as well. I have an appointment with my doctor late this afternoon."

Burns frowned lightly and asked, "Is it with the official doctor?"

"No," Memory shook her head. "This is my personal physician, Dr. Wanda Fairly. Why do you ask?"

"I'm sorry to sound like I've been prying," he said. "I've known about your doctor for a while. I also know her chief nurse, Lena Manfred, rather well. I've worked with her before."

"I see," Memory nodded. "Then you know Wanda's specialty."

"Yes, I do," he replied evenly.

"Then I ask you to keep it to yourself," she said, her voice taking on a tinge of the solid confidence she exuded when in a public situation.

"I will not say a word to anyone," he agreed with a nod.

"Okay," Memory said and pushed her chair back a bit. "Then I believe this meeting is concluded and adjourned. Thank you all for coming and for the information you've provided. I'll keep you informed of our next steps."

CHAPTER TWELVE
Arrival

T he old Greyhound bus pulled alongside the narrow, blond brick building on the south side of the downtown district of Pine Ridge, close to the railroad dividing the town into two unequal sections a short while after sundown. The driver, a man in his middle forties, looked back in the wide mirror above the windshield for another look at the woman seated in the back seat, in the aisle, with her legs spread as they had been since she'd boarded the bus in Baton Rouge. When the lights were on and he happened to look, he could easily see that she wore nothing beneath her tiny denim skirt and kept herself cleanly shaven. He expected her and her six companions to get up and disembark at every stop the bus made, but they'd remained aboard during the entire, long, and boring ride until they reached Pine Ridge. It was there that she finally stood up, the motion flashing him one final time, and his body reacted as it should and he squirmed in the seat a bit, trying to make himself a little more comfortable.

She wasn't exactly the type of woman he typically found attractive, but there was just something about her that drew his attention, something other than the fact that she wore no underwear beneath the shortest skirt he'd seen in a long time. Her long, dark hair hung limply around her bare, lean shoulders, skin tanned evenly above the dark gray halter top she wore that exposed her taut midriff and, though her breasts were a little smaller than he liked, he did like the way the bus's air conditioning affected them, telling him that she also wasn't wearing a bra. He did like that.

It was her six companions that left him confused and somewhat afraid. Three of the women made him nervous and the two men practically exuded an aura of anger and the potential for violence, seeming almost like the tales he'd heard about biker gang members. It was the other woman, the one that had remained almost isolated from the others the entire trip, who had him feeling a little strange. She wasn't a typical beauty, not like those he'd seen on TV, in Movies, or in magazines, but there was something almost magnetic about her. Had it not been for the one who had exposed herself to him, he would've been drawn to the tall woman with long, dark hair and eyes that seemed to hold something powerful behind them. He couldn't quite place his finger on it, but there was something there that drew his attention when it wasn't focused on the lurid thoughts the other one brought to his mind.

He opened the door as the bus came to a complete stop and he turned on the interior lights, though enough daylight remained for the passengers to see as clearly as he could see the woman stand up and start walking rather sinuously along the narrow aisle. The seven of them were the only ones getting up and were apparently the only ones disembarking in the small town of Pine Ridge. There were rarely any people arriving in the town, but there were typically three or four departing.

He watched in the mirror as the woman started forward and her path was blocked by a slightly shorter woman with short, blonde hair wearing a black wraparound dress cinched at the waist with a wide sash. Once she was in the aisle, they all began moving forward, each of them walking as gracefully as anyone he'd ever seen.

As the first one reached the driver's seat, he held his breath and didn't quite dare look at them directly. He felt intimidated by them and didn't want any trouble.

They moved slowly and evenly down the stairs to the wide concrete walk separating the bus from the building then moved toward the center of town. Once the last one, the big bald guy, was off the bus, the driver let out a low sigh of relief and sat back, waiting to see if there were any passengers to pick up.

Carmen led the group away from the bus station and into the seemingly deserted area around it, a few houses nearby that remained dark, as if uninhabited, with the main business district to their right and a few service industry businesses to their left, leading toward a large building just over a small hill that exuded a strange aroma so strong that it almost overwhelmed their senses. After crossing the wide street and stepping into the shadows growing around the houses, mostly beneath a large tree close to the curb, Carmen turned around, facing the others, and they stopped just a few feet away, forming a half circle with the two men to her left and the women to her right, Katrina remaining a bit separate at the end of the line.

"We must find Moonshadow," she said. "We'll wait until the bus leaves before doing anything. First, let's find a place to hide our clothing. We don't want to run around naked in human form."

They all nodded in agreement, except Katrina. Her expression remained blank as she listened to Carmen, their ersatz leader, begin the operation. She knew it was important to the tribe for them to locate Moonshadow and return him to his roots, but Katrina had her own agenda and plan. She would assist in the search for Moonshadow the best she could, but her plan was quite different and hadn't been revealed to the tribe or the pack.

She did help them locate a place to store their clothing, though her own would not be included. As the others began removing their clothing, Katrina moved away, deeper into the shadows closer to the house. She stood there and watched, waiting, as the members of the pack removed all of their clothing and stood naked before transforming. It was their way. They would do nothing unless instructed by their alpha. At the moment, Carmen occupied that role and stood facing them, her back to Katrina.

Carmen stood almost proudly naked in the cool October air with her hands on her flaring hips and her legs slightly spread. It was the first time she'd been nude in front of the pack and she could feel the eyes of Greyeagle and Scott on her, slowly sliding across her body and taking it all in. The heat of their lust was palpable and a glance downward along their bodies showed her just how much it affected them.

The three women were mostly different. The tallest, Holly, and the shortest, Renee, looked at her indifferently, their facial expressions showing only their attention. The third, Nora, did look over Carmen's body appreciatively and almost analytically. There was something in her dark eyes that made Carmen somewhat intrigued and slightly embarrassed. She knew that Nora had been exposing herself to the bus driver since boarding in Baton Rouge and almost expected Nora to have taken him aside for a brief encounter as she'd done with one of the previous drivers on the journey. Thankfully, it had only been a sexual thing and Nora hadn't followed through with the process of turning them. If she'd done so without the Council's approval, it could've meant her life.

After a moment, Carmen said, "Okay. We don't know this town and it's going to be a little difficult to find Moonshadow and the vampires. We're each going on our own. We'll spread out and take a look around. Stay hidden and don't let anyone see you. If they do, get away as quickly as you can. Do not attack anyone. If you spot a vampire, follow it and find out where they're hiding. If not, return here before sunrise. We'll need to get our clothes and find a place to stay and rest while we're here."

"What about food?" Greyeagle asked. "It's been a while."

Carmen focused on him and shrugged, "Find what you can. Just don't make it noticeable. We're trying to keep our presence a secret. If the humans learn about our presence, it'll be spread around like any other gossip and the vampires will find out. We don't want that. Just be careful and let's get moving. We have all night, but it still won't be enough."

She quickly gave them a direction to take and they began to transform. The process took only a second. Each of them fell forward to their hands and knees. By the time their hands touched the ground, their bodies had transformed into massive wolves. Greyeagle and Scott had become wolves with mottled brown fur. Renee's body was covered with dark auburn fur, a bit darker than her natural red hair, and Nora's fur was almost black. Holly became a wolf with golden fur while Carmen's body was covered with the purest white.

Once the transformations were complete, they quickly bounded away from the house across from the bus station. Once they'd vanished into the night, Katrina stepped forward, out of the shadows, and began her transformation. Unlike the wolves, she didn't need to remove her clothing. As a Feline, she had an ability the wolves knew nothing about. In actuality, she wore no clothing. What appeared as clothing was part of her, the part that became her fur as she lowered herself to the ground and transformed into a sleek, powerful panther. As with the wolves, her transformation took only an instant and she let out a low growl then began pursuing her own mission.

CHAPTER THIRTEEN
First Attack

M onica Halpern walked through the front door of her modest home just over an hour after sundown so tired she was almost staggering. Once inside, she leaned against the door, before turning on the lights, and almost fell back against it to push it closed with a satisfying thud and the reassuring click of the lock engaging. She then closed her eyes for a few seconds and let out a slow sigh of exhaustion and relief. She closed her eyes for a few seconds, trying to gather enough strength to at least remain awake until bedtime, and blindly reached across her body with her right hand to drop the keys she held into the large, beige purse tucked under her left arm, secured with a thin leather strap over her left shoulder.

Finally, she decided it was doing no good just standing there and pushed away from the door, standing up as she reached for the switch beside the door with her right hand. Flicking it up almost languidly, the small lever moved and she was rewarded with fairly bright white light that flooded the room and allowed her to see the mess she'd left over the previous few days. Articles of clothing, a couple of old pizza boxes, and a pile of junk mail spread randomly over the coffee table before the small sofa against the wall opposite the door beside the open doorway leading to her rarely used kitchen.

She turned slightly to her right and leaned her shoulder against the door as she lifted her left foot and began taking off her well-used and slightly scuffed work shoes, moving slowly and tiredly. As each was removed, she dropped it to the floor with a heavy thud then removed the thick socks she wore beneath it. Standing barefoot, she glanced at the sofa and contemplated sitting down for a few minutes, but there were other things to take care of first.

The uniform had to go. With three more in the closet of her cluttered bedroom, it wasn't yet time to do laundry. Living alone and with the windows all completely covered to prevent anyone from seeing inside, she didn't feel uncomfortable at all removing the uniform in the living room. She walked over to the sofa and placed her purse on the coffee table then picked up the remote for her TV from beneath a small stack of bills that needed to be paid. She aimed the remote at the TV and turned it on. It flared to life, set on the news channel she liked to watch, and began removing the uniform. The gun belt went first, the removal of its weight feeling like she was light enough to just float away. Instead, she arched her back, stretching it until it popped and gave her a little relief from the tension that had built up during the day. After dropping the belt onto the sofa, she began removing the shirt and pants. In moments, she stood in only her bra and panties. After tossing both pants and shirt to the sofa as well, she reached behind her back, stretching and grimacing with the effort, to unhook her bra. As the clasp came undone and released the tension on her body, she tilted her head back and let out another sigh of relief as it slid away from her body, falling to the floor at her feet.

She stood there a moment, wearing only her pale blue panties, and considered taking a shower before she did anything else, but the thought of standing even a moment longer felt like it was too much. Shaking her head slowly, her hair tickling a bit as it swept across her shoulders and upper back, she turned around and sat down on the sofa. Leaning back to relish the feeling of no longer being constrained by the bra. She felt comfortable and began to relax. She needed to unwind a bit before taking her shower, finding something to eat without ordering pizza again, and going to bed early. She already knew the next day would be a long one as well and she needed all the sleep she could get.

After a moment, she wished she'd taken the panties off as well, but she was comfortable and didn't want to expend the effort to remove them. She would live with it. Her eyes closed as the drone of the voices on the TV began lulling her toward sleep, but she focused enough so she didn't quite lose consciousness.

She zoned out, losing track of time and everything around her. Nothing mattered other than relaxing and relieving the stress of the day. Instead of rehashing the day and everything that had gone wrong, she focused on her personal life. She was a single woman in her early thirties and was without prospects for the serious relationship she'd been dreaming about since she'd first learned about that type of relationship. She wanted a husband, a couple of kids, and a decent home. The house she lived in was her own, but it had been built for a single person, perhaps a couple, with no children. If she did find the perfect guy and managed to settle down, it would most likely involve moving to a larger house and she hated the idea of leaving that house. It was almost paid for and it was in a decent neighborhood, not quite a block off West Drive with the huge cemetery occupying more land than she could measure, and was one of the quietest areas in the town. She would hate to leave it, but she would make the move if the right man came along.

It was just a dream, something she doubted would ever happen with her job in such a small town like Pine Ridge. At first, it had seemed perfect, an idyllic community with a minimal crime rate. After leaving her home in south Louisiana where crime, particularly violent crime, was growing more predominant every day, she'd learned of the job opening in Pine Ridge and the incentives offered by the town government had been more than enough to convince her to make the move. It had been perfect at first, more like the police work she saw in a ton of old movies, but it had started getting worse, more demanding. The crime rate hadn't increased, but the force had diminished from more than a dozen officers down to four full-time officers, two each shift, during the week, and four part-time officers that worked on the weekends. She was almost to the point of resigning and trying her best to find something else, whether it was in Pine Ridge or not, but her sense of duty and responsibility just wouldn't allow it.

Those thoughts were running through her dozing mind, just short of falling asleep, when the loud crash of someone striking her door with what sounded like a sledgehammer caused her eyes to flash open. She sat up straight and looked at the locked front door and waited to see what happened next. She took a single breath and the sound happened again, louder than before, and it caused the door to crash inward, the lock ripping out of the frame. As the cracked and broken door slammed into the wall beside it, Monica gasped at the sight of the unbelievably massive man standing there, his fists raised as if he'd done that much damage without any sort of tool.

He was almost too tall to fit through the door and he did duck his head slightly, his long hair falling forward and casting his pale face into shadow briefly as he stepped into the light of the room.

"What do you want?" Monica asked almost frantically, definitely afraid, as she fumbled for her service pistol still latched into the leather holster on the wide belt beside her while still watching the man approach.

As he moved forward, she barely noticed the arrival of two others in the doorway, one a rather tall woman and the other a rather familiar red-haired man.

The tall man shot forward, faster than she could follow, jumped gracefully over the coffee table in front of her, and snatched the gun belt from the sofa before she could close her fingers around the pistol.

She gasped, almost screamed, and flung herself to the other end of the sofa, her eyes still wide and her body trembling with fear.

The tall woman, Rachel Thanatos, strode forward slowly with the man she recognized, Ryan Sullivan, almost skulking behind her with an expression of glee on his broad face. The massive man moved to the side, holding her gun belt loosely in his left hand by the buckle, allowing it to dangle at his side.

"What do you want?" Monica asked, frowning and tensing for a physical confrontation.

"It's very simple," Rachel said, her voice rich and smooth with just a hint of an accent Monica couldn't quite identify. "We want you, Monica Halpern."

Ryan moved up quickly on Rachel's left, frowning as he looked at the taller woman, "Wait a minute. She's supposed to be mine."

Rachel looked at him, scowling, and said, "You cannot have them all. The other has already been promised to you."

Ryan snarled, but he said nothing. He knew Rachel was right. He'd already laid claim to Dana Richland, once they were through with her and Alex Chance was finally dead.

"Wait a minute," Monica said and shook her head slowly. "What are you talking about?"

Rachel looked at her again and smiled, "You will be one of us."

"One of who?" Monica asked, frowning.

Rachel smiled broadly, her full lips parting to reveal the long fangs protruding from her upper teeth. Monica flinched and tried to press herself deeper into the sofa, but there was nowhere to go. If the woman could move as fast as, or faster than, the tall man, she wouldn't make it off the sofa. There was nothing she could do.

Rachel took a slow step forward and let out a breath that was more of a hiss. Monica braced herself, ready for what she thought would happen.

She was wrong. She had no idea.

Rachel seemed to glide across the floor and around the coffee table then leaned forward, placing her left hand on the arm of the sofa, and opened her mouth wide, wider than Monica thought possible, but her gaze was locked on the fangs, dripping saliva as she leaned over Monica and placed her hand on the side of Monica's head. She gripped it tightly and gently pulled it to the side, exposing Monica's throat. She placed her lips on Monica's throat, eliciting a whimper of fear, then slowly bit down, pressing the fangs into the flesh as easily and precisely as any physician or nurse.

Then she began to feed.

CHAPTER FOURTEEN
Duty Calls

Patrolling the streets of Pine Ridge was the worst part of the job for Raquel Jackson. Of course, Martino always insisted on driving and that left her in the passenger's seat tasked with scanning the area as the car rolled along each street. Most of the town remained calm and quiet after dark, but there was one area that seemed to bring out the worst the town had to offer.

The Oasis Bar, located on Railroad Avenue at the edge of the downtown district, catered to the working-class citizens, the ones that spent large portions of their incomes drinking to forget their mundane existences and just blow off steam. Occasionally, the revelry spilled over into the streets, and that was when Raquel and Hal entered the situation. It was never a great disturbance and didn't bother anyone since the business district, what was left of it, shut down well before sunset. It was an old town and the remaining business in the small downtown area held onto the traditions of the past, sticking to a typical nine-to-five business day.

After dark, the area was deserted except for the bar, which was often a point of contention with nearby business owners. The sometimes raucous activity was frequently brought to the attention of the mayor and the city council, but there was little to be done about it other than to have the department patrol the area regularly and do what they could to keep the activities contained within the bar.

Raquel sat up straight once they turned onto Railroad Avenue from the south. Faint strains of heavy music filtered into the car and brought a frown to Raquel's face. She didn't mind the type of music, but she knew the volume indicated that the bar's sound system was cranked up more than usual. The alcohol had apparently been flowing freely and most likely meant the bar's typical patrons were celebrating something. She had no idea what that might be until they drew closer and the focus of the five guys clustered together at the corner of the bar, the entrance to the wide alley connected Railroad Avenue to Front Street, told her what she needed to know.

Marly Barnes was the stereotypical party girl, growing older and wouldn't admit it while doing her best to entertain the guys and possibly decide which one to take home. Raquel didn't consider Marly to be anything close to a prostitute, since she never asked for or took money from any of the guys she took home. She also didn't believe Marly took home quite as many guys as the rumors stated. The small-town rumor mill was as active and inaccurate as high school rumors of the same variety.

The raucous behavior was standard for the Oasis, but it rarely left the confines of the building. When it did, the sight of the police cruiser was usually enough to scatter them, but there was something different that night. Hal, behind the wheel, pulled to a stop a few feet behind the group of men and shifted the car out of gear.

"Look at that," Hal said, shaking his head as he focused on Marly.

Raquel shook her head as well, but for a different reason. She watched the scene as well, frowning as Marly seemed to almost dance around wearing tight, cutoff, denim shorts and a black halter top that was a little loose and threatened to fall away from her full breasts. Her long, thick, chestnut brown hair flopped around and frequently obscured her lean, narrow face with full lips and wide, green eyes. Raquel knew she was doing her best to keep the attention of the men while trying to decide which one she would focus on and try to take home.

The guys were loud and obnoxious, obviously drunk, but they weren't causing any harm, other than harassing Marly. Raquel didn't quite feel sorry for her, though. She brought it on herself with her flirtatious nature. The guys weren't trying to do anything physically, weren't even touching her, but the promise of contact, not necessarily violence, was there. They were drunk and trying to get laid, as was Marly.

After just a few moments, something moved in the shadows of the alleyway behind Marly. They were indistinct at first, just additional shadows shifting as if a steady wind was moving things around, but there was no wind and there was nothing visible large enough to create those shadows.

Hal, still focused on the activity, frowned and asked, "What is that?"

"I don't know," Raquel replied, shaking her head slowly and keeping her eyes on both the activity in front of the alley and the shadows within it.

Hal reached for the door handle as he glanced over his shoulder at Raquel and said, "I'm going to check this out. You stay here and be ready on the radio."

"Who am I going to call?" she asked. "Lois is already gone and Walt's probably in bed by now."

"Then try Shafer," he said and opened the door. "He'll answer."

Raquel shook her head and watched as Hal strode confidently toward the group across the street. None of them even looked in his direction and Raquel thought his masculine swagger was going to be an issue, but the others appeared to just ignore him.

Then, as he reached the other side of the street, just before the opening to the alley, the shadows moving through the alley began to take shape. There were five of them, three men and two women. Two of the men led the group, a tall man with long, flaming red hair and a shorter man with long, straight blond hair. Behind them, a man of average height with average brown hair cut in a cut she saw with a number of men in town, was flanked by a tall woman with blonde hair a bit longer than that of the man in front and a shorter woman, thinner with short black hair. They moved forward slowly, emanating an aura of confidence and control Raquel could sense from a distance. The aura brought with it a chill sensation of fear.

She ignored the radio as the new arrivals moved slowly closer to the six standing close to the street, with Hall approaching slowly, now moving almost tentatively with his right hand open and loose, hovering close to the pistol at his waist. Instead, she reached into a small pouch on her belt and pulled her cell phone free of it. With practiced familiarity, she tapped the screen with her thumb, bringing the device to life, and shifted her thumb to the icon on the screen to call up her emergency contacts.

She glanced down to make sure she had the right number and looked up as the attack began. The five new arrivals moved more quickly than anyone she'd ever seen and it elicited a sharp gasp from her. The shortest of the three men went for Marly, grabbing her by the shoulders and pulling her back into the alley. The big man with red hair waded into the other five, pushing them aside, and focused his attention on Hal. The two women each went for one of the men while the third man shot after one trying to run back to the safety of the bar, but the third man was much faster and caught him after just a couple of steps.

Raquel was in shock, her mouth hanging open, and stared at the new arrivals began their individual attacks, each of them leaning closer to their target and pressing their mouths to the throats. Raquel was at a loss and tapped the screen with her thumb to initiate the call then held the phone to her ear.

The call was answered on the second ring and a familiar, if gruff and raspy, voice said, "Shafer."

"It's Jackson," she said, keeping voice low to try and draw as little attention to herself. "We have a situation here at the Oasis. Martino is out of the car, trying to settle a situation with six individuals. Five others arrived and are attacking. They're faster than anything I've ever seen."

She looked toward the alley again and saw the man with red hair lowering Hal to the ground. Hal wasn't moving.

"Martino is down," she said sharply, her voice starting to tremble. "What should I do?"

"Are they still attacking?" he asked.

"Yes," she said quickly and nodded sharply. "All five are still moving. The six others are all down."

"Get out of there," he said. "Get back to the station. I'll get on the phone with Barker and Jackson. We'll meet at the station. Give me fifteen minutes."

"Copy that," Raquel said and disconnected the call.

Dropping the phone on the seat and struggling to climb over the central console laden with equipment including a small computer, she dropped into the driver's seat with a heavy sigh. Refusing to look at Hal and the scene taking place around him, she shifted the car into gear and drove away.

CHAPTER FIFTEEN
Planning Session

Jonathan Cardwell was pleased with the progress that had been made on the new facility, the old hospital building at the edge of Pine Ridge's downtown district at the bottom of a steep hill across a narrow street from the strangely triangular parking lot of an old bank. He found it a little strange that a building in fairly decent shape so close to downtown with a low rental rate had remained unused for so long that it had fallen into a state of disrepair. It had taken only a little work, just a couple of days, to get the building into shape, at least enough for the purposes of the task force on what Cardwell hoped was a temporary basis. He missed having the resources of the federal government close at hand, but he would do what was necessary to continue the mission he'd designed for the task force.

Sydney and Jana had done a remarkable job of setting up their lab in the space that had been the small laboratory facility of the hospital. It wasn't quite the space they'd been afforded in Washington, but it would hopefully be enough for the time they would be there. It wasn't quite complete, but it would be ready before it was needed for testing of Dana Richland once she was released from the hospital, which was at least another day away. With the others there, he'd tasked Caroline with keeping track of Dana's status and in contact with the physician in charge, Ross Brinson, or his nurse, Angelica Norris. From what he'd seen so far, those two were highly professional and were doing their best, but they didn't know what they were dealing with. They'd never encountered anything like it before and he hoped it wouldn't get out of hand, that they wouldn't start spreading details before the overall situation could be controlled.

As he entered the large room that had been and was once again a conference room, he wondered if the task force would actually be able to contain the situation at all. The vampires were on the move, growing their numbers more rapidly than ever before, and the new Masters, the Virate, were unlike the previous Master. They were more brazen and determined to do more than simply survive and maintain their status than Davros had been. From what little Brewer had been able to decipher from the Book of Aranos, it seemed that their plan was to take over the entire world. The logistics of doing so and maintaining that level of control was more than daunting. It seemed nearly impossible to Cardwell, but he had learned to never underestimate the lengths to which a vampire would go to accomplish its goal.

The large table at the center of the room, found at a local store specializing in used furniture, was surrounded by chairs, no two alike, with a padded, black leather office chair at the head of the table. They'd also been purchased at the used furniture store, the owner offering a substantial discount just to get the things out of his store, and would suffice in their current situation. They weren't concerned with appearances, just functionality.

He lowered himself into that chair and waited for the others to arrive. Some of them were finishing a late meal while others continued working on the facility. Merina was one of those, having brought along or acquired more equipment than the others, with the possible exception of Sydney and Jana in the lab. They still had a few minutes and he liked having a little time alone to mentally prepare himself and get his thoughts in order for a meeting. He had to be certain he had everything lined up and focused to help keep the rest of them focused. He tended to lead by example, but those days were starting to fade away. He was getting older and definitely much more cynical than he had been, but at least he could keep everything in perspective and could explain his intentions to the others. Part of that, he knew, was due to their sincerity in handling the job. They were as focused on eradicating vampires as he'd been since first encountering them years earlier.

As he sat down, a light smile crossed his face as he saw a neatly typed agenda already on the table. Caroline was already on task and took care of things before he even mentioned them. She also seemed to know what he had in mind even before he did and he appreciated that detail. He picked up the single sheet of paper and was looking it over, making sure everything was in the proper order, when the door behind him, still slightly ajar, was pushed open wide and Paul Sandusky entered the room.

Cardwell looked up as Sandusky walked over and took his usual seat to Cardwell's right.

As he sat down, Sandusky looked at Cardwell and said, "I'm not really sure about all this. It seems like we're just sort of drifting."

Cardwell placed the paper back on the table and looked up, "We're getting there, though. The details are starting to fall into place. We just need to tie them all together and find a few more. I'm hoping Dana Richland can give us a few details that'll help."

"I don't know," Sandusky shook his head. "That's really thin. We need to have the team out patrolling and actively searching for the main vampire nest."

Cardwell sat back and shook his head, hands on the arms of his chair, "We're working on that. Right now, the team isn't at full strength and that's something we're going to address in this meeting."

As Sandusky nodded his understanding, his eyes narrowed a bit as he contemplated what needed to be done and how he could possibly do what was necessary without all the pertinent information. Just a couple of seconds later, the others began filing into the room. Unsurprisingly, the first to arrive were Alex and Sydney. Sandusky knew about their relationship and how it had grown over the years, but it had become quite a bit more complicated with the return of Dana to Alex's life. Sandusky knew a little about his relationship with Dana and how it had ended with the emergence of his abilities and his departure for the military, but he still didn't know why he hadn't made contact with her once he'd settled into a routine.

They took chairs side by side on the opposite side of the table, the side typically reserved for the insertion team, but their numbers had diminished and there was room for Sydney beside Alex. Before he could do more than nod in their direction, the others began filing in and took their seats around the table.

When the last of them, Merina, entered quickly, breathing a little rapidly with her eyes wide with intensity and showing her level of exhaustion, Cardwell sat up, ready to begin the meeting.

"Okay," he said as Merina took her seat between Caroline and Bonnie. "Let's get started. We have a lot to discuss and some serious planning to do."

Once they settled into their seats and focused on him, he picked up the sheet of paper in front of him, glanced at it, then said, "The first order of business is dealing with this book we were given by Father Tourigney in New Orleans."

He looked to his right, toward Patrick Brewer seated across from Alex, and asked, "Do you have anything?"

Brewer nodded and sat forward, "Not a great deal, but we do have something. DeAnna has an uncanny knack for written languages and has been greatly helpful in deciphering some of the older vampire tongues."

"And what does this mean?" Cardwell asked, sounding a little frustrated.

"Sorry," Brewer nodded and continued. "We have translated a portion of the book, sort of an overview of the plan created by Aranos. Consider this was written with the ancient world in mind, well before this nation was founded or even discovered. At the time, there were no real centers of government or large cities as we know them today. The various nations, as they were, had been nothing more than a loose collection of villages and communities. The book indicates that the plan involved conquering one of these villages at a time. They intended to turn a large portion of the population while retaining some, primarily children, as a source of food. Once one village was conquered, an occupying force would remain behind while the majority of their forces would move to the next, and so on. It would've been a slow process, each village taking days or weeks to infiltrate and conquer, and potentially decades to take over the world as it was at the time."

Cardwell nodded thoughtfully for a few seconds then asked, "Are you saying this is their plan now, that they intend to move city by city until they've taken over the nation and eventually the world?"

Brewer shrugged, "I'm not completely certain. If they're using the plan as it is, then I would say so. However, it's possible that they're updating the plan to consider current conditions and modern technology as well as government and military situations. In fact, I think it's highly likely that they're doing just that."

Cardwell continued to nod for a few seconds then drew in a deep breath and said, "That's not really a stretch. These three new Masters, the Virate, aren't doing things the way Davros had and they're trying to change it all. But I want to know why they chose this place, other than the obvious."

"You mean Alex?" Brewer asked. "I believe I can explain that."

"Please," Alex said coldly. "Explain."

Brewer glanced across the table at Alex then turned to Cardwell again, "Part of the book we've managed to translate involves some details concerning a ritual necessary to put this plan into motion. It seems that there is an ancient power hidden somewhere in the Earth that must be released and absorbed by the Master to begin the process. I believe this power is located within this town. I also believe it to be the source of Alex's abilities."

"Wait a minute," Alex said and sat forward, his eyes narrowing slightly as he glared at Brewer. "You'll have to explain that."

Brewer looked at him and nodded, "Of course. It's not exactly clear, and I'll need to check some other sources, but this power seems to have two sides. One side, the portion the vampires are looking for, is darker in nature. The other side, the portion I believe is responsible for your abilities, Alex, is in opposition. The two are similar, though the lighter side is probably not quite as powerful, almost as if it's incomplete. That would explain the similarity between your abilities and those of a vampire. With it being more focused on opposing the darkness, it has taken away the hindrances, such as extreme sensitivity to sunlight and the need for human blood."

Alex nodded slowly, accepting the information.

Cardwell sat forward, glaring at Brewer, and asked, "Is that all? Do you know where this power could be hidden?"

"Not really," Brewer looked at Cardwell and shook his head slowly. "The only hint of a location is one aspect of the power. It will affect the very nature of the plant life around it. It corrupts the very nature of plants and, while they continue to grow and function, they are not quite the same."

Cardwell shook his head, "How can we find out? Is it in the book?"

"I don't know," Brewer shrugged. "We'll keep working on it, but this book is so ancient that I doubt Aranos was able to determine a precise location."

Alex sat up straight and looked from Cardwell to Brewer, "Hold on. I have an idea."

All eyes turned to him as he continued, "This power affects plants, right?"

Brewer nodded and Alex said, "Then I think I know the general area where this power might be."

Brewer frowned, "What are you thinking?"

Alex leaned forward and said, "The black pines, the ones in the Darkwood Cemetery. They aren't found anywhere else. I even asked a couple of teachers, Biology teachers, back in high school when I heard about them. They said they don't grow anywhere else in the world."

Cardwell frowned, "What are you talking about?"

Alex looked at him and said, "There's a spot in the Darkwood Cemetery, the huge place on the south side of the high school, where these trees grow. They're called black pines and there is a grove of them near the center of the cemetery. That's the only thing I can think of around here that makes sense."

Cardwell nodded, his gaze intense as he said, "Check it out."

He looked at Brewer, "Any idea of a time frame? When do they plan on getting to this power?"

Brewer shrugged," Nothing yet, but we're working on it."

"Do that and let me know when you have something," Cardwell said and, without missing a beat, looked at Sydney. "What's the status of the lab and what are we going to do with Dana Richland?"

Sydney nodded and said, "The lab is ready. We finished the last of it this afternoon. We expect Dana to be discharged from the hospital tomorrow. The physician in charge has agreed to let us know the time and we'll transport her here. Once she's settled in a bit, we'll start testing."

"What about the serum?" Cardwell asked.

Sydney shrugged, "We're still not sure. The formula is the best we can do. We'll test it with her blood once she gets here, but I can't guarantee anything."

"Right," Cardwell nodded. "Just do your best."

He paused long enough to draw in a breath then placed his hands on the table, "We have another situation that needs addressing immediately. The team is down two members. The five of you remaining are among the most capable operatives I've ever worked with, but you can't do all of this alone. We need to replace the two we lost in New Orleans."

"I have a suggestion," Alex said and looked at him. "I believe we should increase our total numbers. I think we should find three or four more."

"And where are we going to find four more people?" Sandusky asked. "We don't have time to go back to DC and recruit."

Alex shrugged, "I don't know. I would suggest bringing DeAnna in as the first. She's more than capable and has a unique ability that should be beneficial."

"And what is this ability?" Cardwell asked.

Alex looked at DeAnna. She nodded slowly, giving him permission to explain, and he said, "DeAnna is invisible to vampires. She has such strong faith that it protects her from the vampires by somehow making her completely unnoticeable. I've been training her for a couple of months and I think she's ready to join the team."

Brewer looked at DeAnna, on his right, and frowned, "DeAnna, you didn't tell me about that. This changes things."

"How?" she asked, frowning as well. "I didn't think it had anything to do with translating the book."

"It doesn't, not with the translation," he said. "But there is something I learned long ago when I first discovered the prophecy of the Nemesis."

Alex opened his mouth to say something, but Brewer held up a hand to stop him and continued, "You see, DeAnna, this prophecy indicated that the Nemesis will have an associate, one with different abilities, and will join his fight against the vampires. That person is known as the Holy Warrior and it now seems likely that you will fill that role."

"Okay," Cardwell interrupted, pulling his chair closer to the table. "You guys can figure all that out on your own. Right now, we need to figure out where we'll find more recruits, the right ones, and get everything in order."

The others all nodded in agreement, their expressions stern and focused.

He looked at Alex and said, "Get the team together, including DeAnna, and get started on the search for the vampires. I'd rather find them and take them out before this ritual happens than wait and see if we can stop it. I'd like to have two groups out there, but we don't have enough at the moment. Just get out there and find something."

"Right," Alex said with a nod and pushed his chair back.

"As for the rest of you," Cardwell began and was interrupted by the ringing of a cell phone.

Merina knew it was hers and pulled it from the back pocket of her pants as she said, "I had the comm system connected to the standard phone system then transferred all calls to this cell during the meeting."

Cardwell nodded and sat back as she activated the phone and took the call on speaker phone.

"This is the DSA task force, Merina Janek speaking," she said sharply. "What can I do for you?"

"My name is Neil Shafer," the tinny voice replied. "I'm the Chief Detective of the Pine Ridge Police Department. The Chief, Walt Baker, said I should call you guys. There've been a few attacks this evening and two of our officers are missing. One was taken by attackers down by the railroad. The other isn't answering her phone and we haven't been to her home yet."

Cardwell leaned forward and said, "Detective Shafer, I need you to tell me where you are right now."

"We're at the police station," he replied. "We're locked in and armed, but we don't know what we can do."

"Stay there," Cardwell said. "We're sending a team right now."

"Thanks," Shafer replied. "We're not going anywhere."

Cardwell nodded and Merina disconnected the call. He looked at Alex and said, "Scrap the search. Get to the police station and bring those people here."

"We're on it," Alex said and pushed his chair back, gripping the arms as he looked at the others and nodded toward the door.

As they began to stand up, Sydney looked at him and said, "Be careful."

He nodded and said nothing as he turned and walked quickly toward the door with the other four following him.

CHAPTER SIXTEEN

Converts

The massive box truck, a battered and barely functional former rental vehicle, pulled off the highway onto the narrow dirt drive through thick trees leading to the old hotel. As it turned, the headlights were turned off and the truck continued toward the hotel, its top brushing through overhanging tree branches. Behind it, a small, black car with darkly tinted windows turned off the highway, and its headlights vanished as well. The vehicles rolled slowly forward and stopped several yards away from the hotel's entrance.

As they stopped, the doors opened and the occupants climbed out quickly. The first out of the car was Gerrit Jaeger. He stood up and looked at the dark hotel for a second before turning his gaze to the truck. Colin and Dylan climbed from the cab of the truck and moved quickly to the back. Colin stood aside as Dylan unlatched the door and shoved it upward with ease.

Rachel climbed from behind the wheel of the car and closed the door. Jade and Kim emerged from the back seat, their eyes wide with anticipation.

Gerrit looked over his left shoulder and said, "Help them get the food inside."

"Of course," Jade said and started toward the truck as Kim moved around the back to join her.

Rachel walked to the front of the car and faced Gerrit, "Are there enough or will we need more?"

"I counted twenty-three," he said and smiled lightly. "With the six of us and the one who should be arriving before sunrise, we will have enough."

"What about those five you singled out?" she asked. "Particularly the one I've already bitten?"

"The police officer," Gerrit said and nodded. "Along with the nurse, the paramedic, the coroner, and the girl at the bar, she will provide just what we need. I have no doubt this DSA group will bring in the local officials, especially after two members of their insertion team having been taken in New Orleans. They'll join us soon enough. But the police officer will give us an advantage in dealing with the local authorities."

He shrugged and smiled, "As for the girl, I just like her."

Rachel shook her head and started for the hotel's entrance as she said, "That does not surprise me at all."

Gerrit chuckled and took a step forward as he looked at the truck and said, "Bring them in. Get them prepared."

Colin, coordinating the other three vampires as they herded the captives toward the hotel, nodded and grinned. Gerrit returned the nod and walked toward the hotel quickly.

They were all brought into the lobby, where Rachel and Gerrit waited for them, standing with their backs to the long counter against the wall opposite the entrance with Ryan Sullivan standing a few feet away. The group of victims was herded to the open space before them and the vampires lined up along the counter as well.

"There is no point in trying to escape," Gerrit said as he looked them over. "We are much too strong and fast for any of you. Now, you will be prepared and tomorrow night you will join us. You will live forever if you follow the rules you are given."

He stepped away from the counter, moving slowly across the front of the clustered people. Monica was the first he spotted, noticing her blond hair and short stature as well as her exposed flesh. She'd been taken without being allowed to dress and still wore only her panties. Marly stood beside her, the halter top she'd worn now ripped and loose, exposing her breasts. Gerrit took Marly by the hand and led her forward, taking Monica by the arm as he backed past her.

"You two will come with me," he said and stopped close to the counter.

He glanced over his shoulder at Colin and said, "Take these two to my room."

"Of course," Colin agreed and led the women toward the staircase.

Gerrit then faced the group and looked them over carefully, his eyes narrowing slightly, until he located one of the others.

"Jade," he said and nodded toward a woman near the back of the group with short, dark hair. "Bring the nurse to Colin's room."

Jade moved to comply as Gerrit looked again and spotted the medical examiner near the center of the group.

"Dylan," he said. "Take the coroner to Rachel's room."

As Dylan moved to comply, Gerrit shifted his gaze until he spotted a woman wearing a dark blue uniform. He nodded and held his hand out to her.

"You," he said. "Paramedic. You will go with Kim."

Frowning, Kim took a step forward, not sure what Gerrit wanted her to do with the woman. She'd already fed enough during the attack outside the bar and she wasn't prepared to participate in the turning process.

Gerrit then turned around and stood in front of her, stopping her progress. He looked her in the eye and said softly, "You will secure her for the night. She will not be turned after all. She will be the first meal for our new converts."

Kim nodded and stepped around him. She still didn't want to participate, but she would continue following Gerrit's orders while Moonshadow wasn't around to provide her with a measure of safety.

"Now," Gerrit said and clapped his hands together, turning to face the group. "The rest of you will remain here. The others will arrive in a moment and the process will begin."

As he stepped back, returning to the counter, Ryan moved closer and stopped a few feet from him.

"What is it, Ryan?" Gerrit said without looking at him. "What is it that you want?"

"I want to be like you," Ryan replied, trying his best not to sound desperate. "You gave me your word that you would make me like you."

"I did," Gerrit nodded. "But the time is not yet right. Your services are still needed in the form you inhabit now. But one day, when you have completed what is needed, you will be given all that you've earned."

Before Ryan could respond, feeling anxious and grateful at the same time, the front door opened and another vampire strode confidently and rather flamboyantly into the hotel. She was a bit shorter than the other female vampires with long, blond hair framing a soft-featured face that remained smooth and ageless, but there was an aura around her that seemed to radiate an ancient wisdom and ultimate confidence.

She took three steps into the lobby and looked to her right, easily locating Gerrit. She stared at him for a couple of seconds then started toward him, only glancing at the gathered humans cowering in silent fear.

"What is this?" she asked. "Are you finally preparing for the ritual?"

"Yes, Lady Sharia," he said with a respectful nod. "And I am grateful for your presence."

Sharia Lorman, the oldest and most powerful Mystic in the vampire world, stopped in front of him and looked at him with her soft brown eyes.

"Of course you are," she said coldly. "You cannot perform the ritual without my power and knowledge. You may have taken the power of the Master from Davros, but you did not take it in the customary way. It is divided among the three of you, young Masters, but the great power will only attach itself to one. Though you do share the power as Masters, it is you, Gerrit, who will become the true Master of the world. After centuries of struggle, the dream of Aranos will come to fruition and the vampire will rule the entirety of the planet."

"Yes," Gerrit said with a single curt nod. "I will not fail."

Sharia chuckled, "With my assistance, you cannot fail."

Other vampires began entering the lobby from the stairs and from a door at the end of the counter away from the staircase. They moved quickly and pulled the humans away. It took them only a few moments to do so and both Sharia and Gerrit watched with great interest and pride. Their army would be born the following night and there was little to stand in their way.

Sharia then looked at Gerrit again and asked, "You have followed through with the plan for the Nemesis, I assume."

"Yes," Gerrit replied, nodding slowly. "He has not yet been taken, but it is only a matter of time. It has all been planned."

"Good," Sharia said and took a step to her right. "Now show me where I will reside while here and bring the other two Virate to me and we will discuss the details of the ritual."

"Of course," Gerrit nodded. "They are preparing our special converts. It will take a short while."

Sharia nodded, "The army of the Virate must take precedence."

"Sullivan," Gerrit said and looked at Ryan. "Show Lady Sharia to the suite on the top floor, the one at the center of the building that has been prepared."

"Of course," Ryan replied, feeling cowed, and gestured toward the stairs. "If you'll please follow me."

Sharia smirked, "A human servant. How quaint."

Ryan remained in place until Sharia turned and said, "Show me the way, human."

With just a touch of anger in his mind, Ryan turned and led the way up the stairs.

Gerrit remained where he was a moment longer then turned and made his way into the depths of the hotel, toward the back stairs and the easiest path to the room he'd chosen as his own where Monica and Marly awaited his attention.

CHAPTER SEVENTEEN
Sunrise

As the sun began to rise and dim light began to filter into the town of Pine Ridge, well before the town came to life and the day of most residents began, a sleek black panther moved slowly and carefully through the streets, pausing and hiding at any sign of movement and the potential for being spotted by one of the citizens.

It had taken all night for Katrina to determine the location of her destination. With no scent to follow initially, she'd first had to determine the particular smells and aromas of the people who lived in the town and push those aside to focus on different scents, those coming from recent arrivals. Those people had not been very active and hadn't yet moved through the town a great deal and she'd searched diligently for hours before picking up a faint trace of one such person.

The scent told her everything she needed to know about the person, a man named Alex Chance, except for his precise location. She drew his name from the scent as well as his physical description and a bit of his personal history. He was a native of Pine Ridge, but he'd been away so long that the local scent was almost completely covered by his travels across the world. Still, some details weren't contained within his scent. She did know of his connection to the Domestic Security Agency and the task force dedicated to opposing the activities of the vampires and a bit about the abilities he possessed. He would be a valuable ally if she could convince him and his group to align with her, the Tribe, and the Feline Family. First, though, she had to reach their current headquarters and meet them then convince them that she was not aligned with the vampires in any way.

She didn't know exactly where she was going, but the scent of Alex Chance was growing stronger as she moved slowly toward the downtown area. She also knew little about the town other than the old bus station where she'd parted ways with the pack. She'd told them nothing and owed them nothing. She was there of her own volition, despite having been asked to join the pack in tracking down one of their own. Katrina knew nothing about the one renegade named Moonshadow, but she'd heard the others discuss him and their belief that he had entered a life debt with one of the vampires. If this vampire was in Pine Ridge, it meant that she was in the service of the Virate and, by proxy, Moonshadow was in their service as well. If that were the case, the pack would find it difficult to remove him from their control, and could possibly cost more than they were willing to pay.

Katrina saw the potential connection with the task force as serving more than a single purpose. First of all, she could possibly bring new allies into the fight against the vampires with both wolf and feline factions, but it could also help in removing the vampire's control over Moonshadow. Doing so would generate a bit of respect within the Tribe and would strengthen the relationship between wolf and cat. It would be ideal, but she considered that the humans would be leery of her presence and wouldn't quite believe what she brought to them. It would take a bit of convincing, but she was no negotiator or public speaker. She would speak the truth and let them decide. If they chose not to work with her, she would rejoin the pack and aid them in locating and freeing Moonshadow.

The scent led her first to the local hospital, but she could tell as he approached the huge building that he wasn't inside. He'd been there recently, within a couple of days. His scent was still strong, but it was starting to fade. From there, she followed a path through the residential area near the hospital, taking a circuitous route through the town, but it led her to the town's primary thoroughfare, Bolling Avenue. There was more traffic there, more human presence, and she didn't want to be spotted. Moving just a block off the street, into another sedate residential section, she traveled a block at a time, making her way in the shadows back to Bolling Avenue to ensure she was still on the correct path.

As the sun began to rise and her presence became more noticeable, she moved a bit more quickly, hoping she didn't follow his scent on another tangent that took her away from her target. Before long, the scent grew strong once again and took her into the depths of the residential areas and she moved much more quickly toward her destination. She reached an old building just as the upper arch of the sun rose above the buildings of the town and the strength of Alex's scent, mingled with several more that weren't locals, she knew she'd reached the destination.

The building at an odd corner where three streets seemed to converge looked much older than she'd expected and the few bushes planted along the wide walk leading from the sidewalk to the building that was accessible from the side rather than in a direct line from the wider street the building appeared to face. Katrina wasn't overly concerned with it and approached, walking silently up the few steps to the wide porch before the door. As she reached the top step, she saw a woman standing inside the door wearing tactical clothing and body armor with a large rifle held at an angle across her chest. Katrina stopped there and watched for a few seconds, remaining in the shadows cast by the building's corner, and finally decided it would be best to approach the door as a human rather than a panther.

She pushed off with her forepaws, just enough to propel her upper body a few inches off the concrete step, and her body transformed in an instant. She took on her human form with the shiny black fur shifting into clothing. This time, under her control, it shifted to black pants and a loose black top with long sleeves. After taking a quick breath to adjust to the diminished sense of her human form, she stood up straight and climbed the stairs. At the top, she stopped and faced the door as the woman inside noticed her presence and her dark green eyes opened wide.

Katrina held her hands up in surrender and stood her ground as the woman unlocked the door and pushed it open.

"This is a government facility and access is restricted," Krista Deninger said as she left the building.

"I know," Katrina nodded. "I need to speak with Alex Chance."

Krista shook her head, "You're going to have to explain that."

"Alex Chance leads the team fighting the vampires," Katrina said. "I'm here to offer my assistance and hopefully bring another faction, possibly two, into the fight."

"I'm going to need you to wait here," Krista said and took a step back. "I'll have to get the director."

Katrina nodded, "I'll wait right here."

Krista stared at her a second longer then backed into the building and locked the door before she turned and hurried farther into the building. She walked quickly through the building to the conference room where she knew Cardwell was meeting with a portion of the town's police department and the town's mayor. They'd been there for a few hours, discussing what had happened and what needed to be done.

The door of the conference room was slightly ajar and Krista walked in without breaking stride, pushing the door open farther with her left hand.

Cardwell sat at the head of the table, facing away from the door, with the mayor and Lois Cashlin on his right beside Sandusky and Alex on his left with the two remaining officers and Neil Shafer. They all looked up sharply as she walked in, Cardwell, turning to his left to look at her.

"I hope this is important, Deninger," Cardwell said as she stopped a couple of feet to his left.

She nodded and replied, "I believe so. A woman just showed up at the front door looking for Alex. She knows about the vampires and says she can help."

Cardwell frowned then looked at Alex and said, "She knows you. Check it out and see if it's valid."

"Right," Alex said and rose from his chair.

Deninger backed away, turned toward the door, and walked out of the room with Alex behind her. He strode quickly along the central corridor of the building, past several rooms that had been offices and examination rooms, now serving as offices and workspaces for the task force then to the lobby and an open space with a tall counter set at a right angle with desks and gear behind it, the domain of Merina and Caroline. Alex ignored the vacant area and focused on the glass door at the entrance. He saw the woman as he angled toward the door and frowned, having never seen her before. He didn't understand how someone he'd never met would know his name and what he did.

Krista resumed her post as Alex pushed open the door and stepped outside.

Katrina took a step forward as the door opened and asked, "Are you Alex Chance?"

She sniffed the air once as Alex let the door close behind him and said, "I'm Chance. Who are you?"

"My name is Katrina Bentley," she said. "I'm here to bring the potential for additional assistance in the fight against the vampires to your attention."

"What additional help?" he asked, folding his arms across his chest.

"I must explain," she said and took a step forward. "I represent a collective of feline lycanthropes."

"Lycanthropes?" he frowned. "Like werewolves?"

"Similar," she nodded. "The wolves and the cats are separate entities, though we do have a connection. The felines do not exist in a social construct as the wolves."

Alex shook his head and held up his hands, "Hold on. You're telling me that werewolves and werecats actually exist."

"Yes," Katrina nodded and stopped moving. "Both factions exist. The wolves exist in a more tightly controlled social structure. The felines are not so structured."

"But how?" he asked. "We should've encountered them by now."

She shrugged, "Lycanthropes are typically rather anti-social, wolves in particular. They exist in small groups, called villages, while the majority of them live in a single large community in Colorado and refer to themselves as the Tribe. Felines, such as myself, exist primarily on our own, but we do maintain regular contact, more of a support group than an actual community. It helps us better integrate into human society. Wolves are more feral and rarely interact with humans."

"I see," he said. "Now what does this have to do with me and the task force?"

"We can help," Katrina said and took one more step closer to him, clasping her hands together at her waist. "I traveled here with a pack of wolves from Colorado. They were tasked by the Chief Elder of the Tribe to locate a renegade wolf by the name of Moonshadow. He has been taken in by one of the vampires currently residing in this town. I was given the task of assisting them and determining the truth behind their activities. It is believed that the vampires have acquired an ancient text that details a plan to conquer humanity. If that is so, an ancient treaty between lycanthropes and vampires has been broken. This will mean war between the two groups and the Chief Elder has decided to bring the resources of the Tribe, as well as the Feline community, into the conflict on the side of humanity."

"Okay," Alex nodded. "I get it. But you should discuss this with our director. He's inside meeting with local officials and they have reported attacks within the town."

"Vampire attacks?" she asked, frowning and tilting her head slightly to the left. "Are you certain?"

He nodded, "Yes. We haven't seen them, but one of the officers witnessed an attack that claimed several people, including another officer."

Katrina righted her head and asked, "Was this done in a public place, in view of others?"

"Yes," he said. "It was within a few yards of a downtown bar. Others were in the area."

She nodded slowly and said, "That's the first indication that they've broken the treaty. I believe the Tribe will soon declare war on the vampires."

"And we'll do the same," Alex said with a curt nod. "Now, let's go in and meet with the director."

"Of course," she said and moved forward as he turned around and opened the door.

"We can't handle this any longer," Walt Baker said, leaning forward and looking at Cardwell with a deep frown on his face. "There are no other officers in this town and I don't have the resources to bring in more."

"Hold on," Jay Downing said and sat back, holding his hands up. "This town is almost bankrupt. I admit, you've done a great job of lowering the crime rate, particularly violent crime, but we just don't have the money to pour into bringing in more officers, especially if these other two turn up and we have to keep paying them."

"Let me assure you, Mr. Mayor," Cardwell said and turned slightly toward him. "Those two will not be returning to duty. Actually, they're most likely already dead and will soon be a part of the larger problem."

Downing shook his head, "Then what are we supposed to do?"

Cardwell looked at Baker and said, "Chief, I have an option for you. It's a drastic one and you might not like it, but I think it'll be best in this situation."

"Let's hear it," Walt said and sat back with a sigh.

Cardwell glanced at Sandusky, received a nod from him, then looked at Walt and said, "I want to absorb your department into the DSA. We have a bit of funding, with more promised, and we have the physical resources to continue your work and incorporate it into our own. I've explained the situation and, whether you believe any of it or not, something is happening in this town. Right now, this task force is the best hope you have of resolving it."

"Okay," Walt nodded. "Give me some details."

Cardwell let out a slow breath and said, "First, we'll incorporate your personnel into the task force. We have three positions open on our insertion team. Your two officers and detective will become part of the team under the command of Alex Chance. You, Chief Baker, and Ms. Cashlin, will be part of the task force itself."

"What could I do?" Lois asked. "I'm just a glorified secretary."

Cardwell turned to her and said, "My current administrative assistant, Caroline Parrish, is overwhelmed with work and she's also handling a great deal of our intelligence. With you taking on some of her duties as administrative assistant, or glorified secretary, it'll free her up to handle more of the intelligence duties, which we desperately need."

Lois nodded, "I think I can do that."

"What about me?" Walt asked, holding his hands out in a shrug. "I'm getting too old for all of this stuff. Hell, I've been thinking about retiring at the end of the year."

"Then retire," Downing said. "Pension payments will be less than your salary."

Walt shook his head and scowled, looking at the mayor, "Fine. I'll have the paperwork on your desk later today."

"Hold on, Chief," Raquel said, frowning. "We haven't agreed to any of this. What if we don't want to shut down the department?"

"It doesn't matter," he shrugged. "If the mayor agrees to it, your contracts shift to the DSA. You become federal employees and I'm pretty sure the pay will be much greater."

"It will," Cardwell agreed with a nod. "It'll also include housing, food, and clothing. You won't have to worry about any of that."

"And I agree to it," Downing said. "It'll be a load off the city's pocketbook."

Raquel glared at him, "You're a jerk."

Downing shrugged, "Maybe so, but I'm saving this city money and that's what needs to happen."

She shook her head and tried to think of a response, but she could only focus on anger and frustration. Before she could focus and think of a response, the moment was gone as Alex returned to the room with the tall, lithe form of Katrina Bentley behind him.

He quickly introduced her to the others and she began to explain her position and what she could offer to the effort. Before being accepted, though, she was requested to prove that her claims were true. She quickly shifted into the form of a panther, walked a tight circle in the open space beside the table, then reverted to human form.

That was enough for Cardwell. He simply nodded and said, "We'll need to discuss this further and adjust our plans accordingly. For now, though, we need to get our new recruits prepared to join the team."

Alex frowned, "What new recruits?"

Cardwell nodded toward the officers and he understood.

Alex looked at the three and said, "Come with me. We'll start getting you situated."

CHAPTER EIGHTEEN
Roaming

Nora Burman loved the idea of roaming through the town as a wolf, but she loved it even more doing so as a naked human. There was little activity, human or otherwise, in the area where she'd been sent in the pack's search for Moonshadow, and she frequently shifted into her human form and moved around, walking brazenly along the darkened sidewalks of the residential area a few blocks from the town's hospital. There seemed to be nowhere in the area that was likely to be a place for a group of vampires and one renegade werewolf to be hiding and preparing something major. Even with her senses dulled while in human form, they were still sharper than an average human and she would be able to discern the faintest trace of a lycanthrope's scent.

At one point during the night, a couple of hours past midnight, she'd wandered toward the main street, Bolling Avenue, and approached an old shopping center. She'd arrived just as a drug deal was taking place and she'd hidden in the shadows, still in human form, in a cluster of overgrown bushes behind the bank adjacent to the shopping center as the deal had taken place. She felt a slight thrill at the thought of being naked in such proximity to the few men involved in the deal, but she knew she would never be seen. If any of them gave even a hint of noticing her presence, she would quickly transform and leave the scene. In the darkness, the men would most likely think she was just a very large dog and ignore her. They didn't notice her and she stayed crouched in the bushes until they'd completed the transaction and left in two vehicles, each of them going in a different direction.

She spent the rest of the night simply walking through her assigned area and felt like she'd been sent to the one area with no chance of finding Moonshadow or the vampires. At the first hint of sunrise approaching, a faint glow in the sky to the east, she transformed into wolf form and made her way back to the old house near the bus station.

It took her a while, making her way halfway across the town, but she arrived just as Holly and Renee arrived and shifted into human form in the house's unkempt and dying front yard. Nora was once again taken aback by the two women. Holly was tall and perfectly shaped with the look of a model, or at least one that would appear in a certain type of magazine. Renee, while a bit shorter than Nora, had light red hair and a taut, lithe body. None of them were ashamed of their body or afraid of being seen, but it wouldn't help their cause to be seen and reported to the authorities. It would hinder their search and they needed to find Moonshadow before it was too late.

Holly led them to a spot at the corner of the house's porch, raised a little higher than Nora thought would be typical and higher than the other houses in the area. A small opening had provided access to the space beneath it and had proven to be perfect for hiding their clothing. Holly leaned over, exposing more of herself to Nora and Renee than either wanted to see, and began pulling out their clothing. While she was doing that, groping around in the dark, the others returned. Greyeagle was first, followed a couple of moments later by Scott, with Carmen being the last to arrive.

She walked to the corner of the house slowly and casually, as if she didn't have a care in the world. She stopped and waited until the others were dressed before donning her own clothes. The others gathered around and watched as she dressed, the guys taking in her smooth, soft body while the women waited a bit uncomfortably. She dressed quickly and looked up at them when she was finished.

"Okay," she said. "I'm going to assume we've found no trace of Moonshadow."

"Nothing," Scott said and shook his head, folding his arms across his chest. "I covered the area on the other side of the railroad as thoroughly as I could and couldn't locate his scent."

Carmen nodded, "He is here somewhere. Let's get some rest and we'll start again."

She looked at the house and continued, "This place will be good. It's not perfect and doesn't look exactly comfortable, but it will keep us from being noticed."

"Let's go," Greyeagle said gruffly. "I'm exhausted."

He turned and started for the rickety steps at the center of the porch as the others slowly and tiredly followed.

Inside, they spread out, each finding a spot to rest. Carmen waited until they were settled before sitting down just inside the front door, across the room from Scott, the protector of the pack. He remained close to the entrance, ready to do what was necessary to keep the pack from harm. Carmen understood his position, but she knew it wasn't necessary in Pine Ridge. No one knew they were there, with the exception of Katrina, but she'd gone off on her own and would most likely find somewhere to sleep away from the pack. Carmen appreciated Scott's position and dedication, but it wasn't exactly what she needed. She needed them all to fall asleep, a sleep deep enough that they wouldn't notice her departure.

She'd located Moonshadow, but she hadn't been able to reach him during the night. He was with the vampires in an old abandoned hotel on the south side of town, a location hidden from the view of anyone passing on the road in front of it. The property looked as if it hadn't been visited for decades prior to the arrival of the vampires.

She remained seated beside the door, her legs crossed and her hands resting on her knees, until she was sure the others were asleep. Once she was certain and the sun was high enough to cast away most of the shadows, she rose silently to her feet and made her way outside. Standing on the porch, she drew in a deep breath. Even with her diminished senses in human form, she could smell the scent of Moonshadow. He was still in the same location, the old hotel, and it would take her a while to get there without transforming into wolf form, but it needed to be done. She had to make sure and find out what she could.

After just a moment, she walked down the steps and began her walk toward the hotel.

It took nearly two hours to walk the distance from the downtown district to the wide highway that was essentially the town's southern border. There was plenty of traffic at that time of day and it took her a while to cross the five lanes and reach the gas station on the opposite corner. From there, she followed the narrower highway leading to the south and reached the hotel less than twenty minutes later.

She paused at the entrance to the driveway and looked around carefully for a moment, waiting for a break in the traffic before she hurried off the road and onto the driveway. From there, it only took a few moments to reach the open space before the hotel and she paused at the edge of the trees, concealing herself the best she could behind one of the thick tree trunks as she looked around the property and waited to see if the vampires had posted any human guards.

Once she was sure there were no guards, the vampires apparently believing their location to be completely secure, Carmen removed her clothing and transformed into a wolf. Using her strong sense of smell, she followed the scent of Moonshadow to the entrance, but the door was locked. The vampires might've felt secure about the property, but they weren't so sure about the building itself.

Carmen backed away and moved around the building until she found an opening on the back side, a window frame with no glass on the second floor. She couldn't quite reach it as a wolf, but she could climb as a human. She reverted to that form and climbed the cracked wooden wall of the building, pressing her naked flesh against it as she struggled to find handholds and footholds. Finally, after a few moments, she reached the window and climbed inside.

With the sun out in a clear sky, light filtered into the room and left it uninhabitable by a vampire. She was alone in the room and crossed the broken floor, taking care to avoid the few fairly large holes, and reached the door. She eased it open and walked out into the hall.

Feeling a little tentative and nervous about her nudity, she made her way along the hallway to the central staircase climbed up two floors, following the scent, and found the room where Moonshadow was sleeping.

He wasn't alone. Carmen could feel a cold presence beside him, sharing a bit of his body heat, and Carmen knew he was in bed with one of the vampires, the one that had supposedly saved his life years earlier.

Shaking her head, she backed away and walked slowly through the remainder of the building and did her best to figure out what the vampires were doing, but there were few signs and nothing left out in the open.

Frustrated and still anxious, she made her way back to the room with the open window. She looked back, frowning with concern, then dove through the window and transformed as she fell, landing on four feet before sprinting back to the front of the property where she'd left her clothes. Keeping an eye on the hotel, she dressed as quickly as she could then began the long walk back to the old house.

Once back on the state highway and headed in the right direction, she began thinking about the situation and planning what should be done next. If Moonshadow had been rescued by the vampire and the life debt was in place, it would be difficult to get him to leave her. If the life debt wasn't in place and he was either controlled by the vampires or had willingly joined them, there was nothing she could do short of actual combat to break the connection. It was something she had to consider and had to find out. Whichever it was, she and the pack had a great deal of work to do.

CHAPTER NINETEEN
Discharged

Dana was tired of lying in the narrow bed practically naked and being poked and prodded by doctors and nurses. They'd claimed the frequent drawing of blood was to run tests to find out just what had happened as a result of the attack, but none of the results had been given to her. The physician she saw most frequently, Dr. Brinson, was a little more forthcoming with the information, but he said there wasn't much there, that the tests were inconclusive.

Late the previous afternoon, Dr. Brinson had informed her that the tests were complete. There was nothing else for them to do, no more tests to be performed. Healing from that point was beyond their ability and would just take time. She'd remained through the night for a little more observation and would be discharged sometime that morning. She'd awakened early, just after sunrise, and had been given breakfast then waited for the official declaration of discharge.

She'd begun to wonder if she would be forced to leave the hospital still wearing only the gown and panties since the clothing she'd been wearing the night of the attack had been taken from her and had never been discussed. She was relieved when Tiffany and Ben arrived a short while after she'd finished her meal. They'd brought a change of clothing for her: a pair of jeans, her favorite sweatshirt, and the only pair of tennis shoes she owned.

As they entered, Tiffany placed the neatly folded clothes on the rolling table beside the bed that fit over the bed to provide her with a surface for the hard plastic trays the meals were served on and stepped back, shrugging.

"Sorry," Tiffany said. "I couldn't find any underwear."

"It's okay," Dana nodded and smiled warmly. "It's all in the laundry. I intended to take care of it that night."

Tiffany nodded and asked, "You want me to go get something? It won't take long."

"No," Dana shook her head slowly, keenly aware of the bandage remaining on the left side of her neck. "It'll be okay. I'll take care of it when I get home."

Tiffany frowned, "Are you sure you're up to that?"

"Yeah," Dana replied. "I feel fine. I'm tired of just lying in this bed. I need to get up and do something. Laundry shouldn't be too demanding."

Ben, sitting in a chair beside the door to the bathroom, sat up straight and said, "Just be careful and don't overdo it."

Dana looked at him and smirked, "I'm not an invalid, Ben."

He shrugged and sat back as the door opened and Dr. Brinson walked in holding an aluminum clipboard to his chest. His white lab coat, traditional garb that had changed in decades, was slightly rumpled and looked less than pristine. His hair was slightly mussed and uncombed while his eyes seemed a little bloodshot with dark circles beneath them. The only thing missing from the standard doctor's appearance was the stethoscope around his neck.

He entered the room and moved to the side of the bed, a tired smile on his face as he looked at Dana.

"Well, I guess it's about that time," he said. "You're ready to get out of here, but I don't think you'll be going home."

"What do you mean?" Dana frowned. "I don't have anywhere else to go."

He nodded slowly and said, "I've talked with that group from the government, the ones that visited you. They're going to take you in. The one in charge, Mr. Cardwell I believe, said they have a series of tests they want to run., but they will need your consent."

Dana tilted her head to the left and asked, "You mean the group with Alex? I'll give my consent to that."

Brinson nodded, "That's all I need to hear. They're already here and on their way up. I'd have my nurse escort you to the door, but she didn't show up for work today and the hospital is unusually short-staffed today. They'll take care of it."

"Thanks, Dr. Brinson," Dana said, relaxing and smiling lightly. "I'm sure they'll take good care of me."

He smiled again, nodded once, and left the room. As the door began to swing closed behind him, it was pushed open by Alex as he entered the room with Bonacci just behind him. They were both dressed in black, but neither appeared armed.

Within a few minutes, she was out of bed and had gone into the small bathroom to dress. While she was in there, Bonacci stood at the door almost as if he was guarding it and Alex stood closer to the bathroom while Tiffany joined Ben in sitting against the wall beside it.

Tiffany looked up at Alex and asked, "Where are you taking her?"

He looked at her and said, "We have a facility in the old hospital building downtown. It's fully equipped and secured."

"We're going with you," Ben said sharply. "I want to make sure before you do something to hurt her again."

Alex looked at him and frowned, "That's fine. Just don't try to interfere with what we're doing. You don't understand it and it won't make a lot of sense to you."

Ben scowled, "I just want to make sure she's safe."

Alex nodded as the bathroom door opened and Dana walked out, fully dressed, with the gown wadded up in her left hand.

"I've had enough of this thing," she said and tossed it onto the bed then looked at Alex. "Can we get out of here?"

"Of course," he nodded and turned toward the door.

A few moments later, they reached the ground floor and started through the lobby with Bonacci taking the lead. He looked around carefully, but he felt slightly off-kilter without a weapon in his possession. It made him self-conscious and almost afraid though he knew there would be no vampire attack during daylight hours. Alex and Dana followed a few feet back, walking close together. Alex kept his right hand on Dana's left arm and he looked around carefully as well, though he was distracted by her proximity. It had been a long time since he'd been so close to her and actually touched her. It was a strange feeling and it confused him a bit. He did still care for her, but he wasn't sure there was anything else there.

Tiffany and Ben stayed close to them. Ben held her hand tightly and they struggled a bit to keep up with the rapid pace the others set.

"How are we getting there?" Dana asked, glancing up at Alex.

He replied, "Melissa Dyson is waiting in a car outside. She'll drive us back."

"Yeah," Bonacci said and glanced over his right shoulder. "I don't particularly like being just a passenger, but she's as good as they come."

"I'm taking my truck," Ben said. "We'll follow you."

Alex nodded and said, "That's good. There isn't much room in this car."

Bonacci reached the door and the automatic mechanism was triggered by his presence and the doors slid open. He continued forward and paused outside, looking around for any sign of someone watching them. When he saw nothing, he nodded to Alex and continued toward the parking lot.

As Tiffany and Ben walked through the door and it closed behind them, a shadow appeared in the hallway to the left of the door, moving slowly toward the lobby. As the group moved toward the parking lot, Ryan Sullivan walked around the corner, looked out the window beside him, and nodded slowly with a light smirk on his face.

CHAPTER TWENTY
Examination

Behind the wheel of a small rental car approaching Williamsburg, Virginia, Martin Raymond frequently checked the rearview mirror for any sign of being followed. With the President of the United States in the back seat, cowering with a royal blue hooded jacket covering her brilliantly blonde hair, he was more than a little nervous as he transported the woman he'd been charged with protecting to a small doctor's office on the outskirts of the city for the results of an examination that had taken place a little more than two weeks earlier. He'd driven the course twice before and had planned ahead all three times, preparing a route that would hopefully not be detected by the press that always seemed to be waiting to observe and report on every move the President made. He knew enough about her situation, that she was facing a serious medical condition of some sort, and didn't want it leaked to the press and revealed to the general public until she was ready to do so on her own terms.

He'd picked her up at her home shortly before sunrise, the time when the media presence at the house in Georgetown was at its lowest. The rental car had been chosen because it was the same style several couriers in the area used and his arrival at the rear entrance, one typically reserved for deliveries made by those couriers, made her exit from the house quite a bit less noticeable.

The roundabout course took much longer than the simple journey should've taken, but Memory Hutchins thought it was necessary to keep anyone from discovering where she was going and the reason for her visit. Martin knew the course well and didn't resort to using a GPS unit for fear of it being hacked or detected. He saw the President and everything about her as his personal responsibility and would take every measure available to ensure her safety and privacy.

Once they were well away from her home and on the interstate taking them to the city of Williamsburg, Martin glanced at the cowering President and said, "I think the coast is clear, ma'am. No one seems to be following us."

"Good," Memory said through a tired sigh and slowly sat up. "This is all a bit much and too much like those old spy movies. I'm sorry about this, Martin, but I definitely appreciate all that you do."

"My pleasure, ma'am," he replied with a nod, his eyes hidden behind dark sunglasses scanning their surroundings. "And we should be there in less than twenty minutes."

"Okay," she said and let out a sigh, sitting back in the seat. "I'm going to close my eyes. If I fall asleep, just wake me up when we get there."

"Yes, ma'am," he said and tightened his grip on the steering wheel.

As she closed her eyes and tried to push the fear of what she would hear from her doctor out of her mind, she began to think about Jonathan Cardwell and his task force. He'd been upfront with her about the entire process, even trying to convince her that vampires did exist and that they were trying to take over the county, possibly the world. The whole thing just seemed crazy to her and she wondered about Cardwell's mental state with his belief that it was all real. She'd been generous in giving him funding to that point based on their past relationship and his assistance in keeping her safe while campaigning for her first office, a state senator in Texas. It had supposedly been during that time, when he'd first been recruited by the

DSA, that he'd been sent on a mission in Texas that he claimed had been the beginning of his obsession with vampires. She didn't know for sure, but his belief and her faith in him had been enough to justify, at least in her mind, the creation and funding of his task force.

With his insistence that the battle against the vampires wasn't over, even though he'd declared the beginning of the end with the destruction of the one he'd referred to as the Master Vampire, named Davros, he still wanted more funding. After having funneled additional funds through the DSA and with the assistance of Director Kevin Burns in creatively shifting those funds around, Cardwell wanted more and the only way to get it was to bring the Senate Financial Allocation Committee into the mix and had subsequently involved the Chairperson of the committee, Theda Howland. Now, to appease Senator Howland, Cardwell had to provide proof that vampires exist and present it to the senator. Memory doubted he would be able to do that and there would be no additional funding. It also most likely meant that Cardwell's entire task force would be shut down. She would give Cardwell time to make the presentation happen, but she couldn't hold off the senator forever.

She opened her eyes as the vehicle slowed and turned into a parking lot, the small lot in front of the small building that housed the office of Dr. Wanda Fairly.

Despite having an official Presidential physician, Memory preferred to visit Dr. Fairly for more personal matters. She'd known Wanda for several years and they'd developed a solid friendship as well as a somewhat clandestine professional one.

Only two vehicles were in the parking lot as the car entered and Memory recognized them both. The more expensive BMW was Wanda's car and the small, older Mustang was the car of her nurse, Lena Manfred.

Once parked, Martin climbed out of the car and opened the back door for the President. She climbed out carefully, feeling a little tired and she knew that was something to be concerned about. Hopefully, Wanda would give her the results of the test she'd performed a couple of weeks earlier and there would be good news involved. She doubted it, but she could hope.

Martin led the way up a set of brick steps to the front door and opened it, standing aside as Memory entered the building and pulled the hood away from her head. To her right, was a small counter with the wall behind it consisting of white-painted shelves filled with files and a few binders. Seated behind the desk, as Memory had expected, was Lena Manfred.

Lena was tall and a bit fleshy with several tattoos showing on her arms and hands. Her long, black hair hung perfectly straight to just below her shoulders and framed a soft face with an easy and almost permanent smile.

"Good morning, Madame President," Lena said cheerily. "We're all set up for you."

"Good morning, Lena," Memory replied. "Thanks. The usual room?"

"Of course," Lena said and gestured toward a closed door across the small waiting area from the entrance. "Dr. Fairly is ready and waiting."

"Thank you," Memory nodded and started for the door.

Martin closed the front door and stood there in his usual pose, ready for anything. Memory didn't look back, knowing precisely where he would be if anything should happen. She doubted it would and focused on what Wanda had to say rather than her personal safety.

Once through the door, she entered a short hallway, one leading to a room at the back that was a smaller version of an operating room, the room where Wanda would perform smaller-scale procedures. She closed the door behind her and took only a few steps before she reached the first door on her left, the only door in that part of the building that stood open. It was the examining room she'd become very familiar with.

Entering the small room, she smiled as she saw Wanda seated on a rolling stool beside the narrow padded examination table at the center of the room. Two walls were lined with counters and cabinets while the third held an array of instruments with a sanitizing station beside a sink in the corner directly to her left.

Wanda was a fairly tall woman with long, lightly curly, light brown hair, an almost triangular face and deep, soft, brown eyes. She wore a lab coat over pale blue scrubs with gray tennis shoes. She smiled broadly as Memory entered and gestured toward a chair in the far corner on the left.

"Good morning, Madame President," she said. "I don't think we need to worry about all that undressing stuff and we can skip the table."

"Good," Memory said and nodded, moving toward the table as Wanda rolled her stool around the far end of the table.

Memory sat down and Wanda stopped the stool a couple of feet away.

"Let's get right to it," Wanda said. "This is rather serious."

"Okay," Memory nodded and sat up straight with her hands clasped together between her knees. "Let me have it."

Wanda's smile faded as she leaned slightly forward and said, "I'm sorry, but it's exactly what I thought it was."

Memory shook her head, casting her eyes downward, and Wanda continued, "The biggest problem is that it's systemic and not localized. That means it's not operable. I can't just go in and cut it out. We'll have to set up more tests and determine the extent of it, but I think we can treat it. The good news is that it's not overly aggressive at this point. That should give us plenty of time to figure something out."

Memory nodded slowly, fear coursing through her, and she finally looked up, her eyes rimmed with tears.

"When can we get started?"

Wanda shrugged, "It depends on your schedule, I guess. I want to perform these tests at Bethesda. I know it won't be quite as private, but their facilities are much more advanced than what I have here. Depending on those results, we'll figure out what our next step will be."

Memory drew in a deep breath and said, "Whatever it takes."

Wanda pushed her stool back a bit and said, "I'll make the initial arrangements and have them standing by when your schedule permits."

"Sounds good," Memory said and placed her hands on her knees, ready to stand up. "I'll let you know as soon as I can."

Wanda nodded and Memory stood up, wondering just how long she had left to live.

CHAPTER TWENTY-ONE
Recruits

The conference room was quiet. The eight people seated around the table, clustered at one end, were waiting for the man at the head of the table, Cardwell, to begin explaining the next step with the four seated to his left. Raquel Jackson, Evan Barker, Neil Shafer, and Lois Cashlin sat back in their chairs, anxious expressions on their faces. Across from them, Sandusky, Alex, and Caroline sat leaning forward with their eyes on Cardwell as well.

After a moment, Cardwell sat up and began, "Okay. This is going to be a little tricky. We need to make this happen quickly."

He looked to his right and said, "We need to get these three outfitted, equipped, and ready to go today."

Sandusky nodded, "We have a few spare uniforms and they might fit."

"That's a start," Cardwell said.

Alex added, "We have plenty of weapons, plus what they already have. There's more than enough ammo to go around."

"Wait a minute," Raquel said, shaking her head. "What sort of weapons? The pistols we have aren't enough?"

"Not even close," Cardwell said and looked at her. "It takes special firepower to deal with these things."

Alex leaned forward, lacing his fingers together on the table as he looked at her, "You have to understand that vampires are no longer human. They're corpses reanimated by a virus. It gives them greater strength, speed, and senses than a human. They feed only on blood. We're not sure if it has to be human, but we haven't had the opportunity to examine one closely. So far, the only way we've found to damage them is by using silver. It won't kill them, but it'll slow them down a bit. They can regenerate any other wounds, no matter how many times you shoot them with standard ammunition. And the only ways we've found to kill them is to sever the spine. It's quicker if you remove the head, but any break in the spine is fatal. It takes a while, but they will develop armor, a sort of thicker spine, along their back, but the head remains vulnerable."

"What about a stake through the heart?' Evan asked. "That always works in the movies."

Alex glared at him and said, "This is different. The movies take certain liberties and they are all based on myths and fiction. A stake through the heart will temporarily paralyze them, but it's damn near impossible to get close enough. They don't suddenly become kung fu masters, but they are strong and fast, much faster than anything you've seen yet."

Evan nodded and Cardwell cleared his throat then continued, "So, we have uniforms and weapons. What about armor?"

"Same with the armor," Sandusky said. "It probably won't be a great fit, but it'll get the job done."

"Good enough," Cardwell said and looked at Lois. "You won't have to worry about that, Ms. Cashlin. You'll be here with Caroline, coordinating the field efforts."

He shifted his gaze to Caroline and said, "I think you'd best get started preparing her."

Caroline nodded and pushed her chair back, "That's a good idea. There's a lot to get done."

She started to stand and said, "Come with me, Lois."

Lois shrugged and stood up, "The sooner the better."

Once Caroline and Lois were out of the room, Cardwell looked at the remaining three new recruits and said, "I want you to understand the situation and how it changes what you've known and done."

Shafer looked at him, frowning, and said, "I thought we were just shifting to another organization."

"In a way," Cardwell agreed with a nod. "But there's more to it. Once you're completely outfitted, you'll have to fill out some paperwork. It's basically standard employment forms with a few little extras. You'll be officially employees of the federal government and you'll work for me, through Alex. You'll be part of our insertion team, the group that handles all the dirty work, and Alex is the team lead."

He leaned forward again and continued, "I won't lie to you. This is an extremely dangerous job, more dangerous than anything you've dealt with before. You'll become highly trained combat soldiers, though the combat is unlike anything you'll see in the traditional military. There is a lot more to it, but we don't have time to go over that right now. We need to get you outfitted and armed then get the paperwork done. I know it sounds kind of trite, but the paperwork is essential. There is a strong chance you won't survive too long with this group. We lost two on the way here. So, the paperwork will set up a life insurance policy that will guarantee financial security for your beneficiary. I know that doesn't compensate you, but it's one thing we can offer."

Shafer nodded, "I understand. But what about the town? Are we going to continue as police officers, or at least with that function?"

"In a way," Cardwell nodded and sat back. "You'll continue to patrol, but you'll be looking for vampire activity as well as the standard lawbreakers."

"Okay," Shafer nodded. "I can live with that."

"Good," Cardwell nodded. "Now, let me explain the situation a little more clearly. I want you to know everything. If you can't handle it, you're free to leave."

"We can handle it," Raquel said with a sharp nod.

Cardwell cut his eyes toward her and said, "There is something going on in this town and we're not completely sure what it is. The vampires have some grand plan they've just put into action and we need to stop them. We've also recently learned that there are also werewolves and werecats. One of them, a werecat, has warned us about the involvement of the wolves, but they are apparently on our side. They want to stop the vampires as well. Hopefully, we'll be able to connect with them soon and add their particular strengths to our efforts. But understand this: vampires are vicious, evil creatures and their main purposes in existing are to feed and make more like them. There's a process to that and I'll let Alex explain. He understands it much better than I do."

He looked at Alex and Alex nodded then looked at the recruits and began, "It's also not like in the movies. They don't bite you and you die then three days later you rise from the dead. It's much quicker than that, but it can be slower. First of all, it takes three bites for a person to turn overnight. If a single vampire bites you three times, in one night or over several, when you turn, you'll be bound to that vampire. If two or three different vampires bite you, you'll be a bit like them, but you won't be under the control of another vampire. Also, if you are randomly bitten and not bitten again, you will turn into a vampire, but it'll take much longer, possibly as long as two months. There is no cure and no way to stop it. Once you are bitten, that's it. You will become a vampire. However, if you are bitten a second time, after a few days, you'll start developing some of their abilities. In this state, you'll be known as a dhampir, or half vampire."

He took a breath and continued, "Now, we do have a couple of people, Sydney Lawson and Jana Hendricks, working on figuring out how this virus works and looking for a cure. So far, they haven't had much success, but we're all hopeful. That's why we go through full inspections after each encounter. So, you'll have to get over your insecurities and embarrassment."

Raquel frowned, "You mean, full-body searches?"

"Yes," he said and nodded. "It's the only way we can be sure. Sydney has been working on a detector, to find the bites without having to stand around naked while someone else looks over every inch of your body, but she's been a little busy with other things and hasn't quite gotten around to finishing it."

Raquel nodded, "I guess I can live with it."

Evan looked at her, grinning, and said, "I think I'll like it."

She glared at him and Alex sat up straight, "We won't have any of that. This isn't for your gratification. It's for the safety and security of the team and the task force. That's it."

Evan nodded, looking downward, "I understand. Sorry."

"Okay," Cardwell said. "I think that covers the basics. Let's get these people set up and get things worked out so we can be ready when the sun goes down."

CHAPTER TWENTY-TWO
Loss of Control

Carmen stood naked beside a large tree facing the old hotel with her right hand resting against the rough bark of the tree's trunk as she watched for activity inside the building through the few windows showing sources of light inside. Nora, also naked, stood on the other side of the tree, hidden by the shadows cast by the overhanging branches and thick leaves that remained attached to those branches. Her dark eyes were narrowed as she scanned the area around the buildings, looking for any signs of activity around the building while they waited for the remainder of the pack to arrive.

After waking them up, once she'd slept a few hours, she'd instructed them to meet at the hotel to complete their task of locating Moonshadow and returning him to the Tribe. It was still early in the evening, not long after sunset, and the presence of six wolves traveling together through a small southern town would be noticed. They didn't need the attention and definitely didn't want to reveal the presence of lycanthropes to the general public, at least not yet. She'd sent them to find a vehicle, a van or SUV, large enough to transport them all once they achieved their objective.

"I don't think they have any outside security," Nora said softly after several moments of watching.

"No," Carmen shook her head. "They don't. They think they're secure and hidden. We should have no problems."

Nora nodded slowly and sniffed the air then looked over her left shoulder.

"They're here," she said. "They're coming through the trees, but they haven't changed."

Carmen nodded and looked to her right, "Yeah. It'll be fine. Give them a minute."

It took just a few seconds for the remainder of the pack to reach them, walking quickly and silently through the trees. Scott led the way with Greyeagle at the rear of the group.

As they approached, Carmen turned to face them and said, "Get ready. Transform and follow me. We're going in the front door. The vampires should be waking up any minute. I'll go after Moonshadow. The rest of you handle the vampires."

Without a word, they began removing their clothing. Nora stepped forward slowly, shifting her hips almost seductively as she prepared herself for combat, and took three steps before she leaned forward and began the transformation.

Behind her, the others quickly removed their clothing and changed, leaving their clothes on the ground behind them. Carmen was the last to change, taking a look over her shoulder to make sure the others were behind her and ready to go. Once they were ready, she looked forward and fell forward, transforming as she dropped. Carmen then bounded forward until she was beside Nora and slowed down. She cast a look at Nora and growled lightly, telling Nora to hold back and join the others. Nora returned the look, but she did as Carmen wanted.

As the pack formed into a group, a triangle of fur and muscle, they picked up the pace and followed Carmen toward the door.

They were within twenty yards of the door when it opened and the massive form of Dylan stepped out wearing only a pair of loose, black leather pants. His massive chest, pale and smooth, stood out in the dim light coming from inside the lobby of the hotel.

Carmen didn't stop. With a low growl, baring her teeth in the equivalent of a snarl, she charged forward. The others followed suit and they rushed toward the vampire as he stepped forward and was followed by several others. They shot through the doorway in streaks of multi-colored light that coalesced into human form in an instant, appearing as if they'd materialized out of thin air.

The last to leave the hotel was Gerrit and he stopped in the doorway, grinning and showing his fangs as he looked at the approaching wolves. Carmen increased her speed, running as fast as she could push herself, and focused on Gerrit. She knew him, knew he was one of the Virate. He had the scent of power about him and his posture told her he was the one in charge.

She sprinted between a few of the other vampires and sprang at him as she drew within range. Her jaws opened wide as she aimed at his throat, tilting her head to the side, ready to clamp down and rip his throat out. Hopefully, he hadn't yet fed for the day and would be at least somewhat weakened, giving her a slight edge. She wouldn't be able to destroy him unless her jaws snapped together with enough force to sever his spine.

Her forepaws spread wide, ready to wrap around him the best she could and drive him to the ground as she tried to gnaw through his throat and spine. A quick thought flashed through her mind, thinking that if she was able to take down one of the Virate, their apparent leader, she would effectively end the conflict between vampires and wolves before it truly began.

Just as the thought entered her mind, Gerrit's left hand shot out and grabbed her by the throat as if she weighed nothing and hadn't been moving at all. The sudden change in direction and loss of momentum shocked her and she hung limply in his grasp for a second before she started struggling to be released.

Gerrit tightened his grip, cutting off her flow of air, and she looked into his eyes. As she did, she stopped moving, feeling his power flowing, and there was nothing she could do.

"Now, now, little wolf," he said and shook his head slowly, still grinning. "It is such a surprise for this little pack to have shown up here and you, their leader, are an even bigger surprise. You actually found us without too much effort, I imagine."

The other wolves pulled up short when they saw Gerrit grab Carmen as if she were no more than a rag doll. The other vampires remained stationary and stared at the wolves, waiting for them to make a move.

Gerrit pulled Carmen a little closer and said softly, "Let me see you, the true you."

Before she could attempt to block his power, she felt herself change. In an instant, she'd reverted to her human form and hung naked in his grasp.

Still looking into her eyes, he said with a little more volume, "Now the rest of you. Show yourselves and come to me."

Reluctantly, the wolves transformed and moved slowly forward, their eyes watching the vampires around them. None of the vampires moved, standing still like statues, until the group of naked humans stood in front of Gerrit. They all turned around and waited.

Gerrit pulled Carmen a little closer, their gazes still locked, and his eyes began to glow a faint, sickly yellow as he said, "It has been too long since I've encountered members of the Tribe and even longer since I've seen what can be done with them. You, Carmen Pauling, temporary alpha of this pack, will become my servant. In turn, you will all serve me."

As his eyes continued to glow, he tilted his head to the right and focused on Carmen and her mind. Her breathing began to slow and she relaxed.

After a few seconds, she said, "I am yours to command."

The ones behind her, the pack, repeated those words in unison.

"Good," Gerrit nodded. "You will now join us in completing our plan."

Behind them, Colin and Rachel glared at Gerrit. He'd taken complete and sole control of the wolves.

CHAPTER TWENTY-THREE
Diagnosis

Dana was anxious and frightened sitting alone in the lab. She'd gone through a number of tests with Sydney and Jana drawing more blood than she thought she had, but she wanted to know the truth of what was happening as much as anyone, possibly more. It was her life they were all talking about and she felt she deserved to know all the details.

Sydney and Jana had left her less than fifteen minutes earlier to bring Cardwell and Alex to the lab for the discussion of the results, but it felt like they'd been gone for hours. She couldn't help reflecting on the expressions the two women had borne as they'd left the lab, frowns that told her it was more serious than she'd imagined. Thankfully, they hadn't left her in one of those flimsy hospital gowns and had allowed her to dress once they were done with the tests. For most of the testing, she'd worn only a bra and panties, which had been provided for her after reaching the facility, but they'd given her jeans and a sweatshirt with socks and shoes. She'd been left sitting on a low stool against one of the gleaming metal counters along the back wall of the room while the two women went to find the two guys that she hoped would handle the situation.

The fear hadn't really set in until she was left alone. As long as the two women were there and the tests were continuing, she wasn't worried. The isolation and time to process what had happened and what had been done to her brought the fear to a higher level, to the point where she began shivering involuntarily though the room wasn't overly cool. She just didn't know what was going to happen and she quickly began thinking of the worst possible outcome.

Without her watch and with no clock in the room, she had no idea how long Sydney and Jana had been gone. It felt like it had been an eternity, but she knew it couldn't have been more than ten minutes. She tried to relax, but knew quickly it wasn't going to happen, so she sat there with her back to the counter and her hands clasped together between her knees. Tears threatened to spill from her eyes, but she'd held them back for so many years another few minutes wouldn't be a problem.

She sat up when the door finally opened, her eyes opening wide. Sydney and Jana walked in quickly, their expressions now almost blank, and were followed by Cardwell and Alex. Dana looked up and kept her eyes on them and she was surprised that Alex didn't look at her. That told her just how serious the situation was and the fear she was already feeling grew by an order of magnitude. She trembled and clasped her hands together more tightly as she waited for them to tell her something.

They lined up along the wide table running down the center of the room. Alex at one end and Sydney at the other leaned back. Alex folded his arms over his chest while Sydney held her hands together in front of her. Jana stood close to Sydney and placed her hands on the table, almost leaning back. Cardwell had his hands stuffed into the pockets of his pants as he looked at Dana carefully.

Dana drew in a deep breath and let it out slowly as she said, "Let me have it."

Sydney looked at Cardwell, a questioning expression on her face. He looked at her and nodded.

Sydney then looked at Dana and said, "Okay. Let me start by saying that we've run every test we have and they're all saying the same thing. The vampire that bit you transferred a virus into your bloodstream. We've isolated the virus, but we haven't been able to find an antivirus. Right now, it's incurable."

"What does that mean?" Dana asked weakly, fear causing her voice to shake.

Sydney looked at her sympathetically and said, "I really hate this, but you're in the process of becoming a vampire."

Dana frowned, "I thought it happened a lot more quickly."

Sydney looked at Alex and said, "You can probably explain the process better."

He nodded and looked at Dana, "The big thing is that he didn't draw much blood. Vampires don't need much to keep themselves going. Less than half a pint will keep them active for nearly a week. The bite wasn't enough to do much damage, but it did infect you. Turning is a slow, strange process. In your case, with a single bite, it could take up to a couple of months for you to turn, but you will turn. It takes three such bites for the process to happen quickly and it will then happen overnight. A second bite, like the first, will speed up the process. It'll only take about ten days after that, but during that time you'll start developing some of their abilities, but they won't be quite as strong."

Dana shook her head, "So, what if another vampire bites me? Or two more?"

Alex nodded slowly, "That's where it gets a little tricky and weird. If the same vampire bites you three times and draws blood each time, you'll turn and become his or her servant, more or less. They'll control you. If it's even two different ones, you'll be more or less on your own."

"I don't think I like this," Dana said. "Isn't there anything that can be done?"

"I'm afraid not," Sydney replied. "We've been trying to develop a serum, a sort of antivirus, but we just can't figure it out. We're missing something and just can't seem to find it. I'm sorry, but there's no way to stop this."

Dana felt ready to collapse and the tears began to flow. She leaned her head forward and a low sob came from her.

Cardwell shook his head and took a step toward the door, "This isn't the time to talk about the rest of it, but she does need to know."

Alex looked at him and said, "I'll talk to her. She'll know everything."

"Good," Cardwell said and left the room.

Alex walked over to Dana and knelt beside her, placing a hand gently on her back.

As he started talking to her in whispered tones, Sydney watched carefully. She felt a bit of fear as well, but a different kind. Alex had told her about his previous relationship with Dana and how it had ended. He'd told her several times that he had no intention of trying to find her and the relationship was definitely over. She'd believed him at the time, but seeing them together and the way he was treating her had Sydney worried that Alex would change his mind and try to rekindle what they'd had in high school.

And that would leave Sydney out in the cold once again.

CHAPTER TWENTY-FOUR
On Schedule

Inside the hotel lobby, the vampires and pack stood in a loose cluster in the open space between the entrance and the main counter. The pack members had not been given clothing, but they stood almost transfixed and unaware as Gerrit faced the others with the Mystic, Sharia, beside him and the other two of the Virate a few feet to his right. The other vampires, nearly a dozen of them, stood between the pack and Gerrit, a few of them glancing back suspiciously, as if they didn't trust the pack or Gerrit's control over them.

Moonshadow had joined them and was the only one dressed, wearing black leather pants, jacket, and boots with his arms folded across his chest as he stood rather close to Carmen. His posture suggested a bit of protection, but confidence as well. His dark eyes were focused on Gerrit and he didn't notice Kim standing off to the side, almost glaring at him. She felt almost betrayed by his sudden change once the pack had been brought into the operation. He'd shifted his allegiance to them and to Carmen in particular. Kim knew a little of his history with the Tribe and that he'd at one time been betrothed to the daughter of a tribal elder. She wasn't sure, but Kim assumed that Carmen was the one by the way they stood so close and seemed so comfortable together.

Once they were all assembled, Gerrit held his hands up as if he were an evangelist ready to begin a faith-healing session. He looked over the assemblage briefly then began.

"Tonight, we begin the next phase of our plan," he said loudly enough to be heard though the room was silent. "We have located the building where the DSA task force operates."

He leaned his head back and lowered his hands, "I can sense the presence of the woman and her presence will take us to the Nemesis."

He looked forward again and continued, "We will go to this facility. Our new allies, the wolves, will lead the charge. They will breach their defenses and allow us into the building. There will be a battle and you must all be careful to avoid certain people. The woman, Dana Richland, is not to be harmed. She will be the bait to draw the Nemesis to us. There is another, the one doing her best to destroy us through scientific means, and she is to be brought to me as well. Also, there are two others, the closest friends of Dana, Tiffany Gardner and Ben Mills. They are to be found and brought to Colin and Rachel."

He nodded toward them and looked forward as he continued, "Once we have them, the battle will end. The Nemesis will submit to us once he has made a decision that will affect the remainder of his life, and the lives of others. He will choose which one lives and which one becomes one of us. We will then bring our prize here to prepare him for the ritual tomorrow night. The others in the building, all of them, are fair game. You may turn or kill all that you can. We will leave a pile of bodies for them to sort out."

The others all nodded in unison, Gerrit having assumed control for the moment. He wanted to maintain that control and coordinate the battle himself, but even with the power of the Master, he wasn't yet strong enough to control that many vampires and wolves simultaneously. He wouldn't let them know that, of course. He had to maintain an air of superiority and could show no weakness.

After a second, letting the information take root, he held his hands out wide and smiled, "Prepare yourselves. We will leave within the half hour."

With a nod and a mental command, he dismissed the group and they began to disperse, preparing to leave and begin the attack. Kim didn't quite understand what they were doing. It should've been a simple matter of leaving the hotel and making their way to the building the task force was using. After a moment, she saw they were gathering in groups almost as if forming attack squads. It didn't make a lot of sense to her. There would undoubtedly be a single way to enter the building and the vampires, with their exceptional speed, would attack en masse and spread out once through the door. They didn't need squads or groups. She also didn't know the exact numbers in the task force facility, but she was almost certain the vampires outnumbered them even before adding in the presence of the pack.

She understood why those seven would congregate around Moonshadow. They weren't part of the vampire force and would be operating somewhat independently. They had their own mission and she wasn't sure how they would act once they reached the facility.

She was also a little confused by the way the others deferred to Moonshadow so quickly. She knew he had been the alpha of the pack before taking off on his own less than a year before she'd met him, but their loyalty had been to the Tribe and the alpha appointed to them. She assumed it had been Carmen when they'd first arrived, but even she deferred to Moonshadow without question.

As she watched the pack conferring and the other vampires gathering together and getting each other worked up for the attack, she couldn't help thinking that it just didn't seem right, at least not for her. She'd joined the Virate shortly after they'd received the power of the Master from Davros, days before he'd then been destroyed by Alex Chance, the man they all assumed was the Nemesis. Moonshadow had, of course, gone with her and had seemed to fall in line with what the Virate wanted. She'd done the same thing, but she'd realized once the Mystic arrived and the overall plan had been discussed that she wasn't going to receive any of the ancient power they were seeking and wouldn't be an important part of their future. She would just be another cog in their machine and not given any special treatment. It no longer seemed worth the effort to follow them so blindly without being part of the operation as anything more than a foot soldier.

She felt it was time to leave, to strike out on her own, and merely survive rather than attempting to secure a place in the vampire hierarchy. But she didn't want to leave without Moonshadow. At the moment, she didn't think he would leave, not after reconnecting with and taking charge of the pack. He claimed he owed her a life debt and she thought that might take precedence over the pack, but it didn't look that way. He'd barely glanced at her since making the connection with them, particularly Carmen. Still, she had to try. She had to know for sure.

A few moments later, the group of lycanthropes began to disperse, getting ready to follow Gerrit's instructions, and Moonshadow turned toward her. He paused and looked at her for a few seconds, his head tilted slightly to the left. The expression on his face was one of confusion and she could see by the tightness around his eyes that he was assessing his loyalties. He remained that way no longer than two seconds then started slowly toward her.

He stopped in front of her, no more than a foot away, and looked down at her.

"Moonshadow," she said softly as she looked up at him, her eyes wide. "I really don't understand what's going on. It looks like you've taken over as pack alpha."

"I have," he nodded. "Gerrit brought the pack in and has given me the position. They've all accepted it and I have to lead them."

Kim nodded slowly, her eyes still on his, and said, "I understand that. Now, tell me about Carmen. What's going on there?"

He drew in a slow, deep breath then leaned just a little closer and said, "Kim, you have to understand. Carmen is the daughter of a tribal Elder and I was the abandoned child, an orphan, and I was taken in by another Elder. Carmen and I sort of grew up together and spent most of our time together, especially once we were of age. I won't say we were exactly in love, but we were close and, with our connection to the Elders, it was the logical thing to do, to become betrothed. Now, after everything that's happened and with Gerrit's influence, it's only natural that we work closely together. I don't know what's going to happen when this is over, but we'll just have to go through it."

Kim reached out and touched his arm, "Moonshadow, come with me. Let's get out of here and go away, on our own. We'll find our own life somewhere."

"I can't," he said and shook his head. "I have to do this. I have to honor my heritage. I still owe you a life debt, but this has to take precedence right now. Once this is over, once Gerrit has what he wants, we'll see what happens."

She stared at him for a few seconds longer then finally shook her head and took a step back.

"I don't know what to do," she said and set her jaw firmly. "But I'll figure it out. We'll see if you're going to be part of it or not."

He opened his mouth to say something, but his thoughts were blocked by the call from Gerrit to begin the attack. Without another sound or gesture, he quickly pulled his clothes off and transformed with the pack behind him.

The wolves fell into a formation and started for the door as Kim stepped back, shaking her head. She watched as they left and wondered if she would ever see Moonshadow again.

CHAPTER TWENTY-FIVE
Invasion

Krista Deninger didn't mind the outdoor patrol as much as the others, especially with the current situation. The new recruits hadn't been fully trained in their methods. They were experienced police officers and understood the duty, but she didn't think they quite grasped that dealing with vampires was different than dealing with standard human criminals. It would take time and she hoped they had enough.

Once the sun had gone down, they'd prepared for the night. A watch schedule was set up with one person outside and one inside, though the inside patrol wouldn't begin until the others had retired for the night. She was alone on patrol until that happened and had at least another hour or more until she was relieved by Bonacci and one of the newbies began the interior watch. Not expecting much to happen, no one inside was armed, but Cardwell insisted on full tactical gear for everyone, including those with positions that kept them in their headquarters.

Krista wore the same black clothing as the others, but she'd added the body armor specially designed for the team by Sydney and Merina that included a flexible and impenetrable neckband. She didn't really understand how the material worked, but it could withstand a vampire attack and that was enough to give her the confidence she needed to do her job.

She was also fully armed. Multiple weapons were placed within easy reach and she carried one of the massive rifles, also designed by Sydney and Merina, that had been given no designation. It was just the team rifle and each member of the team had one with several in reserve, though those had been distributed to the new team members. On the wide belt attached to the armored bodice, a large holster held the massive .50 caliber pistol, a long knife with a blade coated in silver, and a pair of grenades Sydney had designed to simulate a brief flash of sunlight. Those grenades had a limited range and only lasted for an instant, but they provided a brief distraction, hopefully enough to give her a moment to regroup or to escape. The final addition to her armor was a helmet that looked a great deal like a standard motorcycle helmet, but it was much more. It was filled with electronics, also courtesy of Sydney and Merina, that included night vision, communications gear, and additional protection.

She felt confident and secure as she patrolled the grounds around the facility with the rifle, loaded with the high-powered ammunition designed to do the most damage to a vampire, she moved back to the porch in front of the building and stopped in front of the door at the entrance. She stood there for a few moments and began to feel a bit complacent, doubting that anything would happen. She checked the watch on her left wrist, easy to read in the light coming through the door behind her, and saw it was still another hour before Bonacci would relieve her. It was going to be a long, boring hour, but she would do her job and stand her ground.

The day itself had been boring and she was growing tired, but she had the determination and drive to remain on duty, though she began to grow less alert as the night progressed. She remained in front of the door and used the night vision attenuated to the particular biological signatures of vampires. She was expecting a vampire presence, as they all were, and the system didn't register anything else. She was caught completely off-guard when the massive black wolf leaped over the railing beside her and landed on top of her.

The force of the impact knocked her helmet off and, without the standard earwig, the communication system was removed. She tried to scream, but the huge muzzle of the wolf began snapping at her face while its claws began digging into her arm. She squirmed and tried to get away, swinging her fists toward its head, but the sturdy strap of the rifle wrapped around her hands and the weight of the wolf pinned her arms to her abdomen. Her head whipped back and forth to avoid the snarling mouth of the wolf, its thick saliva dripping onto her. She felt the claws on the armor and trusted it to protect her, but the wolf found the weak points, the straps that held it tightly against her body, and a precise swipe of one paw ripped through the straps and shoved the heavy plate away along with her rifle. The force of the blow that sent the rifle flying caused the strap to rip through the thick sleeves of her shirt and the twisting motion snapped the bones in both arms. As she began to let out a scream of pain, she was briefly immobilized and provided the opportunity the wolf needed. Its mouth, already open wide, snapped forward and closed on her face as one paw tore through fabric and flesh. Her final scream was released into the mouth of the wolf and was barely audible over its deep growl.

As her blood flowed slowly across the concrete of the porch, the wolf pulled back and turned its head to the left, looking at the other six wolves waiting just past the edge of the light coming from the building's door and windows. With that signal, they moved forward.

Seated at her console behind the counter just inside the door, Merina frowned as she looked at the communications system. She'd lost contact with Krista's helmet system and she shook her head, thinking that something had gone wrong with the helmet. She knew it was a delicate system and hadn't been fully integrated into the helmet's protection and was prone to failure. She shook her head and pushed her chair back to go outside and make sure the helmet was in working order when the front door was shattered by a dark shape diving through the glass. Merina let out a sharp gasp and stood up, looking over the counter. When she saw a massive furry body rolling to its four feet in the wide space of the lobby, she knew they were in trouble. She reached back to the console as more of the wolves approached the door and began to enter. Merina drew in a sharp breath and slapped a control on the desk that would sound the alarm to the others. As a loud buzzing sound began to intermittently fill the air, Merina backed away toward the office behind her where she knew a weapon waited.

She kept her eyes on the creatures moving slowly into the building and forming a group in the lobby. She recognized them as wolves and frowned, thinking there weren't any wolves in that part of the country, at least not in that particular area. She wasn't sure about that, but it didn't matter. They were there and she had to do something. She backed into the office, the one occupied by Sandusky, and quickly found the pistol he kept beside the door just in case of such a situation. With it in hand, help in the shooter's grip she'd been taught, Merina moved forward and raised it toward the largest of the wolves, the one with its muzzle still dripping Krista's blood.

Before she could fire, a man appeared in the doorway and walked through, his black boots crunching through the broken glass littering the floor. He wasn't overly tall and his blond hair was pulled back from his high forehead. His startlingly blue eyes were narrowed slightly as he turned his head to look at her. His pale skin, almost an alabaster white, told her this man was a vampire and she turned the pistol toward him.

He took a step away from the door, making room for the others to enter, and held up his hands, grinning as he looked at Merina.

"I would suggest you drop the pistol," he said. "It will do you no good."

"I don't think so," Merina shook her head. "I know who you are and what you want."

"Do you?" he asked, tilting his head to the right. "Do you really know what I want?"

Merina nodded, "You're here for Dana."

He straightened his head and lowered his arms as he laughed and said, "You have no idea, little woman."

Upstairs, in the room designated for housing, the team members began flowing out of the rooms, finishing the process of dressing and arming themselves. Alex was, of course, the first one out and looked from left to right along the hallway.

"Bonacci," he said as he saw his deputy exit the room across the hall. "You and Dyson get downstairs and judge the situation."

"Right, boss," Bonacci nodded and hurried away to his right, toward the front stairs and the room at the end of the hall where Melissa Dyson rushed out, fully dressed and ready.

Bonacci took her by the arm and pulled her toward the stairs.

Alex looked to his right and saw DeAnna striding toward him, ready as well. He nodded and said, "DeAnna, find Brewer and keep him safe. That's your priority."

"Got it," DeAnna nodded and turned around, moving quickly toward the other end of the hall.

Bonnie Stowers walked out of her room, a few doors to Alex's left, and looked around, confused. She spotted Alex and started toward him.

He turned to her and asked, "Where are Sydney and Dana?"

Bonnie stopped and turned her head briefly over her left shoulder then looked at him and said, "They were in the lab the last I saw them."

He nodded, "You go with DeAnna. Help her take care of Brewer."

Bonnie frowned for a second, but she knew the importance that had been placed on the former teacher and hurried along the hallway.

As he took a step toward the stairs, Raquel Jackson walked out of her room and looked at him.

"What do we do?" she asked, trying to sound more confident than she felt.

Alex nodded and said, "Get the others, Shafer and Barker. Wait for me at the top of the stairs."

She nodded and took a step back, "Got it."

As she walked away, he turned around and saw Katrina walking slowly down the hall. She moved so fluidly and gracefully that the others moved around her, making her seem almost like a ghost moving through them. Sandusky stood at the far end of the hall as Caroline and Lois made their way to him with the others scrambling to get into position.

She reached him and stopped a couple of feet away, looking up at him, though she was as close to his height as any of the women.

"What do you need me to do?" she asked.

"Come with me," he said and started to turn. "You should be able to help."

As he started for the stairs, Katrina followed.

Downstairs, Merina stood her ground and kept the pistol trained on the man facing her. She'd never seen him before, but she could tell he was a vampire and was most likely the leader of the Virate and the one that had attacked Dana. He stopped several feet from her as several more vampires entered the building, moving so quickly she could barely see their movements. She'd seen it before and it wasn't a surprise, but she was surprised at the number. She counted more than a dozen and that was way too many for her to handle on her own. She'd sounded the alarm and hoped the others would respond quickly.

"You see, Ms. Janek," Gerrit continued. "I have created a small army here in this tiny backwater town. We are more powerful than your pitiful little team and I will have what I want."

She shook her head slowly, "We'll see about that."

"Yes, we will," he nodded. "I've been waiting to test their mettle. Two of them have already joined me, but they couldn't make it to this meeting. They will, however, find you if you should survive this night."

As Alex reached the bottom of the stairs with Katrina practically beside him and was followed by Raquel, Evan, and Shafer, the door to the lab just ahead opened and Sydney looked out, turning her head sharply to look both ways before settling on Alex.

She let out a sigh of relief and frowned as she asked, "What's going on?"

"Not sure," Alex replied almost coldly. "We'll find out. You stay there. Lock the door and protect yourselves."

She nodded, "Jana and I are yarmed. We'll be okay, but Tiffany and Ben are here."

"Good," he said. "You take care of them and we'll take care of this."

Sydney shook her head at his bravado, but she knew him well enough to know it wasn't an act. He started moving toward the lobby with the others following him and she closed the door quickly, locking it and sealing it the best she could.

At the corner, Cardwell emerged from his quarters at the other end of the small hallway with a pistol in his right hand. His hair was mussed and he was dressed, but was without armor.

"I was asleep with earplugs in," he said grumpily. "What's going on?"

Alex shrugged, "Someone hit the alarm."

"Let's go," Cardwell said and started toward the lobby.

Alex fell in step beside him, drawing his own pistol and flipping the safety off with his thumb. Raquel, Evan, and Shafer prepared their weapons as well while Katrina balled her hands into fists, not having a weapon.

"Ah, the cavalry has arrived," Gerrit said as the six of them entered the lobby. "And it is time to begin."

"You're Gerrit," Cardwell said and stopped several yards from him, pistol raised and aimed. "You're the one calling the shots."

As he nodded, Rachel and Colin shot closer, flanking him, and he said, "We act as one, Mr. Cardwell. This is our way. And have come to claim what is ours."

"And what exactly is that?" Cardwell asked, his eyes narrowing as his jaw set firmly, ready for the fight to begin.

Gerrit held his arms wide and grinned as he said, "I know you will not give it to us, so we will take it ourselves."

With a nod, Colin and Rachel shot forward, rushing through the six as dark blurs, and the force of their passage knocked the three newest members of the insertion team aside.

"Enough," Alex said and fired a single shot, the report thunderous in the confines of the lobby, then glanced back. "Go after them."

His shot missed Gerrit and struck a tall male vampire behind him, knocking the newly revived back a couple of steps before dropping him to the floor. Raquel and Shafer spun around and ran after the other two vampires.

The wolves moved forward with a pair, one black and the other white, leading the way.

"I have this," Katrina said and stepped forward.

Alex nodded curtly and shook his head, knowing he wouldn't be able to shoot Gerrit. He would have to take him at close quarters. He holstered his pistol and started forward as Katrina fell forward and transformed into a panther once again.

As she moved on the two leaders, a third moved to the side, staying low, and leaped toward her as she neared the two leaders, Moonshadow and Carmen. Greyeagle wanted to be the pack alpha, or at least gain favor, and thought he could do that by attacking and killing Katrina, the representative of the Felines, and showing their superiority.

155

As he leaped toward her, Katrina moved quickly and perfectly, having easily seen his movements. Once he was in the air, Katrina pounced. She rose on her hind legs and twisted her body just a bit. Then, with a single powerful swipe of her right paw, she did what was thought to be impossible. Her claws, with the force of her blow, tore through his throat, and she followed through, showing her true strength. Her claws lodged in his flesh and she drove him to the floor, but she didn't stop. With a single flick of her wrist and pushing her foreleg upward, she ripped his head from his body and sent it flying across the room in a spray of blood and bits of tissue.

Without missing a step, Katrina landed on her back feet and shifted directions, springing back to land between the two wolves and the insertion team. She focused her glittering green eyes on Moonshadow and growled a warning. They stopped as she turned to face them with a low growl warning them to stop. They did and the other wolves fell into formation behind them, staring at her and waiting.

Entering through the office to the right of them beyond the counter, Bonacci and Dyson moved in with their weapons raised. Dyson held a large pistol similar to the one Alex held and Bonacci held a rifle identical to the one Krista had held outside. As they did, a group of vampires led by Hal Martino and Dr. Ross Brinson turned toward them, moving to attack.

"Take them," Alex said without shifting his gaze from Gerrit.

Bonacci and Dyson opened fire, filling the room with rapid claps of thunder. Gerrit shook his head as the vampires fell like bowling pins under the steady fire from Bonacci and Dyson. After a few seconds, once more than a dozen of the newly turned vampires had fallen under the assault, Gerrit held his hands up.

"Enough," he said loudly, his voice rising over the sounds of gunfire. "This does no good."

"Hold!" Alex called out and the two ceased firing.

"This is almost over," Gerrit said and lowered his hands. "It is time for you to face the future, Nemesis."

Alex frowned, "What do you mean?"

Gerrit smiled wryly and said, "It is time for you to make a choice."

Alex shook his head, frowning.

Gerrit smiled broadly as Colin and Rachel returned, now with Monica and Angelica with them. Each of the women held one person in their grasp while Colin held two. Rachel walked behind Sydney with a hand gripping each of Sydney's upper arms tightly. Angelica did the same with Jana. Monica held Tiffany and Colin had a hand on the neck of Dana and Ben, gripping tightly. Their faces were twisted in a rictus of pain and remained that way until Colin delivered Dana to Gerrit. Sydney struggled to free herself, but Rachel was much too strong and pulled her to Gerrit as well.

Once he had both women in his grasp, Sydney on his right and Dana on his left, Gerrit looked at Alex and grinned.

"Now is the time to make a choice, Nemesis," he said almost gleefully. "You cannot move fast enough to stop me. I will bite one and snap the neck of the other, but I will allow one of them to survive, to remain as they are. It is up to you."

Alex holstered his pistol and took a slow step forward as he asked, "What do you want?"

"I want you, Alex Chance," Gerrit replied, sounding almost incredulous. "That is why we're here, to give you the most difficult choice you could make. Now, if you do nothing, I will bite your long-lost love for the second time, bringing her that much closer to being one of us, and I will snap the neck of your new love, the one you consider your true love."

"I can take him," Bonacci said, holding his rifle at the ready a few feet away.

Alex cut his eyes toward Bonacci and shook his head sharply, the movement barely perceptible. Bonacci let out a soft sigh and lowered the rifle.

Gerrit briefly tightened his grip on the woman, causing Dana to cry out lightly with the pain while Sydney merely winced.

"To save one of them," Gerrit grinned maliciously. "You will surrender yourself to me. If you do so, I will release one of them. If you choose Sydney, Dana will come with me. If you choose Dana, I will snap Sydney's neck. If you refuse, Dana will be closer to being one of us and Sydney will die. You must choose now."

Alex scowled, his eyes narrowing as he contemplated his choices. He couldn't let Sydney die. She was too important to the task force and to him. Dana would be taken by the vampires, but he would be taken as well and there was a chance he could save her. If he refused, they would both die and he couldn't live with that.

"Fine," Alex said and took another step forward. "I'll go with you. Let Sydney go."

Gerrit laughed loudly, throwing his head back briefly, then looked at Alex and continued to grin as he said, "Excellent, Nemesis. You have made a decision. Now, you will come with me of your own free will."

Alex nodded slowly, his expression grim, and moved toward Gerrit.

"Lose the weapons," Colin growled, still holding Ben by the neck.

Alex cut his eyes toward the red-haired vampire then nodded and complied, unfastening his gun belt with his left hand, and dropped it to the floor with a heavy thud.

"Excellent," Gerrit nodded. "And I will keep my word."

With that, he released Sydney and she staggered forward, the ghost of the pain remaining in her neck. She reached up to rub it as she stood up straight and looked at Alex.

"You can't do this," she said, almost crying. "They'll kill you and we need you. I need you."

Before he could respond to her, Dana struggled against Gerrit's grip and said, "Alex, you came back for me and now you're abandoning me."

He looked at her and said, "I'm sorry. This is the best I can do."

"Enough," Gerrit said and looked at Cardwell. "We will leave you as you are. I am sure we will meet again."

"Count on it," Cardwell said through his clenched jaw, holding in his anger and the desire for violence.

Gerrit turned toward the door, still holding Dana by the neck, and looked Monica to Angelica as he said, "Bring the woman. Leave that one."

Angelica nodded and shoved Jana to the floor then moved toward Tiffany. Rachel pushed past Angelica and grabbed Tiffany, sobbing silently with tears running down her cheeks, by the arm. Jana fell limply to the floor, landing on her right side with her back to the group of humans.

"I'll handle her," she said, glaring at Monica. "You just make sure we aren't followed."

Monica nodded submissively then followed. Colin pulled Ben roughly toward the door and they were followed by the other vampires with the wolves behind them, guarding their escape.

One of the wolves, Carmen, remained at the back of the pack, moving slowly and almost tentatively. She looked to her left, toward the gathered group of task force members, and Katrina, still in panther form, moved slowly and almost menacingly forward.

"What is it?" Merina asked, frowning. "What's happening?"

Katrina took two more steps then pushed herself upward and transformed into human form. As she rose to her full height, she looked at Carmen and said, "Transform now."

Carmen drew in a breath and transformed, rising to two feet, and stood before Katrina, still naked.

Unabashed, she looked at Katrina and said, "You were supposed to help us."

"I have my own agenda," Katrina replied. "I was not sent to help you. I was sent to observe you and ascertain whether or not the Felines will join the wolves. At this point, I don't believe that will happen."

"You weren't there," Carmen said. "Gerrit took control of us, all of us. He brought us here to help him get what he wanted, and he got it."

Cardwell stepped forward and asked sharply, "Are you saying their entire reason for being in this town is to kill Alex?"

"Not kill him," Carmen said, looking at him. "At least that's what I've gathered. They didn't really talk about all the details. There's some sort of ritual taking place and he's a big part of it."

"Why are you still here?" Katrina asked. "Shouldn't you go with Gerrit and the pack?"

Carmen took in a deep breath and said, "I don't know what happened. I was going along with what Gerrit wanted, but when we attacked and what Moonshadow did to the woman outside, I started sort of thinking for myself again. It took seeing you destroy Greyeagle so easily that finally snapped me out of it. Now I need to figure out how to do that with the others."

"We'll work on that," Cardwell said and moved closer. "For now, stay here."

He looked to his right and said, "Bonacci, you and Dyson take care of Krista."

"On it, boss," Bonacci said and glanced at Melissa as he started toward the door and she followed.

Sydney then moved closer and asked, "What are we going to do about Alex?"

Cardwell looked at her and said, "We're going to figure that out. We have to find out where they took him."

"I can tell you that," Carmen said. "They're staying in an old hotel on the south side of town."

"Then that's where we're going," he replied and turned around. "Sandusky, get this woman some clothing."

Sandusky standing at the back of the lobby, nodded and said, "Right away."

Cardwell looked at Sydney and said, "We won't go after him tonight. We need to take care of Krista and Jana. We'll regroup, get our act together. We also need to know what they're planning. If they wanted to simply kill him, they could've done that here."

"I think I have an answer," Patrick Brewer said as he entered the room from the stairwell with DeAnna and Bonnie behind him.

"Tell me," Cardwell said and looked at him, eyes narrowed.

Brewer moved forward and said, "I've translated a bit of the Book of Aranos. His plan involves a ritual that will unleash a greater vampire power. I've known about the power for a long time; it's what gave Alex his abilities, but I didn't know about the ritual until now."

"Okay," Cardwell nodded. "Keep working on that. We'll gear up and go after them in the morning, when they're asleep."

Brewer nodded, "DeAnna has been helping. She's really good at this."

Cardwell looked at her and said, "Do what you can. Now, let's all get busy."

As Cardwell stepped away from Brewer, Sydney looked at the prone form of Jana, her assistant and friend, shaking her head as she wondered if the vampire holding her had done something more before dropping her. She moved slowly to her side and crouched down behind her. She reached out slowly with trembling fingers and placed her hand on Jana's shoulder.

"Jana," she said softly and gently pulled her shoulder, rolling her onto her back.

As she fell back, her head flopped to the side, her long hair falling out of the way to reveal the twin puncture marks on her neck and the thin line of blood trailing along the contours of her pale skin to the collar of her shirt.

CHAPTER TWENTY-SIX
Regrouping

J ana was dead. Sydney had tried for more than half an hour to revive her, but she hadn't moved or shown any signs of life after being transported into the lab with the help of Sandusky and Caroline. Neither of them had any medical training or background and they'd left her alone to try and keep Jana alive.

She'd failed. There'd still been breath in her body when she'd been placed on the steel examination table at the center of the room, but it hadn't lasted long. Her eyes had never opened and she hadn't gone through the death throes Sydney thought would've happened. She'd simply taken one last breath and let it out slowly as her heart stopped beating.

Tears flowed freely from Sydney's eyes, rolling down her smooth cheeks and along her sharp jawline to finally drip from her chin. She was distraught over the death of her colleague and friend, the woman who had been at her side for more than five years after surviving her own initial experience with vampires.

Most of the people involved with the task force had their own experience with vampires, but Jana had been one to survive an attack. She'd been in college at the time, graduate school at the University of New Orleans, in medical technology, and had been working in a forensics lab with two fellow students and a test subject while learning to use an MRI scanner and analyze the results. Jana, with some experience, was leading the group and the others were figuring it out when a pair of vampires entered the building looking for the small blood bank the building contained. Jana hadn't been able to explain how she'd done it, but she'd managed to get out of the building unscathed while the other two students and the test subject had been taken. Somehow, Cardwell had found out about the incident and made contact with Jana then brought her into the task force.

She'd been a great help in the lab and had learned things that weren't part of her training and education. She'd picked up some of the things Sydney had taken on herself to do, such as designing weapons and technology to fight the vampires while both had done their best to learn about vampire physiology. Now, Sydney was alone in that part of the operation and would either remain on her own or find someone else to bring in and train. The idea of training someone to fill Jana's position was daunting, but she knew she wouldn't be able to do everything the task force needed on her own. She just didn't know where to look for someone to assist her.

After a brief period of mourning and allowing her emotions to flow freely, Sydney sniffed back her tears and placed her emotions in check. She was a professional and there was no place for tears and regrets in dealing with someone who had been bitten by a vampire, even a great friend.

She knew what had to be done, but she wasn't quite ready. The analytical portion of her mind analyzed the situation and brought a deep frown to her face as the truth struck her. Jana had died shortly after having been bitten and she knew how vampire bites worked on humans. A single bite, like the one Dana had received, would make a person weak and anemic, but the process of turning could take weeks. A second would just shorten the process, hastening the turning, and could happen within a few days. A third bite would bring about almost immediate death and they would rise the following night.

When the vampires had invaded the lab and taken the people hiding inside, Jana had only been out of her sight for a few moments, but it must've been long enough for three of them to bite her. She had died and would rise the following night as one of them. Sydney knew it was her duty, her responsibility, to make sure Jana didn't rise as a vampire, and definitely not within the confines of their facility. But she didn't think she could do it. There was very little information concerning the turning process and she didn't know if the Jana that rose as a vampire would be the same Jana she'd known before. One of the legends stated that the virus that killed the host opened the body to possession by a spirit, an evil spirit, and was no longer the person that had previously inhabited the body. If she did return as the person Sydney knew, it would be very difficult to dispatch her. She couldn't see herself destroying a woman that had been a friend and she wasn't yet trained well enough to fight off a vampire.

It was a dilemma and one that was solved a short while later.

Sydney remained seated on the low stool she used frequently and looked at the body on the table, naked and covered with a thin sheet after attempts to revive her and final confirmation that she was dead. She was so intent on the body and the possibilities that she barely registered the opening of the door behind her.

Jonathan Cardwell entered the room slowly and quietly, almost reverently. He paused just inside and slowly closed the door behind him as he looked at Sydney, her back to him, and stood there until she sat up straight and looked over her shoulder.

"I still can't believe it," she said and looked at him, her voice even and almost without the emotion he expected. "How did this happen?"

Cardwell finally moved forward, frowning as he asked, "How did they get in here? The door doesn't look like it's been damaged."

She rotated the stool and frowned, "I don't know. I locked the door with both physical and electronic locks. They should've had to break the door down to get in here, but they just opened it."

Cardwell nodded, "We have a traitor. I don't know who it is, but I think it's one of our new arrivals."

Sydney nodded, "Right. You vetted all of us before we took the job. You would've known if one of us wasn't totally dedicated to the operation."

"Yes," Cardwell nodded in agreement. "And there are four possibilities, but two of them were absent from the conflict. Lois Cashlin and Neil Shafer weren't there. Of course, Lois was with Caroline and she has had access to certain details and the communication equipment."

"I don't know," Sydney shook her head. "She hasn't really had the opportunity. I know she doesn't have a cell phone and she hasn't left the building or been alone since she arrived."

Cardwell shook his head, "I'll have to check into this. It has to be one of the two, but we will find out."

Sydney nodded and Cardwell moved to the side of the table, looking down at Jana.

"I know she's going to turn," he said. "The right thing to do is stop that from happening."

Sydney frowned, "You want me to take care of her?"

"No," he shook his head and turned toward her. "I want you to make sure she's secure and can't get out. Senator Howland wants proof that vampires exist. She wants us to bring a vampire to Washington and show her. I think Jana will be the perfect one for that."

"But how do I do that?" Sydney asked. "How do I keep her locked up? She's going to be stronger than anything we have here."

He started for the door and said, "You'll figure it out. I have some planning to do."

She shook her head as he quickly crossed the lab and left, closing the door behind him.

He walked away from the lab slowly, too many concerns were flowing through his mind and he knew he had to focus. He had to do something to stop whatever the vampires were planning. First, he needed more information from Brewer. He'd mentioned a bit about having translated some of the Book of Aranos, a portion concerning a ritual that involved the blood of the Nemesis, Alex Chance. He hadn't understood why the vampires would want Alex to submit to them, other than to kill him and get him out of their way, but it was starting to make a little more sense. Of course, he chided himself for letting them take Alex without resisting them, but it was done and he could only move forward. He would do his best to get Alex out of that situation and stop the vampires from doing what they seemed to be planning.

The remainder of the task force was in the lobby, most of them behind the high counter with Bonacci and Dyson at the entrance. They'd taken a door from a room in the building and secured it over the opening. The glass that had littered the floor had been swept up and the pair stood beside the door with the blind over the window beside it raised.

Behind the counter, in the primary work area, Sandusky stood beside the desk Merina used for her equipment and she sat behind it with her small computer active. Caroline and Lois sat at a second desk, looking through a stack of paper, notes printed from the research Caroline had already done. Patrick Brewer and DeAnna Jones sat at the third desk with the Book of Aranos open on its surface. Bonnie Stowers sat in a chair beside that desk, alternating attention from their research to what Sandusky and Merina were working on.

Cardwell walked through the narrow gap at the end closest to the hallway and stopped beside the nearest desk, the one where Brewer and DeAnna worked. They were all intent on their tasks and didn't notice his arrival for a few seconds. Cardwell liked that. It gave him a moment to watch them and let the feeling of pride wash over him, the pride of knowing he'd found the right people for the jobs that needed to be done.

After just a few seconds, Bonnie looked up and her eyes opened wide when she saw him standing there silently with a grim expression on his face.

"Jonathan," she said and sat up straight. "What's the story?"

He shook his head slowly, looked at her, and said, "Jana is dead. She'll turn the next time the sun goes down."

Sandusky looked up sharply and said, "We need to take care of that."

"No," Cardwell said and looked at him, taking a step forward. "We can use her. We need a vampire in DC to convince the President and Senator Howland. It'll be easier if we take one that we know."

"How?" Caroline asked, looking up and frowning. "Is it even possible?"

Cardwell moved to the center of the room and stuffed his hands into the pockets of his pants as he said, "Transporting her won't be an issue. We can travel at night. I know we haven't checked, but I'm hoping at least one of the choppers is still serviceable. The difficult part is going to be containing her here."

He focused on Sandusky and said, "Paul, work with Sydney and Merina to get something figured out before sunset."

"We'll do our best," Sandusky nodded and cut his eyes toward Merina.

She looked at him and shrugged then said, "I have an idea, but it might not work."

166

Cardwell looked at her, "Do whatever you can. Now, what about Krista? Has she been taken care of?"

Bonnie nodded and said, "Her body was brought inside and taken to a storage room. We don't know if she was bitten or just killed."

"I doubt she was bitten," he said almost coldly. "We'll take care of her in the morning."

He then looked at Brewer and said, "You said something earlier about having translated a portion of the book and something about a ritual."

"Yes," Brewer nodded. "According to what we've found, the ritual will be performed tomorrow night at the place of power."

"Right," Cardwell nodded. "Alex figured that out. It's in the cemetery where the black pine trees grow."

"Yes," Brewer nodded sharply. "If what we've found is correct, they need the blood of the Nemesis, a portion of the power, to release its opposite side. They won't kill him. That would defeat their purpose. They'll need to drink some of his blood, not enough to do any damage, just enough to give them a taste of the power. Once the third bite takes place, the power will be released and the Master will accept it. I don't know how it'll work with the three of them sharing the existing power, though."

"Not our problem," Cardwell said and shook his head. "We're not going to let it go that far. Now, I wanted to attack them during the daylight, since we know where they are, but we're not ready for that. We need to rest, heal up the best we can, and plan to stop the ritual."

Brewer nodded, "That's pushing it, but I agree that it's probably the best."

"Yes," Carmen said and entered from the back with Katrina beside her. "The pack will be guarding the hotel during the day. They are not as easy to kill as Katrina made it look."

"Of course," Cardwell said and looked at her, seeing her dressed in tactical clothing that didn't quite fit. "We'll still have to deal with them, but I think the cemetery will be a better battleground."

Sandusky nodded and said, "We can prepare for that during the day, since we know the precise location."

"Good," Cardwell said and looked at him. "Make that happen."

He then turned to Bonacci and Dyson, "Where are our three new recruits?"

Bonacci took a step toward him and said, "They're patrolling the perimeter."

Cardwell frowned, "All three of them?"

Bonacci shrugged, "I thought it would be safer for them since they're all newbies."

Cardwell continued to frown and looked at Bonacci. The armed man paused and could tell Cardwell wanted more.

He shrugged again and said, "They're experienced cops and this is their town. They can handle a patrol."

Cardwell finally nodded and said, "I doubt the vampires are coming back tonight. Bring them in."

"On it, boss," Bonacci said and opened the door with Melissa's help.

Once the door was open, leaning against the wall beside the opening, Cardwell looked at the others and said, "Let's shut it down for the night. We need to rest and recover. I think we can do away with the watches for tonight. We'll just lock the place up and get some rest."

Merina looked at him and said, "I've set up a security system. I can tie it into the alarm system and we'll know if someone tries to get in."

"Make it happen," he said and turned to the door as Melissa rushed in.

"We need a little help?" she said. "Two of them are down, knocked out. The third is nowhere around, but Bonacci is doing a perimeter sweep."

"Which one is gone?" Cardwell asked.

"Shafer," she replied. "The detective."

He nodded slowly and said softly, "That's what I thought."

He took a step toward the gap and said, "Paul, DeAnna, come with me."

The three rushed out of the building and were gone for only a few moments. They returned with Raquel supported between Bonacci and Melissa with Evan between Cardwell and Sandusky with DeAnna following them and keeping an eye out for Shafer.

Once inside the two injured team members were seated across from the counter in the hard plastic chairs left by the previous tenant.

As they were lowered into those chairs, Cardwell looked at DeAnna and said, "Go get Sydney."

DeAnna nodded and hurried toward the back of the building while Cardwell crouched in front of Raquel, her eyes wide and her jaw slack.

"What happened?" he asked.

She drew in a deep breath then said slowly, "It was Neil. He attacked us. He hit Evan and knocked him down then hit me in the back of the head. He didn't say anything, just ran away."

"That's what I figured," Cardwell said. "He's our traitor."

Raquel frowned, "What do you mean?"

"I'll explain it later," he replied and stood up. "Right now, you rest and let Sydney take a look at you. We're going to need you two tomorrow."

He turned and looked at the others, "Let's all hit the sack. Sydney can handle this. We need to be up early and get a jump on this."

There was no argument. The others began shutting down equipment and closing books then rose from their seats and began making their way out of the lobby as DeAnna returned with Sydney carrying a large plastic case Cardwell knew was her emergency medical kit.

As Sydney moved to the two injured people, Cardwell took a step back and waited until Sydney was finished and they were on their way to their bunks before he left the lobby and returned to his own quarters.

CHAPTER TWENTY-SEVEN
Morning Light

G ina Filmore was afraid to leave her office on the hospital's fourth floor. She didn't know exactly what was going on or what had happened the previous night, but it had sounded like a war going on. Of course, she'd never been in a war, but she'd seen plenty of movies. The sounds reminded her of a scene in a movie where the bad guys raided an apartment building and captured the residents, going from door to door. She'd heard them coming and did her best to hide. She'd locked her office door and blocked it with a heavy, two-drawer filing cabinet that had taken every ounce of her strength to move. She'd then retreated to the small closet in the corner beside the office's single large window and locked the door as well. The sound continued as she cowered in the corner with an old winter coat covering her almost from toe to chin.

She'd eventually fallen asleep and woke up feeling stiff and sore from having slept in a seated position with her knees drawn up to her chest. It took her a few moments to work out enough of the stiffness to climb slowly and painfully to her feet. She wanted to let out a groan, but she didn't know if the people who had invaded the hospital were still there or not and she didn't want to draw attention to herself.

Once she was on her feet, she stretched her back for a moment, feeling a bit of relief, then carefully unlocked the closet door, holding her breath as she turned the small tab and winced as it clicked once. She waited a moment then slowly turned the knob and pushed the door open just enough so she could see a portion of her office. She could see the office door and the filing cabinet was still in place and nothing looked disturbed. Letting out a sigh of relief, she opened the door and tiptoed into the office, trying not to make a sound.

She was breathing rapidly and it sounded like the wind in a thunderstorm to her, but she couldn't help it. Fear and anxiety had taken control of her mind and body. Her eyes were open wide and she looked around quickly. Noting appeared to be amiss and she stopped at the center of the square room to try and control her breathing. She knew several relaxation techniques and tried a few until one of them helped a bit. Within a few moments, she began to breathe normally again and her mind began to clear.

She walked to the door and stood beside it, pressing her right ear against the narrow gap between the door and the framing, listening to see if she could discern whether or not the invaders from the night before were still there. She remained there for a few moments and heard absolutely nothing, not even the standard daily activities of the hospital. She glanced up at the clock on the wall and saw that it was just after six in the morning, well before any of the others working on her floor would arrive, but there were still sounds of activity that filtered through from other floors. It didn't make sense and it brought a confused frown to her face.

Curiosity got the better of her and she began slowly moving the filing cabinet away from the door, sliding it across the carpeted floor. It was a struggle and her back was still rather stiff, but she finally moved it far enough to allow the door to open.

Before opening the door, she returned to her desk and took her purse and cell phone from one of the drawers, turned the phone on, and hung the purse over her right shoulder, tucking it against her side. Once the cell phone was ready, she pressed the button to put it in sleep mode, tucked it into the purse as well, and returned to the door.

She carefully unlocked the door and slowly opened it a few inches, just enough for her to peer out at the deserted hallway. The silence was unnerving, but Gina knew she couldn't stay there and wait for someone to find her. She didn't think anyone would be coming and she was on her own.

Taking a deep breath to steady herself, she forced herself to leave the office and enter the hallway. Once outside the office, panic flooded through her and she almost just ran for the bank of elevators at the end of the hall. Not knowing the situation, she didn't trust the elevators. If there was someone waiting on a lower floor, they would be alerted to the arrival of the elevator and she wouldn't stand a chance. The stairs were closer and she would at least be able to see if someone was waiting for her on a lower level.

She hurried along the hallway, found the door to the stairs, and pulled it open slowly, looking into the stairwell before opening the door wide enough for her to go through. There was no one visible and she slipped through without opening the door much wider then began her descent.

Taking each step carefully, trying to remain as quiet as possible, looked over the handrail, able to see to the ground floor, and just didn't stop. She reached the ground floor without seeing anyone and made her way from the stairwell to the lobby. She saw no one and still heard nothing as if the entire hospital had been deserted in the middle of the night. It was an eerie feeling and she saw the exit less than thirty feet away. Shaking her head, she moved quickly toward it, not caring if anyone should happen to appear behind her.

The automatic door remained in operation and slid open as she neared it, letting her feel a little relief, but the hissing of the pneumatic opening system was much too loud for her at the moment and she looked around quickly, gasping as she expected someone to come running toward her at any second. When no one appeared, she ran through the doorway and turned to her right, heading toward the parking lot and her car.

The sun had risen and cast a golden glow over the town, but it was eerily quiet as Gina made her way across the parking lot. Her car, a gray Kia, was parked near the back of the lot and she silently cursed herself for having parked so far from even the closer entrance, the doors leading to the emergency room on the north side of the building.

As she scurried across the parking lot, looking around carefully, she didn't see anything or anyone. Nothing around the hospital appeared to be moving. Even the normally busy street barely in view past the Baptist church across the parking lot was without traffic. She expected someone to jump out from behind one of the parked cars to come running and screaming around the rear corner of the building, but nothing moved and everything remained silent. With her left hand, she reached into her purse and dug around for her keys. She let out a light sigh of relief as her fingers felt them and she pulled them out of the purse quickly, too quickly, and they flew from her hand, clattering to the asphalt of the lot several feet away.

She spat a curse and altered her course to retrieve them then stood up and looked around with her eyes open wide, fear flooding through her. She looked around quickly, her head turning so rapidly that her hair flew across her face. Holding the keys tightly in her right hand, still seeing nothing and no one around her, she turned and trotted to her car.

She fumbled with the keys in the lock, the key fob remote's battery having long since died and she hadn't gotten around to replacing it. Finally, after two attempts with shaking hands, she managed to get the key in the lock and opened the door. Tossing her purse to the passenger's seat, already cluttered with receipts, fast food napkins, and assorted change, and climbed in. She pulled the door closed and inserted the key into the ignition. Taking a deep breath to try and calm herself, she pulled the seatbelt across her body and locked it in place. She gripped the steering wheel with both hands and sat there for a moment as she tried to decide what she should do next, where she would go.

She wanted to go home, but the house she'd been paying on for ten years was in a rather affluent area outside the city limits and she felt it might be too isolated if what she suspected was actually going on.

She remembered the brief discussion with the government people when they'd visited Dana before her release and what they'd said. They believed there was something major brewing in Pine Ridge and Dana was at the center of it. She also remembered where they said they'd be taking Dana once she left the hospital. Gina knew about the old building, the former hospital that had closed a long time before she'd arrived in the town. She knew where it was and had even gone inside one time. If it hadn't been refurbished since then, she didn't know how they would be able to operate from there, but it was her best hope.

She started the car, pulled out of the parking space, and drove as quickly as she could across town to the old building. There was absolutely no traffic through the town and that was most definitely out of the ordinary. Even that early there should've been at least a few vehicles moving along the streets, but it was completely silent and deserted. She began to feel like she'd shifted to another dimension, one where she was the only person to exist.

As she parked beside it, she shut off the engine and stared at it for a moment. She didn't see any signs of activity, but she did see that the old glass door had been shattered and replaced with another door that looked more like an interior door than one typically used as an entrance. It looked like a haphazard replacement with the aluminum frame of the previous door still in place. If the government group was still there and they were still active, she would have to go inside.

Taking a breath to prepare herself, she pulled the key from the ignition and started to open the door then remembered her cell phone. There had to be someone somewhere to answer her call. She didn't know the direct number for the police department, but she could call 9-1-1 and could be transferred to them. She punched in the digits and tapped the small circle on the screen to initiate the call then held the phone to her ear.

She waited through a dozen rings and her fear was multiplied when the call wasn't answered. Something had definitely happened to the town. If she went to the building and found it abandoned, she would have to figure out something else to do. It was her only choice at the moment and she finally opened the door as she ended the phone call and grabbed her purse.

She closed the car door carefully, not wanting to make any sounds that might draw attention to her, then hurried around the front of the car and practically ran to the door of the building.

She tried the handle. It turned easily, but the door didn't open. Frowning, she reached up and knocked rather tentatively on the door. She looked around carefully, turning her head back and forth quickly as she waited to see if someone would open the door. She began to think that the government group had already abandoned the building and the town, returning to the nation's capital, leaving her with having to find somewhere else to go.

After a long moment, she finally heard the sound of someone opening a lock on the other side of the door and she became hopeful, but she wouldn't relax until she was inside and the door locked behind her.

The door swung open and Melissa Dyson stood there in full tactical gear with body armor and a rifle slung over her right shoulder. She frowned as she saw Gina standing there wearing only dark blue scrubs.

"Can I help you?" Melissa asked.

"I hope so," Gina said, her feet shifting with nervousness and fear. "I'm looking for the government group that brought Dana Richland from the hospital."

Melissa nodded, "Right. And who are you?"

"Gina Filmore," she replied. "I'm an Occupational Therapist at the hospital. I worked with Dana a bit before she was discharged."

"Come in," Melissa said and stepped back.

"Thank you," Gina said and entered the building.

Melissa closed and locked the door behind her then turned to her and said, "Wait here. I'll get someone in charge."

"Cardwell?" Gina asked, frowning. "He's the one in charge. I met him the other day."

Melissa nodded and said, "Just wait here."

As Melissa walked away from her, toward the back of the building, Gina began pacing nervously across the open area of the lobby near the counter occupying a corner of the spacious room. With the seemingly useless phone back in her purse and the purse over her shoulder, she wrung her hands in front of her as she paced.

It took only a few moments for Melissa to return. With her, Jonathan Cardwell, Paul Sandusky, and Patrick Brewer entered the lobby and they stopped in a line across the space between the corner of the counter and the wall beside the door.

Cardwell looked at her and asked, "What can we do for you, Ms. Filmore."

Gina took in a deep breath and told her story, including the detail that she'd seen no signs of life as she'd crossed the town.

When she finished, Cardwell nodded and turned his head to Sandusky as he said, "It looks like they've already taken the town. This isn't going to be easy."

"No," Sandusky agreed. "But we don't have a choice. If we don't stop them here, there's no telling if we'll ever be able to stop them."

"What are you talking about?" Gina asked, frowning.

Cardwell looked at her and said, "Vampires. This town has been invaded and most likely taken over. I'd suggest you stay here with us. Perhaps we'll find something for you to do. I don't think we really need an Occupational Therapist, but there might be something."

Gina shrugged, "I was in public relations before this. I did that for years."

Sandusky nodded and said, "I think we can find a use for her."

"Good," Cardwell said with a sharp nod. "Let's get her settled in and get started with the preparations for tonight."

"What's tonight?" Gina asked, frowning again.

Sandusky smirked, "Possibly the most important moment in this town's history."

CHAPTER TWENTY-EIGHT
Nightfall

Her dark hazel eyes flashed open in the darkness of the room on the lowest level of the old hotel. She gasped, surprised to find herself awake and aware. The last she remembered was an experience with Gerrit, the leader of the vampires. She'd been afraid when she'd been taken from the old hospital building along with Ben, Dana, and Alex, wondering what would happen to them. Her first thought, and what she thought during the transfer from the task force facility to the old hotel, was that she was simply going to be killed along with the other three, but Gerrit had come to her after she'd been locked in a tiny room that looked as if it had been a storage room at one point and seemed as if he was on her side, that she was going to survive.

He'd seduced her and she'd thought her commitment to Ben would've kept her from even considering the idea, but there had been something about Gerrit that overpowered her senses and she forgot about Ben once Gerrit looked into her eyes. She'd relaxed with him and let him do as he pleased. She hadn't minded at all and not really thinking about it when he'd revealed his fangs and lowered his mouth to her neck.

It all became a blur after that, but she was sure he'd bitten her at least three times. After the third time, she'd closed her eyes and knew no more until they'd opened again and she found herself alone in that small room.

She sat up on the hard, dirty cot and looked around. She knew there was no light in the room, but she could see everything clearly. She could hear the sounds of others moving around and she could tell they weren't just outside the room. They were in other areas of the hotel, and she could feel the presence of more than a hundred vampires, each one with their own distinct aura. She also felt the presence of the wolves, the lycanthropes that remained under Gerrit's control. She'd been afraid of them when she'd first seen them at the task force headquarters, but they were now servants of the Master and they would do her no harm.

She swung her legs over the side of the cot, placing her bare feet on the cold, stone floor, but the cold was just a sensation. There was no pain or discomfort involved. Then, just as she was prepared to stand up and make her way to the others, the door opened and Gerrit entered the room.

He smiled at her and said, "Welcome to your new life, Tiffany. Now, come with me and complete the process. You must feed."

She nodded and stood up, his voice soothing and of utmost importance. She could do nothing other than to comply. She started toward him, walking slowly, almost as if she'd recently learned to walk. He waited patiently just outside the door with an almost beatific smile on his face.

As she exited the room, Gerrit gestured to his left and said, "Come. Your first meal awaits."

Still feeling rather disoriented, she followed the narrow hallway to a narrow staircase just a few yards away that led to a room adjacent to the hotel's lobby. As she entered, her mouth fell open at the sight of so many vampires standing around the lobby with all eyes on her. Most of their eyes held looks of hunger and their posture suggested they were anxious, most likely to get out of the building and find food for the night. Others, though, held expressions of what she could only assume was jealousy. She didn't understand that, but Gerrit was at her side and he kept her moving forward.

Directly ahead of her stood the two remaining Virate with the Mystic standing in front of them.

Sharia took a step forward as Tiffany approached. She tilted her head back slightly and adopted a posture of superiority as she said, "The final phase of your conversion is ready."

She gestured to her right, toward the dining room, and continued, "It is waiting inside."

Without hesitation, Tiffany turned to the left and walked calmly to the double doors leading to the dining room. As she approached, a pair of vampires, one on either side, stepped closer and opened the doors for her and the small entourage following her.

The massive room, nearly twice the size of the lobby, was lit by a number of battery-powered lanterns mounted to the walls in small depressions in the walls that had formerly held electric lighting. The lanterns provided enough illumination for Tiffany to see everything in the room clearly, though her new vision would easily allow her to see with no light at all. She realized that it was for the benefit of those without such a gift.

The first thing she noticed was the group of five naked people and one red-haired man in jeans and a black t-shirt gathered around the bare-chested and bloodied body of Alex Chance, the chains stretched between two massive columns, the second two in a line of four pairs that divided the room into two large open areas with a somewhat narrower space at the center. His head was hanging forward and his massive arms strained the links of the massive chain holding him in place. Tiffany looked at him without emotion, seeing him as nothing more than a problem for Dana, a problem that had lasted more than fifteen years.

It was the man chained to a column of the first pair, somewhat smaller chains wrapped around his arms and chest then circling the column, that drew her attention. She felt a brief twinge of emotion, a distant memory that faded quickly. She knew Ben Mills better than she'd known anyone in her life, but the memory of their years together meant nothing to her. He was no longer part of her world and she was no longer part of his.

He turned his head at the sound of the group's entrance and his eyes widened as he saw Tiffany among them, her skin paler than he'd ever before seen. She loved being in the sun and only felt sure of herself when her skin was darkly tanned. It took him a moment due to the exhaustion of not having slept, unable to sleep in a standing position, to realize that Tiffany had become a vampire.

As the group approached the space between the two sets of columns, Gerrit looked back at one of the two at the doors, Ross Brinson, and said, "Bring the other one here."

Ross nodded and hurried away. Gerrit then took Tiffany by the hand and had her face Alex as the five wolves in human form stood around him.

"Excellent," Gerrit said. "I believe you have done enough for our purposes."

Holly, the tall blonde, turned toward Gerrit and said with a blood-stained smile on her face, "Let us kill him."

"No," Gerrit said calmly as he shook his head slowly. "It is not time for him to die. That will happen after the ritual. Once it is done, I will kill him myself."

Holly glared at him for a second then, seeing the intensity of his gaze, turned away and focused on Alex again, making sure he didn't manage to escape.

"Now," Gerrit said and turned Tiffany to face Ben. "It is your first night as one of us and you are hungry. I can feel the hunger burning through you, a desolate fire, and you must feed."

He gestured toward Ben and said, "I've brought him here for you. Show me that you are no longer part of the human world, that you are completely dedicated to me and to our cause. He will be your first meal. Take him. Drain him completely and the power you've always craved will finally be yours."

Tiffany looked at Ben for a moment, her expression one of curiosity that turned to a frown. She knew him, knew everything they'd been through together, and it still meant nothing to her. He was still human and would never be part of her new life. Gerrit would never allow it and she would do as Gerrit wanted her to do. At the moment, he wanted her to end Ben's life and she had no problem with it.

Drawing in a deep breath she no longer needed, she pulled her hand free of Gerrit's and moved slowly toward Ben. Her frown slowly turned to a snarl and her lips parted, stretching wide to reveal her newly grown fangs.

Ben shook his head and said weakly, "Tiffany, it's me. You know me. Don't do this. I love you, Tiff. Please."

She ignored him and moved forward. Her hands rose and reached for him. She was much shorter than Ben, almost a foot shorter, but Gerrit had planned for that. With a simple nod, two vampires, Hal Martino and Monica Halpern, moved behind him and grabbed the chains binding him to the column. With little effort, the two pulled him down until he was almost kneeling and in perfect position for Tiffany.

She walked over to Ben and her head tilted to the right, her expression cold and blank. She placed her right hand on his left shoulder and her right hand on the side of his head. As she leaned closer, she pushed his head to the side and exposed his neck completely, stretching the skin taut. With a hissing exhalation of useless breath, her head snapped forward and her fangs plunged into his skin, instinctively finding the perfect spot. As she pressed her lips to his skin, hot blood flooded her mouth and she drank greedily.

Ben flinched sharply as Tiffany's fangs penetrated his flesh and his eyes closed a few seconds later as the blood was quickly drained from him.

Gerrit turned to face Alex, a gloating grin on his face, and stared at the limp form of the man they called Nemesis for a moment. He shook his head slowly and turned his attention to Moonshadow standing a few feet to the right with Renee and Nora flanking him.

"You have done well, my wolves," he said. "He is beaten and worn down. Your job here is done. Go now and prepare the cemetery."

Moonshadow nodded then quickly glanced around at the others and transformed. They did the same and five wolves rushed out of the room.

Once they were past the small contingent, Sharia moved forward holding a large leather-bound book in her hands. Dressed in a dark red, hooded robe with the hood thrown back to reveal her loose, blonde hair, she approached Alex and stopped in front of him. She stared down at him for a few seconds then reached out with her left hand and cupped his chin. She lifted his head until his dark hazel eyes were looking into hers.

"You are not the Nemesis yet, Alex Chance," she said. "You have begun the journey, but you are far from completing it. This night will see that you never become the Nemesis. Once the ritual is complete and the true power of the vampire is released, you will be destroyed. Your death will ensure the continuation of our race."

"Yes," Ryan Sullivan said and grinned broadly.

Sharia cut her eyes toward him and Gerrit shot over to grab him by the throat. He looked into Ryan's eyes, his smile gone and replaced with a scowl of fear.

"This is not your time," Gerrit said harshly, his voice thick and raspy. "You are not to speak. You are fortunate that I allow you to observe."

Ryan nodded the best he could while in Gerrit's grasp and said weakly, "Yes. I understand."

Gerrit released him and took a step back. Ryan coughed a couple of times, his face turning bright red, and looked at Gerrit, almost snarling.

"What about me?" he asked. "You said you would make me like you."

Gerrit shook his head and said, "It is not time yet. Your usefulness as a human has not come to an end."

Ryan nodded slowly and took a step back, feeling put in his place.

Gerrit then turned to Alex and said, "Now, Nemesis, it is time to complete the process of preparing you for the ritual."

He looked over his left shoulder toward the door as he felt the return of Ross Brinson holding tightly onto the arms of Dana Richland. She staggered along, her eyelids sagging as if in a daze and she looked pale to Alex as he looked up, but she appeared to be in better shape than he was in. He could see the remains of the vampire bite on her neck, the second bite that Gerrit had undoubtedly administered after leaving the task force facility. His own body was ripped and torn with blood smeared across his chest, arms, face, and back. He knew he would heal, but it would take time and rest.

Ross guided her to Gerrit and she looked up at him, her eyes opening wide.

"Thank you, doctor," Gerrit said and took Dana by the hand.

The former physician nodded and backed away as Gerrit pulled her close to him and they both faced Alex. Gerrit slipped his left arm around Dana's waist and smiled.

"She is mine now," Gerrit said. "She will turn very soon and you will lose her to me forever."

Alex snarled and tried the chains, pulling as hard as he could, but he was too tired and weakened to do more than pull them taut.

Gerrit laughed and said, "Now I will finish the process."

He paused for a second, smiling confidently, and turned his head toward Dana, opening his mouth wide as his fangs extended from sheaths behind his teeth. With a snap of his head, he plunged his fangs into her throat and drank slowly, taking little from her, but it was enough.

As he withdrew from Dana, Tiffany pulled back from Ben with a satisfied sigh. She took a step back and looked at the lifeless body of Ben, the man she'd loved for almost two decades. She remembered the feelings, but they weren't there any longer. Her heart was as cold as her body had been. Now, with the influx of fresh blood, she felt almost human again, but those feelings and memories were part of another life and she pushed them aside easily as she turned to look at Gerrit.

"Excellent," Gerrit said as Tiffany walked over to her. "Take Dana back to her room then join us in the lobby. We will go to the cemetery and complete the ritual."

Tiffany nodded and took Dana by the arm, her eyelids sagging again, and led her slowly out of the room.

Once they were gone, Gerrit looked at Alex again and said, "It is time for you to leave here, Nemesis. You will leave in chains and you will not know another moment of freedom before you receive the ultimate freedom of death."

He then looked over his shoulder again and called out, "Bring the chains."

Instantly, four vampires rushed into the room. Hal Martino, Neil Shafer, Marly Barnes, and Angelica Norris trotted into the room each carrying a heavy chain with a manacle on each end. They went to the columns, Hal and Marly on one side with Neil and Angelica on the other.

"Colin. Rachel," Gerrit said. "Release him."

The two older vampires, scowls on their faces, moved over quickly and one went to each side of Alex as Sharia backed up a couple of steps, turned, and walked out of the room. Rachel and Colin each quickly released the chains binding Alex to the columns. The other four moved quickly to attach the manacles to Alex's wrists and ankles, but his anger and frustration gave him a burst of energy, enough to break free from them just long enough to take care of one thing, the one person who had revealed Dana's existence to the vampires and brought her into the situation.

He rushed forward, faster than a human but still not quite at vampiric speed, and grabbed Ryan Sullivan by the throat. Where Gerrit had simply applied a little pressure, Alex lifted him off the floor and snarled as he held the chubby man at arm's length. Ryan grabbed Alex's forearm with both hands and kicked his legs to try and get away, but Alex held firm.

"This is what you deserve," Alex growled and spun to his left, driving his right hand, the hand holding Ryan's throat, to the floor. He twisted his wrist as he turned and Ryan's neck snapped then his head crashed into the marble floor, cracking the marble and crushing Ryan's skull. With a release of breath that sounded like a pleasant sigh, Ryan fell still and didn't move again.

The four vampires with the chains rushed to him and quickly placed the manacles on him before he could rise from the kneeling position he'd ended in with the motion. He struggled a bit, but the rush of energy faded in an instant and he was unable to do more than rattle the chains.

Gerrit moved closer and looked at Ryan's body for a few seconds then turned to Alex and said, "You have done me a favor. He wasn't worthy of being turned. I would've destroyed him once he was no longer of use. That time was coming soon and I believe we will survive without him."

Alex glared at him and said nothing as the four vampires pulled him to his feet and turned him to face Gerrit.

"Now," Gerrit said. "We are ready to begin."

He turned toward the door and said, "Gather our forces. It is time."

As he started for the door, the four vampires holding the chains guided Alex toward the door as well. The remaining two Virate remained behind for a few seconds, looking at each other and frowning. With the frowns remaining on their faces, they walked slowly toward the door and each began thinking what they would do once the ritual was complete and the power was released.

CHAPTER TWENTY-NINE
Preparations

The pack roamed the wide pathways winding through the Darkwood Cemetery in a V-shaped formation with Moonshadow leading the way. Nora and Renee followed a few feet behind walking close together. Scott and Holly were behind them and were farther apart. The pale light of the full moon overhead was more than enough for them to see their way clearly among the scattered headstones and massive mausoleums with barren tree limbs overhanging the asphalt path casting mottled shadows across the neatly trimmed grass between the graves and along the path.

It wasn't enough to hinder the eyesight of the wolves. While not quite as strong as the vision of the vampires, their vision was capable of seeing things clearly with minimal light. There was, however, enough light for them to be seen by human eyes, but they moved without fear of being observed or reported. The vampires had spread their influence and had taken most of the town with hundreds more of their kind prepared to rise that night. They wouldn't be ready to join the ritual, but their existence would keep the few remaining human residents in fear and away from the cemetery.

Moonshadow knew the location of the ritual site. He'd been there before, but he hadn't known it as the place of power the vampires sought. During one of his hunting excursions that had taken him through the cemetery and past the grove of Black Pine trees, the trees that had given the cemetery its name, he'd been fascinated by the slim, ebony black trunks rising to the sky and had even stopped to stare at them for a moment until the hunger took control of his mind and pulled him away. But he did remember the location and led the pack there unerringly.

They rounded a final sharp curve in the path and the grove appeared on their left, looking more like an open-air chapel surrounded by the black trees. A pair of pristine white benches faced each other across a narrow stretch of grass beneath the canopy of the tree's black needles high above. Two of the trees, the largest of the grove, were on either side of the small clearing, one behind each of the benches.

Moonshadow stopped at the edge of the clearing, his front paws almost touching the raised curb lining the path through the cemetery, and stared at it for a moment. He couldn't quite feel the power that was supposed to be hidden there somewhere, but there was something about the location that seemed a bit out of place in both the town and the cemetery. The cemetery had a chapel, a small building on the south side near the entrance just past the campus of the local high school and he didn't see the need for an outdoor chapel. He did consider that the benches had been placed there for people to appreciate the unique native trees, but it still didn't make a lot of sense.

After a moment, he pushed off the ground with his front paws and transformed into human shape. As he stood up and turned around, the others transformed as well. Once they were all ready, Moonshadow looked them over briefly.

"This is it," he said. "This is where the ritual will take place. Our job is to protect the perimeter. Once they arrive and get started, we'll move out about fifty yards and patrol. But remember, Carmen is with them. I don't know if she's joined them or if they've captured her. Either way, don't trust her."

He pointed to his right, the direction from which they'd arrived, and said, "I'll take that sector."

His arm swung to the left, almost directly away from their path, and said, "Scott and Nora, you'll go that way. It's their most likely path to invade and disrupt the ceremony."

They nodded and he pointed farther to his right, turning until he was almost pointing at the small clearing, "Holly and Renee, you'll take that area. It's possible they'll come in from the other side of the cemetery."

He lowered his hand and said, "Stay in your area, close to any possible entry point you see. If they enter, don't attack. There'll be too many and they also have Katrina on their side. If you see them, come back here and report their arrival. Then, when they come closer, you will do as Gerrit orders."

They nodded and backed away as Moonshadow turned and started toward his position. He took two quick steps then fell forward and transformed, continuing forward without breaking stride. The others turned in their appointed directions, transformed, and hurried away.

As Moonshadow reached a position where he could see the planned entry point for the vampires, a gap in the tall hedges lining the north edge of the cemetery near the end adjacent to the high school football stadium, he stopped and looked around until he found a place in the shadows dark enough to conceal him. He would remain hidden there until he sensed or saw someone approaching, but he didn't have to wait long.

Just a few minutes after assuming his position, the first of the vampires arrived. Gerrit led the way with Rachel and Colin behind him holding the heavy chains that bound Alex as he walked along slowly, his feet dragging the ground. The Mystic approached from behind, still wearing the dark red robe with the hood now pulled up. She looked like a satanic cult member from an old low-budget movie and carried the heavy book holding it to her chest tightly with both hands to further embody the image.

Others followed in groups of two and three. Moonshadow recognized most of them. Jade Hyson followed with Dylan Ambrose at her side. Kim Chandler followed them, walking alone, and Moonshadow stared for a moment, her presence distracting him from his mission and filling his mind with thoughts of their past. Those thoughts were quickly overcome by the memory of Carmen and his betrothal to her. He wasn't sure it was still in effect and they hadn't discussed it during their brief time together since the pack had arrived, but he felt it deeply. He was no longer sure the life debt he owed Kim remained, but his feelings for Kim were diminished by the return of those he felt for Carmen.

Behind them, a large contingent of locals followed. The two former police officers, Hal Martino and Monica Halpern, walked behind Neil Shafer, more recently turned and not quite as integrated. Others included the former Medical Examiner, Mitchell Roth, EMTs Jim Williams and Erin Smith, Tiffany Gardner, Dr. Ross Brinson, the nurse Angelica Norris, and the wild girl, Marly Barnes. A half dozen more came after them, people Moonshadow didn't recognize, and he wondered if they would be enough to hold off the task force with the aid of Carmen and Katrina.

They walked in silence, focused on the task at hand. Gerrit, leading the way, kept his gaze forward and barely registered the presence of Moonshadow in the shadows behind one of the larger mausoleums on his left. He was focused on the ritual and accepting the ancient power that would give him what he needed to complete the plan of Aranos and take over the entire world.

It took them only moments to reach the clearing and the approximation of an outdoor chapel. Gerrit stopped before it and smiled, thinking it was the most appropriate place for the ritual and could almost be seen as a monument to the ignorance humans had of the history of the vampire race.

After a moment of reflection, Gerrit looked over his right shoulder and said, "Chain him to the two trees, between the benches."

Colin and Rachel pulled Alex around Gerrit's right side, almost dragging him forward. His left foot caught on the high curb and he staggered forward, but the two vampires held him firmly and didn't allow him to fall. Gerrit stood and watched with just a touch of glee in his smile. He hadn't felt anxiety or such excitement since before he'd been turned, and that had been quite a long time earlier.

Once Alex was secured to the trees, his arms stretched out wide and his head leaning forward once again, Gerrit moved closer and stood precisely six feet in front of him on a small mound that looked like nothing more than a bump in the ground, a simple topographical feature, but Gerrit knew the truth about it. He'd been informed by the Mystic of the precise place where the power was buried. It was all he could do to refrain from grinning as he nodded to the Mystic and she moved forward with the book in hand.

Sharia stopped a few feet in front of him and turned to face the others as they moved forward to gather around. While they moved closer, Sharia opened the book and quickly found the proper passage.

Once they stopped and all eyes were on her, Sharia began, "Long ago, near the beginning of time, the ancestor of the vampire was cast out of paradise, considered a beast of evil that began the downfall of man. Soon, the first vampire rose from the earth, bitten by the desolate creature. The first vampire created more and began a new race that survived every cataclysm both the earth and man could create. Centuries later, long before civilization rose and nations were founded, the vampire race expanded and explored the world. When they arrived on the shores of this continent, they found a tribe of humans inhabiting this particular region. They were a powerful people, the Anasazi, and they opposed the presence of the vampire. The great Master Malakor was overpowered by the Anasazi wizards and was defeated. His great power was cast into the earth and with it the greatest power of the Anasazi. The two were bound together in the earth, but it was not the entirety of vampire power. The power of the Master remained with Malakor and has been passed down through the ages. Only the Book of Aranos contains the necessary information to locate the resting place of the Greater Power and the method guaranteed to release it."

She placed a hand on the pages of the book and continued, "The Book of Prophecy has given us details on the one who would oppose us, the one known only as the Nemesis. It is stated that he will rise from the land of the ancient power. He will possess similar powers to the vampire, but he will not suffer the vampire's weaknesses. His power is the antithesis of vampire power and he must be destroyed so that our destiny might be fulfilled."

CHAPTER THIRTY
Conflict

Eleven people moved slowly and stealthily toward the old gate at the end of a narrow road beside the high school's vocational center that provided a barrier to entering the cemetery. Scott Bonacci and Melissa Dyson led the way with rifles readied and night vision gear in place over the standard visors of their helmets. The newest members of the team, Raquel Jackson and Evan Barker, flanked them, weapons drawn as well. Cardwell and Sandusky followed them, each with a pistol drawn. Merina and Sydney followed them. Merina held a pistol while Sydney carried a long blade, not quite a sword, in her right hand. Bringing up the rear were the three remaining women. Katrina and Carmen, both unarmed, walked with DeAnna between them. She carried the sword Alex had trained her to use and the small silver crucifix she wore around her neck was visible over the tactical gear she wore. She also had a small pack strapped to her back containing her Bible, a vial of holy water, and a half dozen sharpened stakes. She doubted she would use any of that, but it felt comfortable and safe to have with her.

They moved along the narrow street, lit from behind by a single streetlight on the corner, and took it slow, their eyes scanning around carefully.

As they approached the gate, Cardwell glanced back and said, "Be careful. We know where to go. Brewer gave us the location and the quickest path. Watch for sentries, most likely the wolves."

"Got it, boss," Bonacci said with a nod and continued forward.

He reached the gate a few seconds later and stopped, looking around carefully. He saw no signs of movement and looked over his shoulder.

"Looks clear," he said. "The gate's unlocked."

"Go ahead," Cardwell said. "But be quiet."

Bonacci nodded and reached for the gate, releasing his left hand from the rifle. He placed it atop the gate and slowly pushed it forward. It moved easily, with only a slight screeching sound of a rusted hinge. It wasn't substantial and he continued until it was open wide enough for them to walk through.

DeAnna, the last one through, left the gate open. She didn't think it would be a problem and might be somewhat beneficial should they be forced to retreat quickly.

Once inside and back in formation, they moved more quickly along the path at the urging of Cardwell. He felt they were running late and sent Bonacci and Dyson ahead to clear the way, if there was anything to clear.

Cardwell estimated they were halfway to the site when Bonacci and Dyson stopped and trained their rifles to the left, aiming into the darkness beneath the cover of several trees. As they did, Cardwell looked back at Merina and said, "Give me all comm now."

"On it," Merina said and reached into her pants pocket. She pulled out a small device and touched a control.

"Done," she said and looked up at Cardwell.

He nodded and said, "Bonacci. Sit rep."

"I've got motion to the left," he said, his voice almost a whisper. "It looks like two of the wolves."

"Let me handle this," Carmen said, kicking off her shoes as she moved forward and began removing her clothes.

"I should go with you," Katrina said and moved forward as well, matching Carmen's stride.

"Good idea," Cardwell said as Katrina began transforming.

Carmen tossed her shirt to the ground and slowed to remove her pants as she began to transform as well. The wolf and the panther then sprinted ahead and turned to the left just before reaching the spot where Bonacci and Dyson stood.

Once they vanished into the darkness, Cardwell said, "Let's move. They'll take care of it. We're on a schedule."

Bonacci nodded and started toward their destination at a fast trot. Dyson joined him and the others picked up the pace as well. DeAnna lagged behind for a second, slowing down to pick up Carmen's clothing. She held it in her hand and sheathed her sword then tucked it into her pack while trying to move fast enough to catch up to the others.

Once off the path, Carmen and Katrina moved slowly into the darkness. Their eyes adjusted to the darkness quickly and it took only an instant for them to spot the two wolves nearby. Carmen knew them instantly by their scent. The darker of the two was Scott and the blonde was Holly. As they approached, the two wolves began almost circling, their heads lowered as they anticipated a fight. Katrina moved forward, ready for the confrontation, but Carmen stopped and shifted back into human form.

She held up her hands and said, "There's no need for this. The vampires are influencing you. They did something to control your minds. You didn't come here to work for them. You came here to find Moonshadow and return him to the tribe."

The two wolves paused and stared at her for a second. Scott then backed up and pushed off the ground as he began to transform. Beside him, Holly growled and leaped for Carmen. Before she could react and transform back into wolf form, Katrina shot forward and met Holly.

The two tangled amidst growls and snarls. Holly swiped at Katrina repeatedly, but Katrina dodged the attacks easily. After just a few seconds, Katrina saw an opening and lunged forward. With a howl that was more war cry than anything else, Katrina's mouth opened wide and her massive fangs closed on the side of Holly's neck. She bit down and held on as Holly let out a painful whine and thrashed about to get free of the bite, but it did no good. Katrina felt the wolf's hot blood flooding her mouth and did her best not to swallow. It would cause her no harm, but she didn't like the idea of swallowing blood.

While still twisting her body to get free, Holly swiped with her right forepaw and her claws scraped across Katrina's abdomen. A flash of pain went through Katrina's mind, but it didn't stop her. She bore down on Holly's neck, grinding her jaws and biting down until her mouth closed completely around a large portion of Holly's flesh. Then, with a sharp snap of her head, she ripped fur, skin, and meat away from Holly's neck and leaped back before the arterial spray struck her.

Holly began flopping around, whining and howling, with blood flying freely. Katrina gave her a second and glanced back at Carmen. The blonde woman merely shrugged, telling Katrina that it was up to her. With a sharp nod, she returned her attention to the injured wolf and resumed her attack. She found the right spot and bit down on Holly again, at the base of her skull. She placed her right paw on Holly's back and threw herself forward, gripping Holly's throat tightly. As she'd done with a single blow to the head of Greyeagle the night before, she rolled over the injured wolf and came with another chuck of meat in her mouth as Holly's head fell away from her body and the body collapsed to the ground.

"Okay," Carmen said and looked at Scott. "I'm going to assume you're not going to try the same thing."

"No way," Scott shook his head as Katrina reverted to human form.

With a bit of Holly's blood still on her chin, Katrina looked at Carmen and said, "We should join the others."

Carmen looked at her and said, "You go with the team. Scott and I will find the other wolves and try to straighten them out."

"I don't think it'll be much trouble," Scott said. "They'll understand."

"We'll see," Carmen said and shifted once again.

Scott did the same and followed her into the darkness as Katrina shifted again as well and bounded off in the direction the team had gone.

At the grove of black pine trees, Sharia prepared to read the next passage in the Book of Prophecy and continue the ritual, but she paused and looked up as she saw motion in her peripheral vision. The wolf, Moonshadow, walked along beside a tall, lean woman with long, dark blonde hair wearing pale green scrubs.

As Jana entered the area, the others looked toward her and Rachel, frowning, shot over to her and stopped in front of her.

"You have turned," Rachel said, remembering the attack on the task force and what she'd done. "And now you've joined us."

"Yes," Jana said and nodded respectfully. "What would you have me do?"

"Join us," Rachel said and gestured toward the group facing the Mystic. "Participate in the ritual."

As Jana moved to join the group and Rachel returned to her position, Sharia resumed reading from the book.

"The Nemesis holds a portion of the ancient power," she said. "He holds enough to grant him a portion of the abilities granted to the vampire in undeath. It has also made him the key to the power. His blood, portioned slowly to the Master, will unleash the ancient power. It is now time for the ritual to begin."

She turned around, facing Gerrit, and said, "You are the first. You will begin the process by drawing the first of his blood."

Gerrit bowed respectfully then turned to Alex. With his hands at his sides, he moved slowly toward Alex, opening his mouth and preparing his fangs.

"Now, little Nemesis," Gerrit said condescendingly as he stopped to Alex's right and took hold of his arm with both hands. "This little power of yours will now give me the power to accomplish greater things than any Master has done before me."

Alex turned his head slowly, glaring at Gerrit, but he remained silent, his jaw slack with the exhaustion and pain he still felt from the torture the wolves and Ryan had administered. He continued to stare at the vampire as he opened his mouth wide and his head snapped forward, his fangs plunging into Alex's forearm.

Alex let out a grunt as the fangs penetrated his skin like a pair of cold needles, long needles, and he sucked in a sharp breath, creating a hissing sound, as his blood flowed into Gerrit's mouth. He took two deep swallows and slowly raised his head, grinning almost maniacally as Rachel and Colin moved forward at the urging of Sharia.

Gerrit stepped back and leaned his head back, relishing the tingling sensation that ran through his body, an anticipatory feeling of the power coming to him. Colin took his right arm and repeated the process as Rachel moved to his throat. She placed a hand on his head, gripping his hair, and pulling it sharply to the side. She leaned closer, almost moaning as she first kissed his neck then plunged her fangs into him.

Gerrit didn't watch the others. He moved forward, returning to the small mound several feet in front of Alex, and stood atop it. He closed his eyes and tilted his head back with his hands clenched into fists at his sides. He gasped as energy began to flow from the earth beneath him into and through his body, settling into every pore of his being. It was exhilarating and his jaw dropped as he began to feel stronger, more powerful, and more immortal than ever before.

He laughed heartily and declared loudly, "The power is mine!"

CHAPTER THIRTY-ONE
Resolution

At Cardwell's direction, the team had split up to infiltrate and attack the group of vampires gathered for the ritual. DeAnna was on her own and she wasn't quite confident enough in her ability to remain unseen by vampires to move without a little trepidation. She'd taken a different path, moving around to the area behind where Alex was chained and moved slowly through the black pine trees with her sword drawn and ready. Unlike Alex, she couldn't sense the precise location of the vampires, but she could feel the coldness of their presence. It was almost the same as sensing the source of a fire through the surrounding heat. She felt a large area of deeper cold than the air around her and knew there were many more than any of the task force members had suspected.

Before long, she began to hear faint sounds, voices in the still air, and knew she was drawing close. She adjusted her grip on the hilt of the sword, tightening it as she prepared to face the vampires on her own. Her dark eyes narrowed behind the night vision gear she wore and her long hair flowed from beneath her tactical helmet as she neared the clearing and could see one of the white benches between two trees, including the chain binding Alex in place.

Taking a deep breath, she stepped forward and trusted her innate ability to keep her from being seen. As she moved into the clearing a bit to Alex's left, she saw the tall vampire woman pull back from his throat and the leader step onto a small mound of earth and declare that he'd received the power. DeAnna moved forward slowly, planning to somehow release Alex from the chains, but she didn't quite make it. As she moved toward him in a crouch with the sword held up with both hands, Rachel looked at her and frowned.

"What do we have here?" Rachel asked. "A pesky human leading the task force to try and stop us?"

DeAnna stopped and stood up straight. She had hoped none of the vampires would see her, but the woman did.

The big red-haired vampire near her frowned and asked, "What are you talking about?"

Rachel nodded slowly and said, "We have one of those, Colin, one of the faithful that can hide from those who no longer believe."

Rachel moved toward her, ducking under Alex's left arm, and said, "You see, little human, I was there when he died and rose again. I believe in his deity, but I do not follow him. There is no place in his heaven for the vampire."

DeAnna shook her head and backed away, still prepared for battle. Once Rachel was clear of Alex and DeAnna was almost in the trees again, the task force arrived and the battle began.

Colin moved away from Alex as well, frowning as he moved toward Gerrit. The three had planned to share the power, but Gerrit had claimed it for himself. That didn't sit well with Colin and he shook his head as he lumbered toward Gerrit to confront him.

Once he was clear of Alex, Katrina and Sydney moved in from the side. They moved quickly and quietly to him and Sydney pulled a small tool from a pouch at her left hip. With Katrina standing guard, watching as Colin approached Gerrit, Sydney went to work on the manacles holding him in place. The tool worked quickly and he was released within moments.

She released his feet first then worked on his arms. His right arm was released and fell limply to his side, his head still hanging forward. She moved to the other side and released his left arm and as she did, he dropped to his knees and let out a heavy sigh as he placed his hands on his knees and leaned slightly forward.

Ignoring the attack beginning several yards away, Sydney knelt beside him and placed a hand gently on his shoulder.

"It's going to be okay," she said. "We'll take care of you."

"No," he said weakly. "It's done. He has the power."

Sydney gasped and shook her head slowly, "Then we've failed."

"Not yet," Alex said and looked at her. "He's not invincible. We can take him out. I just need to get my strength back."

Katrina, with her back to them, looked over her shoulder at Sydney and said, "Kiss him. I have a feeling about you two."

Sydney frowned and looked at her, "What do you mean?"

"Just kiss him," Katrina said. "I'll explain later."

Sydney shrugged and leaned closer to Alex, "What can it hurt?"

He turned his head toward her. She placed a hand on each side of his face, tilted her head slightly, and kissed him.

It lasted only a few seconds, but they both knew there was something else there, an energy neither had felt before. Sydney felt something change inside her, a strength appeared that she hadn't known before. It wasn't a physical strength. It was more of a mental strength, a power that gave her the confidence to continue.

As the kiss broke, Alex drew in a deep breath and a snarl crossed his face as his eyes settled on Gerrit and Colin approaching him. He rose slowly to his feet, hands clenched into fists at his sides, and drew in a deep breath.

"Stay here," he said to Sydney. "This won't take long."

As he strode forward, the other members of the task force entered the area from all sides. With so few of them, there were wide gaps between each member, but they covered the area with heavy rifle fire from the four insertion team members entering from the sides while Cardwell and Sandusky opened fire with their pistols from behind the cluster of vampires. The silver-infused rounds they all used did cause damage to the vampires they managed to hit, driving several of them to the ground. Merina remained behind Cardwell and wasn't firing. She held in her right hand the sword Alex had used since shortly after his inclusion in the task force. She was there to keep the communications working and to get that sword to Alex once he was released. The only problem was that the vampires stood between her and Alex. She watched over Cardwell's left shoulder as Alex stalked toward the two vampires, two of the Virate, as they appeared to be in the midst of a verbal argument.

Shaking her head, she tried to think of a way around the vampires, or through them, to get the sword to Alex. Considering he was facing two of the three Masters, she knew he needed a weapon.

"I need a path," she said, hoping the others weren't too focused on their portion of the fight to help her. "I have to get to Alex."

"Hold on," Cardwell said. "We're working on it. Bonacci, you and Dyson move forward and try drawing them to you."

"Got it, boss," he replied. "Give us a minute."

As Bonacci and Melissa moved away to draw the attention of at least a portion of the vampires and Merina looked for an opening, DeAnna continued backing into the grove of black trees with Rachel steadily approaching her, drawing closer as she spat a series of threats and empty promises. She held the sword in front of her and tried her best to look intimidated and frightened until she neared the edge of the grove.

She took in a breath and said into her comm, "Can I take her now?"

Cardwell replied almost instantly, "Do it, DeAnna."

With a nod, DeAnna stopped her retreat and stood her ground. She braced her feet and flexed her knees, just as Alex had instructed her, and lowered the sword until the blade was parallel to her upper arm.

Rachel continued forward slowly and shook her head as she said, "You can do nothing to me, little believer. I have no faith in that little symbol you wear around your neck. I can smell the silver, but that won't stop me."

DeAnna nodded once and said, "It doesn't matter if you have faith, just that I do."

Rachel laughed, "Then do your worst. You are nothing."

"We'll see," DeAnna said and started forward.

Rachel stopped and held her arms wide, smirking confidently and unafraid. DeAnna continued forward, moving evenly, again the way Alex had trained her, and she began her attack.

She feinted to Rachel's head with the sword. As Rachel leaned back to dodge the clumsy swing, DeAnna lowered the sword, spun around, and kicked Rachel's feet from beneath her. She fell onto her right side, surprised that the woman had been able to do even that much, and rolled backward, trying to move out of range, but DeAnna was ready for that and moved forward, turning around as she shifted the sword in her grasp. Her left hand fell away as the tip of the blade pointed downward and she lunged forward just as Rachel rolled onto her back. The sword was already in motion, anticipating Rachel's movements and position, and drove the point of the blade between Rachel's breasts.

Rachel let out a howl of pain and a milky fluid flowed around the edges of the blade as she writhed as the silver blended into the steel of the blade began to burn. DeAnna leaned her weight on the sword and held her pinned to the ground. She held it for a moment, her expression completely devoid of emotion, then made her next move. She stepped over Rachel, pulled the blade free, and swung it like a hammer toward Rachel's neck. Her aim was perfect and the blade drove through her neck and her head snapped away from her body like a cork shooting from a bottle of champagne.

DeAnna stood up straight and looked down as Rachel's corpse, no longer animated by whatever virus or entity had been keeping her moving for centuries, rapidly began to decay. In just a few seconds, her body quickly faded from the appearance of a woman in her late twenties to a decayed corpse with the flesh turning to dust, revealing a tainted skeleton that also collapsed into dust and became indiscernible as anything other than additional dirt on the ground.

Once she was certain Rachel wasn't going to return, DeAnna shifted her grip on the sword, holding it down at her side, she turned and moved through the trees to join the others.

As he moved, Alex caught a glimpse of Merina trying to make her way to him with the sword. With more than a dozen vampires between them, he knew she wouldn't be able to reach him in time. He had to stop Gerrit, to destroy him before he could use the ancient power to complete the plan the vampires had begun following. He didn't know any details of the plan, but he knew it centered on the idea of vampires taking over the world and he couldn't allow it to continue.

His strength had returned and he wasn't sure if it had something to do with the release of the ancient power or if Sydney's kiss had accelerated the healing process. It didn't matter at the moment, though. His strength was returning and he hoped it was enough.

Two of the Virate were standing in front of him, the two males, and he had to get past Colin to reach Gerrit and conclude the issue. With his jaw set, he shot forward with Colin as his target. He moved faster than he ever had before and slammed into Colin an instant later. He wrapped his arms around the vampire and drove him to the ground. As they struck, he rolled over and smoothly rose to his feet.

Before Colin could recover, Alex moved in and struck with a sharp kick to the chin. Colin was briefly lifted off the ground by the force of the blow and Alex followed through, stepping forward and dropping to a crouch. He grabbed Colin's head and, with a snarl and growl, he twisted sharply to the left. He was rewarded with a sharp cracking sound as Colin's neck and upper spine shattered, shards of bone cutting through his spinal cord.

Satisfied that Colin was out of the picture, Alex rose to his feet and turned to face Gerrit. He didn't see the expected anger in Gerrit's eyes. Instead, he saw a faint smile.

"You have done me a great service, Nemesis," Gerrit said. "But it's not enough. I have claimed the ancient power and you will be destroyed."

Alex took a step toward him, ready to engage him in combat, but stopped as someone moved behind him. Jana Hendricks, the task force's lab tech, dove out of the darkness and landed on Gerrit's back. Alex was more than a little surprised to see her mouth open and reveal a pair of fangs that plunged into the throat of the Master. Gerrit let out a scream of surprise and pain as he turned around quickly, thrashing as he tried to throw her from him, but Jana wrapped her arms and legs around his body to hold her in place as she drained him. Within a few seconds, before Alex could get to them, Gerrit's eyes rolled back and he collapsed to the ground.

Jana finally released him and climbed to her feet as Gerrit's body slowly turned to dust.

CHAPTER THIRTY-TWO
Sorting It Out

"This is not over," Jana said, looking at Alex. "This town is now mine. I am the Master and the possessor of the ancient power. I am the strongest vampire on Earth. We will meet again, Nemesis, and when we do, I will destroy you. The vampire race will become the greatest power this world has ever seen and your beloved is now one of us."

Alex glared at her, preparing to attack, but she moved first, more quickly than he'd seen a vampire move before. She shot away so quickly that he saw only a streak of light piercing the darkness like a laser. As she did, the other vampires began to follow, a bit more slowly.

Bonacci went after Sharia as she ran in the direction Jana had taken, moving more slowly without the use of her hands. She still held the book clasped to her chest and tried to run, but Bonacci remained just a few yards behind her. He raised his rifle and fired a shot that struck her in the right shoulder. The silver-coated slug struck her and caused her to cry out in surprise and pain. It also caused her to lose her grip on the book. It fell to the ground and she paused to look at it then glanced up to see Bonacci taking aim again. She made a choice and shot into the darkness, leaving the book behind.

Once Jana departed, Kim Chandler remained, staying in the shadows where she could see Moonshadow and determine his allegiance. She stayed there only a moment, just long enough for her to see another of the pack, Carmen, approach him. With her enhanced hearing, she listened to their conversation and she knew she'd lost Moonshadow to his former love. She watched a moment longer and decided what would be her best course of action. She took a couple of steps back, away from the two wolves, and turned around then shot into the night as fast as her vampiric speed would take her.

On the other side of the area, Monica Halpern was confused. She didn't understand how the Virate had been destroyed. She no longer felt the connection to the Master as she had with them. When the others vanished, she didn't know which way to go. They'd scattered in different directions and she no longer knew which one was in charge.

While she was trying to decide which way to go, Raquel and Evan moved up behind her slowly and quietly with their pistols drawn. Monica was searching for some sign of a vampire presence and felt nothing close, distracting her enough for the two former police officers to close on her.

"Stay where you are," Raquel said, training the pistol on Monica's head.

As she turned to face them, Cardwell and Sandusky rushed over, pistols in hand as well, and moved around until they were effectively encircling her. Monica looked around, confused and a little disoriented. She recognized Raquel and Evan, knew them from her former life as a fellow police officer, but her new life, her afterlife, didn't allow for the camaraderie that had existed previously.

"What are you going to do?" Monica asked, looking at Raquel.

"I think you're coming with us," Raquel replied.

"Yes," Cardwell said and nodded. "You are coming with us. We're taking you to see the President, and a few others, to prove that your kind exists."

Monica nodded slowly and held up her hands, "I surrender. But you need me and that should allow me to make certain requests."

Cardwell shook his head, "We'll give you what you need, nothing more. I guarantee that you will survive, at least until the President has a chance to see you for what you are."

Monica nodded and lowered her hands, "I guess I'll have to prove myself."

"That you will," Cardwell said. "Now, let's get out of here and get this figured out."

As the four began escorting Monica toward the perimeter of the cemetery, keeping her surrounded, DeAnna emerged from the trees and walked toward the asphalt path where Alex stood a few feet away from Katrina. He was looking along the path where Jana had vanished and Katrina was looking at the bodies on the ground as they slowly decayed. Some of them collapsed into dust while others looked as if they'd died recently.

As DeAnna reached the path, Alex turned toward her.

She looked at him and nodded, "I took out the woman, Rachel."

"Good," Alex said. "But we have a new problem."

DeAnna frowned and he started toward her as he said, "Jana, the lab tech, has become a vampire and she took the power from Gerrit. She's the new Master and she has the ancient power."

DeAnna shook her head, "How is that possible?"

Katrina looked at her and said, "When one vampire drains another, they not only take the excuse for a life the vampire has, they take their experience and power, adding it to their own."

DeAnna stopped and her frown deepened, "But Jana doesn't have the experience, the history, Gerrit had. How can she hope to lead the vampire world?"

"We'll figure that out," he said and nodded to his right. "Cardwell and the others have a captive. Go help them."

With a single nod, DeAnna turned and hurried toward the group escorting Monica away from the scene.

Katrina took a step toward Alex and said, "Sydney is waiting."

He nodded, knowing that Sydney had run when the battle began in full, seeking safety far from the action. Alex could feel her presence and knew she was waiting and relieved that the fight was finished.

"She's okay," Alex said. "And I think you know more about all of this than you've told us."

Katrina nodded, "I do, but I can't tell you right now. I need to contact a couple of people, my people, and figure things out on that end before I tell you everything you need to know."

Alex took a step forward, looking at her curiously, and said, "I think that's going to be one very interesting conversation."

She nodded again and said, "For now, let's just say that I'm going to more or less join your task force."

"That's good," he said and stopped a couple of feet from her. "But first tell me about the wolves. Are they going with the vampires?"

"No," she said and shook her head. "Their connection was to Gerrit. With his final death, the control he had over them was removed. They are themselves again."

"And what does that mean?"

She leaned slightly forward and tilted her head to the left, "It means they are free to do as they will. Moonshadow is their alpha and Carmen has some influence over him. The pack was sent here by the Tribe to return him to the pack."

Alex frowned, "I thought the wolves were allied with the vampires."

"No," she shook her head. "They are not. I will explain that later, but first I need to meet with them and explain the situation."

Alex nodded and gestured toward the others as they made their way toward the cemetery exit, "Let's get out of here first. There's a lot left to do."

"Yes," Katrina nodded. "There's more than you know."

Without another word, they started toward the others, a strange sense of calm coming over Alex at the thought of how much they still had to do. The task force he'd thought several months earlier was no longer a viable entity was now more necessary than ever.

He was also a little confused about Sydney. His feelings for her were still there, but there was something else about her that he wanted to understand. She'd kissed him and he'd started healing, his strength had returned and seemed to have increased. He wanted to know what that had to do with her.

The wounds inflicted on him by the wolves, the vampires, and Ryan had completely healed, but splotches of dried blood remained on his exposed skin. The energy that infused him and left him with only a few hours of sleep each night had also returned, but it felt stronger, almost as if he was infused with a constant flow of adrenalin. He would have to talk to Brewer about that and see if they could figure out what had happened.

A moment after they started, breaking his chain of thought, Katrina glanced at him and said, "I hope you have more clothing."

He glanced down and saw the ripped and torn pants and his lack of a shirt. With a light smirk, he looked up and said, "I hope Sandusky brought enough. This look doesn't quite lend itself to leadership."

"No, it doesn't," Katrina shook her head and they continued walking, rapidly catching up to the others.

CHAPTER THIRTY-THREE
Assumption of Control

Kim Chandler approached the entrance to the old hotel slowly and carefully. A few lights burned in the windows, providing illumination for the few remaining inside the building, the ones not included in the ritual, and the smaller number made it easier for her to accomplish what she'd decided to do.

Dana Richland was the connection to Alex Chance and the task force, the people who would stop the new Master. Jana Hendricks had been a part of the task force, but she'd been turned and had taken the power of the Master from Gerrit in the typical way a vampire would gain more power. It confused Kim a bit. Jana was a new vampire, having awakened that night for the first night of her afterlife, she didn't have the knowledge of vampire physiology, and there should've been no way for her to have known that draining Gerrit would give her the power that the much older vampire had developed. Kim was a skeptic and questioned nearly everything and she suspected that someone, another vampire, had sent Jana to attack Gerrit, but she couldn't be sure and had no idea who might have done that.

Dana was her target. Kim knew that Gerrit had been the only one to bite her and, with her turning, she would've been under his complete control. With his demise, she would be free of his control, free of any control, and would be able to make her own decisions. Kim hoped that she still had some feelings for Alex Chance and would jump at the opportunity to do something to further his cause, though it might mean their own destruction.

She knew there would be a guard inside the entrance, but it would be a young one, having been turned within the previous two days, and would be no problem for her at all. With her eyes narrowed slightly, she approached the door with confidence, ready for anything Gerrit or one of the other Virate could have devised.

Setting her jaw as she reached the door, she pushed it open and entered. The guard left to protect the lair, standing just to the right of the door, was Dylan Ambrose, the monster of a man with a penchant for physical combat. He was older than the others in the town, but not by much. He stood there with his massive arms folded over his equally massive chest, stretching the limits of the black leather vest he wore.

His eyes looked down at her, seeming almost drowsy due to his height, and asked, "Where are the others?"

"Finished," she said, her voice sharp and staccato. "The Virate have been destroyed."

He frowned deeply, "Impossible. They are invincible."

She shook her head, "You'll see them soon enough."

"Huh?" he asked and dropped his hands to his waist.

That was all the opportunity she needed. She struck quickly, just a bit more quickly than Dylan's reflexes, and her first blow, to his chest, shattered his sternum and drove bits of bone into his slowly beating heart. Kim could tell by that brief contact that he hadn't yet fed for the night and he was weakened. It didn't matter, though. She would destroy him before he knew what to do.

Her second blow was a powerful uppercut to his sharp chin. She leaped upward to reach him and the force of her jump, her legs pushing her upward and forward, snapped his head back and broke his neck. It wasn't quite the killing blow she'd envisioned, but it was enough to knock him off his feet. He landed on his back and before he had time to recover, she jumped atop him and followed through by grabbing the sides of his head and twisting to the left with every ounce of her strength. It was more than enough. His head separated from his body and only a small flow of the clear ichor that flowed through a vampire's circulatory system before they'd fed seeped onto the faded carpet of the lobby floor.

Kim dropped his head as it began to decay and made her way toward the room where Dana had been sequestered once the third bite had been administered. She knew there were others awake in the building, but they were all recent turns like Dana and would be no trouble at all.

The room was far from any of the others and Kim encountered no one as she made her way into a lower level of the hotel, a small basement beneath a mechanical room located in the southwestern corner of the building. She found it easily and tried the door. It was locked, as she had expected, but it would take little effort for her to break into the room. Dana, being freshly awakened, wouldn't yet know her strength and still held onto a bit of her humanity. She would have seen the locked door and believed she was unable to leave.

Kim held onto the doorknob and leaned back then slammed her right shoulder into it as she lunged forward. The door's frame shattered as she hit it and the door collapsed inward. As it did, she heard a brief yelp from Dana, the only occupant, and she stepped forward.

The room was dark, no light source at all, but that wasn't a deterrent for Kim. Her eyes adjusted quickly and she saw the slightly shorter woman cowering on the small cot against the far wall.

"Dana," she said and stopped just inside the door. "I need you to come with me."

Dana relaxed a bit and frowned as she asked, "Who are you?"

"I'm Kim Chander," she said. "And I'm going to take you away from here."

"But Gerrit said to wait for him," Dana shook her head slowly.

Kim took a step forward and said, "Gerrit has been destroyed. So have the other Virate. Alex Chance is free and he's going to go after the new Master."

"What new Master?"

Kim paused for a second then said, "Jana Hendricks is the new Master. She drained Gerrit and took his power."

Dana sat up, "You can do that?"

"Yes," Kim nodded. "And I don't know how Jana figured that out. She rose tonight, just like you, but she managed to destroy the Master. Now, I want you to come with me. We're going to find another group that I hope will take us in and allow us to help fight against this new vampire regime alongside Alex and his task force."

"You mean it's possible for me to see Alex again?" Dana asked.

"Yes," Kim nodded. "But we have to go now, before the others return. We won't be able to get out once that happens."

"Okay," Dana nodded and stood up. "But where are we going?"

Kim shook her head and took a step back, "I'll tell you on the way. Let's get out of here first."

With a shrug, Dana followed Kim out of the room and the hotel a few moments later.

The two women were clear of the area, heading south, while Jana and the other vampires arrived from the north, traveling quickly and in a tight cluster. Jana led the way with Sharia on her left and Jade on her right. Several others followed in a loose cluster, but there were far fewer than had departed the hotel hours earlier.

Jana was upset about the situation. She'd known the members of the task force and the insertion team for a few years and she'd completely underestimated their abilities. Of course, she'd never seen the team in action and had only heard about Alex's abilities. Thankfully, a large portion of Gerrit's knowledge had transferred to her along with his strength and powers. She knew more about the Nemesis than anyone in the task force, including Alex, and she felt that would give her at least a slight advantage.

They'd lost a number of the vampires, their soldiers, in the fight with the task force, but a large portion of the town's population would be awakening soon as vampires, rebuilding their numbers rather quickly. The issue, as she saw it, was in feeding such numbers. Gerrit and the other Virate had planned ahead and kept a percentage of the population alive, as humans, to provide sustenance for the population and had brought Ross Brinson into the fold to keep the humans alive and producing blood, extracted without biting to keep them from turning. Jana thought it was a smart move and one that would need expansion and a little revision as they continued the plan Gerrit had extracted from the Book of Aranos.

As they left the road and walked along the narrow path toward the front of the hotel, Jana knew it was time for something different and said, "We will not remain here long. This is not the place to begin the next phase of the plan."

Sharia looked at her, frowning, and replied, "We have established a community here. We are in complete control of this town. It is connected to major thoroughfares and the remainder of this nation is accessible."

Jana looked at her and said, "No. We must follow the plan. We will take the larger cities and spread our influence from there."

"But must we begin so soon?" Sharia asked. "We have barely begun. This is a good place to grow our numbers and prepare the army we need for total conquest."

At the door, Jana turned around and snarled as she said, "We cannot start from this small town. Even with the growing population, we cannot follow the plan. We will start with one city and build our base there slowly. That is how Aranos stated in the plan and we will follow the plan. The Virate began it and I will finish it."

Sharia nodded slowly for a second then asked, "Where will we begin?"

Jana turned to the door and looked over her shoulder as she said, "We'll go to the nearest city, one I'm quite familiar with. Once our new converts awaken and are prepared for the move, we will relocate to New Orleans."

Sharia nodded again, appreciatively this time, and said, "New Orleans has a rich tradition of things that thrive in the dark. It will be our true starting point and our haven."

Jana nodded and opened the door, finding the decayed remains of Dylan on the floor to her right and she knew the hotel had been invaded. She shook her head and realized that only one survivor of the battle had not returned with her and the others. She scowled angrily and clenched her hands into fists. She sniffed the air, her eyes narrowing to mere slits, and she quickly discerned what had happened. The power she'd received opened her senses and her mind to the nature and existence of the vampires around her. She could smell their passing and knew what had taken place shortly before their arrival and realized that Kim Chandler had betrayed them.

She moved away from the door, allowing the others to enter, and they all stared at the corpse on the floor, each of them quickly realizing the victim of a vicious was Dylan Ambrose, the enforcer of the Virate.

Jana turned to face them, still snarling, and said, "We have been betrayed. A vampire has destroyed another vampire. That cannot go without retribution. Kim Chandler has done this and she has abducted the one that could allow us access to the task force through a connection to Alex Chance. She has taken Dana Richland from this building. I want her found and brought to me. I will reward the one who brings her to me greatly. She must be destroyed, but she must also be made to suffer for this transgression."

Jade, the last surviving member of the original group associated with the Virate, took a step forward and said, "I know her well. I will find her and bring her to you, but I will need a few to assist me."

Jana looked at her and nodded, "Choose your team and begin the search."

It took her only a moment. She knew the ones she wanted to work with. She nodded once and said, "Hal Martino, Mitchell Roth, and Angelica Norris will accompany me."

Jana nodded once and said, "Feed tonight and rest tomorrow. You'll begin your search tomorrow night."

CHAPTER THIRTY-FOUR
The Next Phase

Cardwell led the way into the old building through the shattered door to find Caroline Parrish and Bonnie Stowers standing just a few feet inside with rifles in hand, ready to defend themselves and the facility from vampire invasion. They both stiffened with a sharp intake of breath at the first sign of motion and relaxed a bit as they recognized Cardwell and the others filing into the lobby and spreading out. Both women lowered their weapons, letting out sighs of relief.

The group gathered in the lobby, dividing into smaller segments. The pack, all in human form and all naked except for Carmen, stood closely together against the wall opposite the door. The insertion team members stood at the center of the room with Monica at the center with five of them around her. Sandusky stood beside the door while Merina made her way toward the counter behind Caroline and Bonnie as Cardwell, Alex, Sydney, and Katrina stood at the front of the group.

"Good," Cardwell said as they all settled into place. "There was no attack here."

"No," Caroline replied. "But Jana managed to escape."

Cardwell frowned, "Did she harm anyone?"

"No," Bonnie shook her head. "I checked on everyone still here. No one saw her leave and no one was touched."

"Good," Cardwell said. "But we know about Jana. She joined them, in a way."

Caroline frowned, "What do you mean?"

He shook his head slowly and Alex looked at her as he said, "Jana attacked Gerrit after he'd received the ancient power. She's now the Master."

"No way," Caroline said. "How is that possible?"

Cardwell took a step forward and said, "We'll talk about that later. Right now, we need to get settled in here and figure out our next move."

He glanced over his shoulder and said, "First, let's get these people some clothes. They'll be with us for a while."

Sandusky moved away from the door and said, "I think I have something that'll work."

He gestured toward the back of the lobby and the hallway beyond it as he said, "Follow me."

Cardwell and Alex stepped aside as the members of the pack walked quickly through the group and followed Sandusky down the hall.

"Next," Cardwell said. "We need to find a place to secure Monica until tomorrow night."

"Wait a minute," Caroline said and frowned. "She's a vampire."

"Yes," Cardwell nodded. "She's going with us to Washington. She's the proof we need for the President and the senator."

Bonnie leaned slightly forward, "We're going back to D.C.? I thought we had to get the vampires out of this town."

Cardwell shook his head, "It's too late for that. This town has been overrun and we don't have the manpower or funding to take care of it right now, but I'm sure we'll come back."

He took a step forward and said, "I have to talk with the wolves. Get this place secured and get everything settled for the rest of the night. Bonnie, you go with them and talk to Monica. I want to know exactly where she stands."

"Of course," Bonnie said and stepped aside as the insertion team began escorting Monica into the depths of the building then followed them.

As they walked off, Bonacci walked forward and looked at Caroline, "Where's Brewer?"

She gestured to her right, "He's in the corner office, still working on that book."

Bonacci took a step forward and held up the book he'd retrieved after Sharia had dropped it, "Then I've got more work for him to do."

As Bonacci moved behind the counter, Katrina looked at Alex and said, "I have a few things to discuss with you."

Alex nodded and gestured toward the counter, "There's an office there we can use."

Katrina took a step forward then looked back at Sydney, "You come, too. You're part of this."

Sydney shrugged and joined them as they walked into the office.

It was Sandusky's office, the hub of the operations center, and Alex closed the door once they were all inside. Katrina walked to the large desk taking up much of the small room and stood behind it as Alex and Sydney stood side by side across from her.

"I need to tell you a few things," Katrina began. "This could affect the future of this task force and your team, at least to a certain extent."

Alex nodded and folded his arms across his chest, "Okay. Go ahead."

Katrina took a deep breath and said, "I first need to tell you about the Feline Nation, as we've been calling it. There is a network of feline lycanthropes spread across the world, but it's mostly centered in the United States. We exist in every state, though some are less populated than others. This state, Mississippi, for example, has one of the smallest factions. There are no more than thirty Felines in this state. Others, such as California and Florida, have as many as two hundred. I can't quote exact figures right now. Keeping up with the population isn't exactly my job."

"And what is your job?" Sydney asked, leaning slightly forward and frowning with her hands on her hips.

Katrina looked at her and said, "I don't exactly have a title, either, but I am the leader of the Feline Nation. We don't use such designations. As the leader, I am connected to every faction across the globe and my word is law."

"Wait," Sydney shook her head. "I was under the impression that you were here working with the wolves."

Katrina nodded slowly and said, "That was my intention. I wanted all of you to think that I was nothing more than an observer. The truth is that I wanted to know where the Tribe stands in relation to the recent vampire activity. I came with them to help find their missing alpha, but I also wanted to see how this task force operates. So far, I'm impressed. I think you're on the right track in your effort to end their threat."

"We do what we can," Alex said. "But we're starting over with this. I thought it was over months ago and walked away, but I didn't know that a new Master had shown up."

"Understandable," Katrina nodded. "I believe, with a little negotiation, I can convince the Tribe to join your efforts. They are a larger, more cohesive community and will be of great help in dealing with them, especially with this new Master. I'll go to Colorado and talk with the elders of the Tribe. I'll also commit the Feline Nation to joining the fight. For now, though. I'll stay with the task force and travel with you to Washington. I believe revealing myself to the President will add credence to the situation and my offer. Once that's taken care of, I'll travel to Colorado and I would like some representatives of the task force to accompany me and help negotiate an agreement that will benefit all of us."

"I think we can arrange that," Alex nodded. "And thank you. Every little bit of help is greatly appreciated."

Katrina shrugged, "We'll see how this all plays out."

Alex lowered his arms and took a step back as he said, "If there's nothing else, we should probably get back in there and see what else needs to be done."

"That's about it," Katrina said and moved toward the door. "I'll explain the differences between cats and wolves later. It's not important right now."

Sydney shook her head, "I'm having a hard time wrapping my head around all this. I mean, I've been dealing with vampires for years, but I never knew lycanthropes of any kind existed until recently, and I thought it was all werewolves. I never considered werecats as well."

Katrina looked at her and smiled warmly, "Don't worry. You'll figure it out quickly. You're a highly intelligent woman."

"I hope so," Sydney said and turned around as Alex opened the door and waited for her and Katrina to lead them out of the office.

Back in the lobby, only a few remained. Rachel and Evan, the newest members of the team, had returned without Bonacci and Melissa. Sandusky had returned and stood at the door once again. Merina had taken a seat behind her desk and was checking her instruments to make sure everything was still in working order. Caroline stood in front of the counter with Lois Cashlin on her left and Gina Filmore on her right. DeAnna stood stoically in the car corner with her sword sheathed at her left hip, ready to be drawn, and held her arms folded across her chest.

Alex, Sydney, and Katrina moved toward the center of the room slowly, seeing the facial expressions of the others, all appearing a little frustrated and anxious, ready to know what was going to happen next. Caroline looked the most disturbed, feeling nervous about an actual vampire being in the building with them. She didn't like the idea at all.

Before any of them could speak, as the three turned around, Cardwell appeared at the far end of the hall and walked quickly toward them.

He stopped at the corner of the counter and rested his right elbow on it as he looked over the few standing there.

"Okay," he began. "Here's the situation. First, Monica has agreed to work with us and will not cause any trouble. She'll be going with us to Washington and will meet with both the President and Senator Howland as soon as it can be arranged. Bonacci and Dyson will handle the transportation."

He looked to his right and said, "Second. We're going to hire Gina as our Director of Public Relations, though the job will entail a little more than that. She'll be coming with us to Washington."

"Thank you," Gina said and smiled wanly. "I'll do my best."

"I know you will," Cardwell said and nodded once then faced forward again. "We don't know what the vampires are planning, if they'll stay here and use this town as their base of operations, but they have taken this town, like I've said. The remaining residents have either been turned or will be used to feed the others. We're going to let them have it for now. There's nothing we can do right now. We've been through a fairly sizable battle and we're tired. We're down a few people and we need to rebuild before we can do anything. But I promise you that one day, we will come back here and reclaim this town."

"Hold on," Sandusky said and stood up straight. "I hear something. It could be them."

"I doubt it," Alex said and turned to face the door as well. "They'd be much quieter."

Caroline picked up her rifle from where she'd leaned it against the front of the counter and Alex held his right hand over the pistol at his hip. DeAnna lowered her arms and took a step forward, ready to handle the situation.

"Open the door," Cardwell said and nodded to Sandusky.

He shrugged and did as he was asked. He struggled with it for a second, but it finally came open and the others, the armed ones, took a step toward the door and stopped as they saw the familiar figure of Mayor Jay Downing standing there looking haggard and tired.

"Thank God you're here," Jay said through a heavy sigh and walked through the door. "They've taken everyone. I can't find a single living soul in this town."

Cardwell nodded and moved a little closer, "Because the vampires have taken over. We'll be leaving within the next twenty-four hours. You'll come with us."

Jay looked at him for a long moment, frowning, then said, "You're just giving up, then."

Cardwell glared at him and said, "We don't have a choice. We're outnumbered and there's nothing we can do right now. But I'll give you a choice. You can come with us and live to fight another day or you can stay here and either become one of them or their food."

Jay thought about it for a handful of seconds then nodded, "I guess I'll be going with you."

CHAPTER THIRTY-FIVE
Nine Days Later

President Memory Hutchins sat in the back seat of the armor-plated limo as it rolled along the highway south of Washington, headed for the DSA task force facility once again. She had a lot on her mind and more was added to her plate every day. At the moment, she needed to focus on the task force and what her old friend Jonathan Cardwell had to show her. She still wasn't sure she believed him that vampires were a real thing and that they were a threat to the United States. She had agreed to visit once again when he had proof and he claimed that it was waiting for her at his facility.

She wasn't alone on the journey. As always, her Chief of Staff, Stephanie Kenton, was seated at the other end of the bench seat at the rear of the passenger compartment. She was sitting up straight, prim and proper as always, dressed in a dark blue dress that reached to well below her knees. She'd brought along her tablet, her connection to the office and the constant flow of information flowing through it. She was never without it, unless she was in her office at her computer.

Seated in front of Memory, his back to the side of the car, was her lead Secret Service Agent, Martin Raymond. He sat ramrod straight in his slick black suit and dark sunglasses. She wouldn't go anywhere without him and trusted him completely. He was dedicated to his job, her safety, and she was more than pleased with everything he'd done.

Across from Martin was Senator Theda Howland, the chair of the Senate Appropriations Committee, meaning she was in charge of funding various government agencies, both on and off the books. She was also the biggest skeptic Memory had ever seen and it had been at her urging that the presentation of proof was necessary. She wouldn't do more than allow the task force to continue operating on the limited budget they had until she was evidence that vampires existed. She hoped Cardwell would come through and show them what Theda wanted to see.

The other occupant of the car, seated across from Memory with her back to the thick plexiglass shield separating them from the driver's compartment, was Vice President Penny Kramer. She sat back on the wide seat, dressed in a black skirt and white blouse with a fairly lightweight black jacket and her dark green eyes looked half-closed, almost as if she was falling asleep. Memory knew better, though. Penny was focusing on what they were doing and getting herself prepared to deal with just about anything.

Penny Kramer was her perfect counterpart. She was as smart and as tough as they came. Very little got past her and she would be able to easily take over when the time came.

Thinking of that brought a frown to Memory's face. She rested her left elbow on the armrest of the door and leaned her cheek against it, covering her mouth with her hand to conceal the deep frown, the worried and frightened frown. The news she'd received from her doctor, Wanda Fairly, had been much worse than she'd imagined.

With a little more than two years left in her term, Memory knew she wouldn't make it that long. The cancer Wanda had detected was farther along than she'd thought and there was nothing to be done. There were treatments that could prolong her life by a few months, but Memory didn't think it was worth the trouble or the expense. It would take her out of office much sooner and she didn't think doing so would give her time to adequately prepared Penny to take over. It was inevitable, but she would bide her time and keep her secret until it became more of an issue and caused her ability to perform her duties to begin failing.

They rode in silence, none of them wanting to discuss the possibilities of what they might or might not see in the DSA facility, and it was a little uncomfortable for Memory, but there was so much on her mind that she didn't overly concern herself with the lack of communication.

Finally, the ride ended as the driver, a man assigned by Martin, slowed the limo to a stop outside the aging building. Martin would be the first to exit the limo and he waited with his small earpiece in place until he was given word by the remainder of his unit that they were all in their assigned positions and ready to cover the President from the vehicle to the building's entrance.

After just a moment, Martin nodded once then looked at Memory and said, "It's all clear. We're good to go."

Memory nodded and replied, "Then let's go. I'm ready to get this over with."

Martin drew in a deep breath and rose from the seat, turning slightly before leaving the padded leather to open the door and climb quickly out of the car. Once he was out and standing in his usual protective position beside the door, Memory followed him and stood up, squinting a bit in the morning sunlight.

Martin stepped aside, toward the rear of the car, and Memory followed him while the others filed out of the car behind them.

Kevin Burns, Director of the Domestic Security Agency, was waiting for them at the door and held it open for them. He was dressed in a blue-gray suit with a white shirt and a black tie. He nodded as they approached with Memory leading and Martin a step behind and off to her right.

"Madame President, welcome," Burns said as she reached the door.

"Thank you, Director Burns," she replied with a curt nod and a brief smile as she crossed the threshold with Theda just behind her as Martin waited at the door. Once Penny and Stephanie were inside, Burns closed the door and joined them in the lobby.

Cardwell was waiting with Alex, Sandusky, Sydney, and Katrina in a line behind him.

"Welcome, Ms. President," Cardwell said. "I guess we should get the festivities out of the way first."

"Yes," Memory nodded. "Show me what you've got."

He turned to the side and gestured toward the hallway behind him with his left hand as he said, "Right this way."

Memory shook her head slowly and said, "You'd better lead the way. This is your place, after all."

"If you insist," Cardwell said and started walking.

The Presidential entourage followed Cardwell and the other four followed them.

As they walked, Cardwell said, "I'm sorry. I should've introduced our most recent addition. Katrina Bently, allow me to introduce the President of the United States, Memory Hutchins."

Memory looked at her and nodded, "Pleased to meet you, Katrina. What is it that you do here?"

Katrina smiled lightly and said, "Pleased to meet you as well, Madame President. I think it'll be better for me to show you than try to explain."

Memory frowned and looked at Cardwell, "What does that mean?"

Cardwell shook his head, "It's something of a surprise. You'll see soon enough."

"Okay," Memory shrugged. "I'll trust you."

A moment later, they reached the end of the hallway and turned to the left. They entered another hallway, a bit narrower than the first, and Cardwell led them to the first door on the right, a massive metal door that looked much like the door of a bank vault. It was flanked by the task force's two security officers, Steve Wolverton and Nicole Jennings. Both were dressed in the standard tactical gear of the task force with the inclusion of body armor and weapons. Their rifles were slung over their shoulders, not expecting any trouble, but they had to be prepared in case something did happen.

The guards didn't move as the group arrived and Cardwell unlocked the door. With Alex's help, he pulled the heavy door open and they entered the small room, a medical lab with a number of instruments and standard equipment spaced around it.

Seated on the small examination table at the center of the room, clad in black, was Monica Halpern with her long, straight, blonde hair hanging over her shoulder and her wide brown eyes, a little bloodshot, staring straight ahead.

The group entered and spread out into a line across the width of the room. Cardwell took a step farther into the room and turned to the side, looking at Memory and Theda, standing side by side, and gestured toward Monica.

"Allow me to introduce Monica Halpern," he said. "Our vampire representative."

Theda frowned and said, "She doesn't look like a vampire."

Cardwell looked at Monica and said, "Show her."

Without hesitation, Monica slid off the table and landed lightly, almost as if she'd floated to the smooth tile floor. She looked at Theda, slowly opened her mouth, and allowed her fangs to slide into position.

Theda shook her head slowly, a skeptical frown on her face. Monica then shot toward Theda, her movement so fast it appeared as little more than a dark blur. In an instant, she stood in front of the slightly taller woman and looked up at her. Theda could feel the cold practically flowing from the woman and seeing the fangs up close was more than enough.

"Okay," Theda said and swallowed heavily. "I think that's enough. I'll have to admit it. Vampires are real."

She then leaned slightly forward, her eyes narrowed as she looked Monica over and asked, "Could you tell me more? How often do you need to feed? Does just one bite turn you into a vampire?"

Monica nodded slowly and replied, "I could feed every night, but I only have to feed about once a week, depending on how much I take. Yes, one bite will turn you into a vampire, but it takes a while. It could take as long as three months. A second bite will turn you in about six days. A third bite will turn you the following night."

Memory looked at her, frowning, and asked, "Is it true that you die then the virus, or whatever, brings you back to life?"

Monica shrugged, "If you want to call this life. I've been thinking about it and I'd call it more reanimation than resurrection. I can't explain it very well. I haven't been a vampire very long at all and I don't know all the details."

Theda nodded slowly, appreciatively, and asked, "How did you become a vampire?"

Monica looked at her again and said, "I was a cop in Pine Ridge. One night, after a long day of work, I went home to relax. Vampires broke in and attacked me. I wasn't given a choice."

Theda shook her head, "So, that means vampires don't have to be invited into your home."

"Right," Monica nodded. "From what I've learned, most of the myths about vampires are things seen in movies and don't actually work. For instance, a cross can't harm a vampire on its own. To do anything, it must be held by someone with faith in its meaning and power."

"I see," Theda replied. "Now, how many vampires are there."

Monica shook her head and Cardwell moved closer, facing Theda, and said, "Let me take that one. The truth is, we don't have an exact number, but we're certain they number in the thousands, especially now."

"Why now?" Theda asked, tilting her head slightly to the left.

"Because they've taken the town of Pine Ridge," he said evenly. "The population of more than ten thousand has either been turned or captured to provide food for the others. Our best intelligence suggests they'll remain there for a while before moving on and continuing their plan."

"What plan is that?" Theda asked.

Cardwell took a breath and said, "Their plan to take over the world."

Her eyes flashed open wide and she drew in a sharp gasp, "Is that even possible? How can they do that?"

"We're not sure yet," Cardwell replied. "We have a document, a book, created by an ancient vampire Master that details a plan to take over the world. We've acquired the services of a translator, a linguist who's part of a group called the Morte Society. They've been around for centuries, tracking vampires and documenting their history. He'd been working on it, but there are a number of vampire languages and it's taking quite a long time."

She frowned, "Then how do you know what they're doing?"

"We don't know all the details," he replied. "We know their overall goal and we're learning more each day. We believe they'll attempt to take over several major cities then spread their influence from there. We need to be prepared for this and that's why we're asking for so much additional funding."

"I see," Theda nodded, glancing at Monica once again, then focused on Cardwell. "I think we can do something about that. I have no doubt that you're serious and I now believe vampires exist and present a major threat to this nation."

She turned to Memory and said, "Madame President, I will put my stamp of approval on whatever budget request is made. You have my word on that."

"Thank you, Senator," Memory replied with a respectful nod.

Theda then looked at Cardwell again and gestured toward Katrina as she said, "I believe this young lady has something to say."

Katrina took a step forward and looked at Theda, "My name is Katrina Bentley and I represent another faction, one group of what you might call lycanthropes."

Theda scowled, "Are you talking about werewolves?"

"Not quite," Katrina replied with a nod. "Though there is a tribe of werewolves in this country. I represent another group. You would probably call us werecats. My society of felines and the Tribe of werewolves both oppose the actions of the vampires and, as leader of the Feline Nation, I have pledged our support to Mr. Cardwell's task force and their agenda. I will soon travel to the home of the Tribe of Wolves and try to convince them to join us as well, working together to finally eradicate the vampires."

"I don't get it," Theda shook her head. "Are you serious?"

"Let me show you," Katrina said and took a step back.

She leaned forward and let herself fall. As she fell, she transformed into the sleek black panther once again. As Theda gasped in surprise, Katrina walked in a tight circle, much like a normal housecat, then pushed off the floor and transformed again, returning to her human shape.

"Okay," Theda said and held up her hands. "This is too much for me. You people just keep doing what you're doing and I'll make sure you have the money you need."

She started for the door, shaking her head, "Can we get out of here now? I need some air."

At Memory's urging, Martin stayed close to Theda as she stormed through the building toward the exit while Cardwell escorted the others from the building.

"This is really something," Penny Kramer said as they walked slowly along the hallway. "I never would've expected any of this to actually be true. I hope you can get everything figured out quickly."

"Thank you, Ms. Vice President," he replied with a nod. "We're going to do our best."

At the door, they said their goodbyes, and the Presidential entourage left the facility. Kevin Burns remained behind and, once the door was closed, looked at Cardwell and shook his head.

"I don't know how you did it," he said. "You convinced the most skeptical woman on the planet, the one with the tightest purse strings of all time, to give you more money."

Cardwell looked at him and shrugged, "We just showed her what she wanted to see."

Burns shook his head, "Well, I guess you'd better start getting your budget together."

"I will," Cardwell nodded. "And I think we'll need an accountant before long."

Burns shook his head and started for the door, "Do whatever you need to do. I'll be back sooner or later."

"Thanks," Cardwell said. "I'll keep you updated."

Burns shook his head and walked out the door.

As the door closed behind him, Katrina and Alex walked over.

Cardwell turned around and said, "Let me guess. You're ready to start this journey of yours."

"Yes," Katrina replied and nodded.

"Okay," Cardwell said and took a deep breath. "Who is going with you?"

Alex looked at him and said, "I am. We're also taking Jackson, Barker, and Bonnie."

"Why Bonnie?" Cardwell asked, frowning.

Alex shrugged, "She'll probably be better at negotiating and figuring out what they really mean when we talk to them."

Cardwell thought about it for a moment. Bonnie had been a great help to the team since she'd joined them, but they were at a point where her services weren't as essential, though he had no doubts she would be needed again before long.

"Fine," he said. "I understand that. But why the two new recruits?"

"They need experience," Alex replied. "I'll take time to work with them on the road and make sure they're both ready for the fight we all know is coming."

"Good point," Cardwell nodded. "When are you leaving? I'll need to make some arrangements."

"Two days," Katrina said with a sharp nod.

"Make it happen," Cardwell said. "Get these two groups on our side."

"I'll do my best," Katrina said and offered a faint smile.

EPILOGUE
Tribal Reaction

A small fire burned bright in a clearing well away from the Tribal village. Small mounds of snow remained at the base of several trees lining the clearing, but the hard-packed earth was clear of snow. The four members of the Tribal Council, the Elders, sat in a semicircle on one side of the fire, each wearing a brown robe of soft leather while Eldon sat across from them wearing black trousers and a loose-fitting shirt. To the right of Eldon and the left of the Elders stood KJ, the Tribal Shaman wearing his ankle-length dark brown robe trimmed along the front seam with a mosaic of green and gold thread. His long, brown hair hung loosely down his back as his bright green eyes stared straight ahead and reflected the dancing orange and red flames of the fire.

With his hands clasped together beneath the wide sleeves of his robe, KJ looked at Danette, the Chief Elder, and said, "I have experienced a vision of the current situation and I must report it to you."

Danette nodded once, looking at him, and said, "Please, tell us of your vision."

He drew in a breath and said, "The pack, the four that survived a great deal at the hands of the vampires, have joined the humans, the DSA task force led by Jonathan Cardwell, and have relocated to Washington. They are allied with the humans and, while not controlled by them, they will assist them in the fight against the vampires."

Danette nodded, "This is not totally unexpected."

He shifted his weight, turning a bit more toward her, and said, "There is more. The task force failed in their task of stopping the vampires from releasing the ancient power of the Anasazi. However, the Master performing the ritual was then destroyed and the power taken by another, one of the task force members that had recently been turned. She is now the Master and is controlling the vampire race, but she does not yet know the full extent of her power. However, something has taken place with the release of the ancient power that could prove to be beneficial. The power has brought the Nemesis to his full power."

"That is good," Danette nodded. "But it also means the vampires have broken the pact. They are on the move and continuing with their plan."

"Yes," KJ nodded. "They are following the plan of an ancient Master, but it will take some time before they are prepared to make their next move."

Danette looked around the group and said, "We must do our part in stopping the progress of this vampire plan."

Levin Gaston, seated on her right, turned toward her and said, "With the pack having been reduced to only four, we cannot ask them to lead the effort. We must make contact with the other communities and begin working together."

As Danette nodded, Carlos Montoya, seated on her right with Melanie Parkman between them, frowned and said, "It has been too long since we have unified the communities. I fear we will not be able to bring them all into line."

Danette looked at him, scowling, and said, "We don't have a choice. We must bring all the wolves together. I would suggest that we coordinate with the task force to plan our efforts carefully."

KJ took a step forward and said, "There is a little more."

As they all looked up at him, he continued, "The Feline, Katrina, is now abroad with the Nemesis and others from the task force. She plans to unite the Felines to work with the task force and will bring the solidarity of the Felines to the Tribe."

Danette nodded then looked around as she asked, "Can we agree to consider this option and join forces with the task force to oppose the vampires?"

"We must," Melanie said and sat up straight, her long hair flowing over her shoulders and fluttering in the light, cold breeze that stirred the flames of the fire. "We must honor the terms of the pact. The vampires have exposed themselves and attacked the humans. It is our duty to end their plan and the task force will bring more strength to our efforts as we will bring strength to theirs."

228

"I concur," Levi nodded. "We must join them."

Then, as Carlos nodded his agreement, KJ straightened, his back stiffening, and looked around. He frowned and finally turned slightly to his right, looking away from the fire.

"Hold," he said. "We are not alone. Others approach."

Danette sat up straight as well and turned her head to the right, "Melanie, you are the stealthiest of us all. Change and find these intruders."

Melanie nodded once and stood up sharply, untying the narrow belt around her waist and threw off her robe. Naked with her pale skin reflecting the light from the fire, she moved away from the group and dropped forward, transforming. As a wolf with light brown fur, she shot into the trees as the others stared after her.

After a moment, Danette looked at KJ and asked, "Can you identify them?"

He shook his head, "No. They are too cold for my senses."

Danette frowned. KJs senses were heightened by his powers as Shaman and it was strange for him to not easily identify even the smallest creature within a hundred yards.

They rose to their feet, expecting a conflict, and stood ready to drop their own robes and transform, but they would wait until they knew the nature of the interlopers. A few minutes later, seeming much longer to each of them, Melanie returned, now in human form, and walked toward the fire leading two women, both with long, blonde hair. Both were roughly the same height and were dressed in black. One had hair a shade darker than the other and had a narrower face.

"Vampires!" Levi said through a snarl and started to open his robe.

"Stop," Melanie said and held up her hands. "There's no need for a conflict. They are here seeking our help."

Danette frowned and shook her head slowly, "Why would two vampires ask for our help while their kind is working to take over the world?"

Kim Chandler stopped and nodded, "I am Kim Chandler. I have been a vampire for more than four hundred years. I served the Virate for several years, but they have been destroyed and a new Master has taken over. I no longer support their plan and cannot justify remaining with them."

She gestured to the woman beside her and said, "This is Dana Richland. She was turned by Gerrit Jaeger, the leader of the Virate, and was under his control. When he was destroyed, the control did not transfer to the new Master, even though she has taken Gerrit's power. She also has a strong connection to the Nemesis and has dealt with the task force. We only seek asylum, a place to hide from the vampires should they try to find us and bring us back into their plan."

Danette frowned, "This is unprecedented. No vampire has ever been to Tribal land. We must discuss this in council."

She looked at Eldon and said, "Take them away, far enough to prevent them hearing our deliberations."

"Of course," Eldon said and stood up quickly.

He was a bit nervous, wondering what a vampire could do to him, but Kim looked at him and said, "We'll do as you ask."

"Come with me," Eldon said and turned around, walking away from the fire.

Kim and Dana followed him obediently and they vanished into the night.

"We have to," Melanie said once they were out of range. "I believe KJ will be able to use them to find out more about the vampires and their actions."

"That's all I need to hear," Levi said.

Carlos shrugged and said, "I don't particularly like the idea, but we can monitor them and make sure they do nothing."

Danette drew in a deep breath and let it out slowly as she said, "Then we will honor their request. We will grant them asylum within the Tribe."

Corruptor:
Reign of Darkness Volume II
COMING SOON

Don't miss out!

Visit the website below and you can sign up to receive emails whenever Jeff Brown publishes a new book. There's no charge and no obligation.

https://books2read.com/r/B-A-VMTK-XMLQC

BOOKS 2 READ

Connecting independent readers to independent writers.

About the Author

Jeff Brown is the author of more than 40 works of fiction. Based in the Deep South, his stories all have a connection to the area.

Milton Keynes UK
Ingram Content Group UK Ltd.
UKHW020243221123
432980UK00016B/1039